Golden Boy

James Gregory Randall

AOS Publishing, 2026

ISBN: 978-1-998662-85-2

Cover Artist: Meredith Lindsay

Visit AOS Publishing's website:

www.aospublishing.com

To Grandmothers and Great-Grandmothers

For picking up the pieces

RIP

Maria (*geboren* Gutschi) Graus

1845-?

Maria (*geboren* Graus) Gutrater, Edler von Puchstein

1885-1965

Elizabeth (*née* Beaumont) Pogue

1866-1941

Isabel (*née* Pogue) Randall

1909-1986

Rise again, rise again—though your heart it be broken

And life about to end

No matter what you've lost, be it a home, a love, a friend.

Like the Mary Ellen Carter, rise again.[1]

[1] Stan Rogers, "The Mary Ellen Carter." Used with permission.

Remember that old saying,

"If you didn't want me to write this, you should of brung me up better!"?

Well, you should have.

Contents

Introduction

To Be

This is not a work of fiction. It is the story of my life written in narrative form.

I tried using the first-person point of view, but couldn't sustain the emotional distance to keep writing. The third-person omniscient is less confessional than the first. It allows me the freedom to traverse the length and breadth of my memory.

Sometimes the pain of human experience cannot be shared in conversation. It is all too much to bear. I once told the story of my life at a Men's Retreat on the shores of Lake Nakamun, Alberta, and am grateful for the compassionate guys who bore my burden. But once was enough. I refuse to allow the story that I told them to define who I am today. I am more than my pain. I am more than my suffering.

I think. I write. I make music. I cook. I do crosswords. I learn languages. I refinish old furniture. I help neighbours. I love bicycles, motorcycles, and the FIFA World Cup. I go to church and take communion every Sunday. The liturgy and comfortable words reach deep into my soul. I love my wife, children, and grandchildren. I cherish my family and friends.

I doubt, second-guess myself, and wonder what in the world.

Writing seems to be the only way I can make sense of my life. It helps to put everything into perspective. However, I refuse to allow the past to define who I am today. Writing in the early hours gives me the hope that something new is dawning.

Golden Boy is a story about how life happens to the best and worst of us. The only thing we can do in the midst of our troubles is to get on with whatever needs to be done in the moment. What happens, happens. We cannot waste our time assigning blame or casting judgement. We may not be able to forget, but we can forgive. Granting mercy is what liberates us from the past, not the response of the perpetrator, or the judgement meted out to him, her, or them.

Forgiveness is something we do over and over again for ourselves. It frees us from those who abused us emotionally, physically, and sexually. Forgiving those midnight whisperers, lurkers in shadows, and smotherers in dark corners neutralizes their power. It sets us on the road to healing. We may never be whole again, but we can stop the cycle of violence in our lives. It does not need to carry on from generation to generation. Forgiveness gives us hope in spite of our wounding.

While this is a true story that includes elements of faith and spirituality, it is not a theological statement. It is not a prescription for how you should get on with your life. That is something you have to discover on your own. How should you then live is indeed the question you have to ask yourself.

I have chosen to be.

Part One

1

A Christmas Story

1955

Over his long and eventful life, with its ups and downs, hairpin turns, and switchbacks, Antony learned one important truth: Eema Mother in Her great mercy sometimes answers the frantic prayers of unrighteous women.[2]

The ramifications of such a pain-filled and begged-for grace, however, are often as long-lasting and as heart-wrenching as a marriage turned sour. In those dire circumstances, when women pray out their anguish to Eema Mother, who sometimes listens, they need to take care.

To their great woe, they may actually receive an answer to their deepest plea. In hindsight, the answer would have been the absolute furthest thing from anything they could have asked for or imagined.

If they had been able to see the hollows, valleys, and precipitous turns down the road ahead of them, they would have kept their mouths shut.

But in their desperation, they knocked, and kept knocking on Heaven's door until Eema Mother, who wasn't blind to their woe, gave them exactly what they wanted—not necessarily what they needed.

Antony's mother Mary Helen had no idea what she unleashed on that far-off Christmas Eve in 1955 when she gave her son to Eema Mother. He had swallowed a Christmas ornament the size of a cat's-eye marble.

---

[2] In the New Testament, God is often referred to as Abba, the Jewish word for "father." I use Eema, the Jewish word for "mother" as a reflection of Antony's impression of the nature of who and what God is: a woman ignored at your peril.

She'd been holding her lovely, ten-month-old baby boy close to the decorated tree. He was just as beautiful as his father James George was handsome. He was just as dazzled by the magical lights as she was by him on that most silent of holy nights.

Mary Helen couldn't have been happier if she tried. Her heart was filled with love and joy. The two of them drew near to the glittering lights and flashing tinsel. Then, quick as a wink, in the blink of an eye, the little boy grabbed one of the ornaments and popped it into his mouth. He swallowed it whole. His eyes grew wide. It lodged in his throat. Stuck tighter than tight could be, it was stolid and unmoving, like a rock rolled across a tomb only an angel of Eema Mother could remove.

The innocent wee boy choked, stopped breathing, and turned blue then grey. His perfect little body grew still and lifeless. Mary Helen screamed and burst into tears.

James George came running. "What the hell?"

As his baby lay dying, he grabbed his only begotten son, pried open his mouth, and pounded him on the back.

Mary Helen prayed to Eema Mother and James George swore all to hell as his temper flared.

"Oh, Eema Mother, wherever you are, please save my son's life. I'll give him to you and the church. Just don't let him die, I beg you."

Mary Helen genuflected and bawled her eyes out. Her face was awash with tears, her heart burst with regret and sorrow, and her conscience burned with guilt and shame.

She was, after all, a married woman with three other kids of her own. Now she was living in sin with the handsomest man she had ever met. After a long, delicious night of indiscretion that she didn't for a single minute regret, she bore him a son.

Life was simply too much. It came crashing down.

"Eema Mother!" Mary Helen swore.

She sure could use a drink.

At her side, James George grew angrier with each chest-hammering beat of his hand. He was so mad he could just about punch the bitch who let this happen.

Then, out of the blue, stopping the two desperate parents dead in their tracks, making them gasp for air and catch their breath, a miracle of miracles occurred.

In a ratty little trailer in Drayton Valley, Alberta, on the coldest night of the year, an angel of Eema Mother God From On High performed an infant's Heimlich on the little gaffer. He once again inhaled the breath of life. His parents retched and heaved; the adrenalin coursed through their veins so.

James George's brand-new candy-apple red 1955 Chevy Nomad was parked out front, and the block heater was plugged in. At -35° that night, it was goddamn cold. Twenty-years old and the youngest tool push for Commonwealth Drilling, James George sure as hell did not want his car to freeze up, in case something happened out at the rig, and he'd be called to work.

"Damn-it-all," he said. He was a family man with responsibilities and a job to do. There was no way he'd let his company down.

Eema Mother, who doesn't always disappoint, answered Mary Helen's anguished prayer. Out popped the ornament, the little boy gasped for air, and his colour came back. Turning red in the face, he wailed like there was no tomorrow.

Mary Helen was so relieved, she burst into another flood of tears.

James George finished his Bloody Mary and reached for something stronger— a Crown Royal, because he could afford it. He had more money in his pocket than he could burn through in a day.

Then Eema Mother said to Mary Helen, "A promise is a promise. I've saved your golden boy's life. Now he is mine. He will go the way I want him to and sure as hell not the way you're raising him."

And that was that.

Mary Helen sat on the floor and sobbed her heart out. She held her son to her breast. She begged her gorgeous, young lover with his Gregory Peck straight-out-of-the-movies good looks to take those son-of-a-bitch ornaments off the tree this very instant and throw them out. There was no way in hell she'd ever allow them into her house again. She bawled and bawled, and the boy suckled all the milk she could give him.

She lit a smoke, and James George handed her a rye-and-ginger. That was exactly what she needed. She downed it with one swallow. The booze calmed her nerves.

"Would you make me another?" Mary Helen handed James George her empty tumbler. "Please and thank you very much, my dear."

They didn't own a piece of cut crystal or a set of matched plates, or even half a drawer of cutlery to go around if they ever had some company, just odds and ends she picked up at the Sally Ann.

Mary Helen settled down. She didn't give her vow to Eema Mother another thought until she and Antony were reunited after they'd been separated for over a decade.

He told her then that he had become a non-genuflecting follower of Eema Mother.

"How could you do this to me?" she asked, crushed with disappointment. Heartbroken. After a lifetime of woe, her vow finally came into play.

She handed over her beloved son to Eema Mother, who saved his life. In the years since she last saw him, he rejected the outward trappings of religion that she feigned at Christmas and Easter. He adopted something else: the heartfelt, transformative faith of personal belief in a loving God.

How could Antony do that to her? Dismiss the ritual that was the sum total of her practice? His was a betrayal that cut to the quick.

She would never forgive him for it.

Grown as tall as he'd ever get, just shy of the six feet he dreamed of— because tall is tall, and women can't get enough of men they look up to— Antony thought that he could have become a nice Catholic boy, had Mary Helen been anywhere near half the woman she could have been. *Believe from the heart and live out your faith in acts of kindness, not simply going through the motions, and live like there are no consequences for your actions.*

As it was, she spent her son's growing-up years drinking and smoking and screwing around. The life she led was unliveable.

Even as a kid, he wouldn't follow in her footsteps.

He made his choice to be.

2

Please And Thank You Very Much

Antony took Izzy to church those wasted Sunday mornings of their mother's second go-around at parenting. Mary Helen was too goddamn hungover to care for anything other than the sorry predicament of a life she made for herself.

The proverbial failed and broken mother who tried her best would have been good enough for Antony. But no, Mary Helen didn't even try.

Antony and his little sister Izzy were so tiny you wouldn't think they'd survive another minute of the hollowed-out emptiness of their parents' neglect. They'd need a lifetime of counselling and therapy for the trauma that Mary Helen and James George meted out to them in unmeasured beats from their hands, mouths, and feet.

Was it too much to hope that she would confess and apologise? Maybe even reconcile herself to her children?

After she escaped the fury of her incendiary young lover, she slept in sex-stained beds with a series of nameless beaus. Her hangovers refused to lessen their grip on her life-wearied soul. She'd be up until all hours partying and this-ing and that-ing, and waking up dry-mouthed and reeling.

Her darling son-of-a-pistol would shake her on a Sunday morning and ask her to take him and Izzy to church, please and thank you very much. He'd stand there at the side of her bed and wouldn't take her cold-shouldered, not-in-your-life answer for a no.

"Mummy's too tired," she'd groan. "Go fix yourself a bowl of cereal and watch some cartoons. Okay? When Izzy wakes up, look after her. I need to rest a bit longer."

Mary Helen would turn over. She'd try to fall back asleep, hoping he'd goddamn disappear for a couple more hours, because God knows she felt about ready to die. She deserved a little sleep-in after the week she suffered through.

This life of hers had not turned into the cakewalk she thought it would be when she boarded that westbound train so long ago. With an express one-way ticket she bought with her own money, she travelled straight to this, her own demise.

Little Antony turned his back on his mother because he knew beyond a doubt that there was no use in waiting a minute longer for her to do that one good thing even he knew she ought to do. Get off the pity pot and go to church. Listen to the words. They make sense.

He rescued Izzy, all potty-trained and happy, from her crib. He sat her on the toilet and got her all scrubbed up and decent. After some milk and cereal and lots of sugar, the two of them wandered off to Sunday school.

Little ragamuffins, hair akimbo, clothes awry, they'd show up at the nearest church down the street. They wouldn't know where to turn when they got there, but some stranger would kneel down to their level and ask:

"Who do we have here, Little Man and Young Lady?"

"Izzy," Antony answered for his shy sister. "I'm Antony, named after the Saint of Lost Things. My mum sure as shooting will have a fit if you try to call me Tony."

"Then Antony it is."

That person, now long forgotten but her grace forever remembered, could not help but wonder "What on earth?" and "Where in the world were the parents?"

Manning the door, womaning the people into the sanctuary, shepherding young mums to the nursery, and showing all who entered the church the way to the Cross, were normal duties assigned to the greeters. They welcomed the ragged, worn out, and broken into the house of God.

He or she, whoever happened to be on duty that blessed Sunday morning as the gatekeeper to the house of Eema Mother, was in a quandary, thinking, *should we call Children's Services, because surely something isn't right?*

But Antony, sensing her hesitation, would answer as quick as you please.

"Mum's still in bed. She knows we're here and that we want to go to Sunday School. You can ask her if you want. We live up the street."

"Then let me show you where your class is." The kind adult, who'd never experienced this literal sort of hungering and thirsting for the kingdom of God in one so young, would ignore their suspicions and shepherd the brother and sister hand-in-hand towards Eema Mother, whose love for children in this harsh world knows no bounds.

In this way, Antony and Izzy, who didn't have a hope in hell, learned how to survive this dark world and wide. When it was snack time, they'd chow down on far more than was their fair share.

The adults didn't mind.

They somehow sensed these cute-as-a-button little strays who had shown up at their church door were all on their own and needed more love and care on this holy day of celebration than they would ever receive at home during the long week ahead of them.

Besides, the good people of this church in the heart of the city knew that there was no greater calling than to look after the least of these, the children of a lesser God—the One who fights tooth and nail for Her charges.

Less is always better, especially when it comes to divinity.

And sure as shooting, back home with red-hot James George long out of the picture, Mary Helen was sleeping with whomever happened to come along, another forgettable man with an emptied wallet. He'd be wrung out from a long night of drinking and carrying on.

The cupboards were indeed bare. The beer bottles were tipped out and drained.

There'd be nothing left in the house for the kids, just the nauseating, stale stench of spilled alcohol and stubbed-out cigarettes in overflowing ashtrays.

Antony and Izzy made sure to stuff their faces full at Sunday School with whatever they could grab. Just to be sure, they jammed a few more cookies into their pockets before they left.

The church people seeing all this would make a note to bring along a few more platefuls for the next Sunday on the off-chance that these little ones who'd always be welcome should show up again.

They'd wave them off and wish most heartily that they could indeed do more, it broke their hearts so. This world is no place for helpless little children whose parents don't give a care. They think only about their next drink and where they'll get the rent money that was due the Friday before.

Since they drank it all up, there wasn't a chance that they'd get another extension. This life is hard enough without people making it worse for themselves.

When Antony and Izzy got home, all churched up and filled to the top with snacks, and happy to have more squirreled in their pockets for later, Mary Helen would be sitting at the kitchen table with a cigarette hanging from her lip.

She'd be in a housecoat with her hair wrapped in a scarf. Her this-time-only lover would have fled the scene, kicked out of her bed, and gone back to his wife and kids, his dinky piece of tail hanging limp and useless between his legs.

Shame on him, Antony thought, *and all the others.*

Mary Helen would breathe out a sigh of relief. Her children, little angels, cherubs from on high, sent from Eema Mother to teach her the lessons she refused to learn, were the only joy she had in this world, wretched and dismal.

From deep down and underneath, these uncomfortable words niggled at her conscience. *You could do better.*

"I hear you, Eema Mother," Mary Helen replied, "but can't you just shut the hell up and let me be?"

One look at her son with his cowlick and hazel green eyes, and Mary Helen would think about how hard she fell for James George, the most beautiful man she'd ever laid her eyes on.

How he'd come to that dance in Rocky when she was there alone in her desperation, her husband Del at a camp working, her three boys at home with the sitter. She was so fed up she couldn't take it any longer—the poverty, the grind, the boys running wild, and not enough money to make it through to the end of the week. She needed to forget all her troubles, if only for one short night.

With Del away all the time, she was so lonesome she could cry.

A girl has to get out sometimes, she pouted as she put on her lipstick, her tightest skirt. My, how she looked even after three kids and her most colourful blouse pressed down, pulled together, straining at the buttons, and bursting forth in wild abandon.

Beige is the death of a woman, she thought as she slipped on her shoes and kissed her boys. "Nighty-night. Sleep tight."

Telling the sitter not to keep them up too late, she ran out the door and down the street to the dance hall. Her heels click-clacked on the sidewalk. She could hear the music playing and the people laughing. The sound of it all carried her away. She hoped in her heart of hearts that she'd never have to return again to her house of broken dreams on its dead-end street.

She drank in straight with no chaser her first sight of James George, and immediately thought she wouldn't mind sleeping with that gangly, big-boned boy. He could be her ticket out of here, so she set about stealing him from his date. He couldn't and wouldn't ever say no to her.

No man had, in fact, ever refused her offer of a lifetime's worth of earthly delight. He was twenty and she thirty-two. Her hips and breasts and legs and hair and laugh and mouth and eyes were everything a man could ever dream about.

James George was just the boy with money to burn and a new car to boot. He was as innocent as a lamb, and she was sexy as hell, and could conquer any man she wanted. And she did.

James George fell as hard for her as she for him. One day he found himself driving her and the boys in his spanking new '54 Bel Air two-door sedan on a trip to Granny's in Gleichen. While he spent the afternoon fixing the leaky roof, the boys fried ants with a magnifying glass and Mary Helen sat with her mother in the kitchen, smoking cigarettes and silently cursing the mess that was coming their way.

Granny's resentment burned in her throat. *This won't end well*, she worried.

That evening, Mary Helen and James George drove into Calgary. They promised that they'd return in the morning. James George had some business to attend to and some papers to sign. They'd be back around ten with bacon and eggs and bread and butter and a couple gallons of milk.

Except they never did. Granny was left to pick up the pieces that Mary Helen left behind.

"Goodbye, Del," is all Mary Helen wrote on a piece of paper before they left Rocky. "The boys are at Mother's. Pick them up. They're yours. I'm out of here."

And that was that.

The two had married in a fever in Victoria in 1943 where Del was stationed with the navy. She was nineteen and he twenty-seven. They lived from hand to mouth. Their kids were born one after another. When the war ended, they moved to Alberta, because that's where the jobs were. But nothing turned out quite as they expected.

Eema Mother, who shows mercy to all but not in the way Mary Helen expected, once again left her out in the cold.

Ten years later, poor Del, broke, beside himself, and with nowhere to turn, closed up the dump in Rocky. He drove to Gleichen, picked up the boys, and headed east to Winnipeg.

His sons had a rough childhood, of that there's no question. They somehow survived, but they never forgot. Mary Helen abandoned them. Motherless children, they needed more love and care than anyone else could ever have imagined.

How could anyone ever get over such a desertion? A runaway parent leaves an emptiness in a child's heart that can never be filled.

Even in his old age, Antony knew this to be true because that's exactly what she did to him and Izzy a few short years later.

She must have had her reasons, which Antony tried to fathom in his lifelong attempt to forgive her. No matter how hard he tried, though, the pain of his childhood was never more than a half a twain (six feet)[3] below the surface. It coursed from the very centre of his being into every aspect of his life.

It's a pain that ebbs and flows but doesn't go away.

---

[3] From Antony's reading of *Huckleberry Finn*. A mark twain is two fathoms, twelve feet, or 3.7 metres deep.

3

Run Away

Eighteen-year-old Mary Helen couldn't stand for a minute longer the grief and the sorrow that laid her out level and sobbing in that godforsaken prairie town where she was born and raised. As soon as she could, she followed the trajectory that her father Sigmund *von Gutrater*—which the immigration official wrote as Goodwrath—*Edler von Puchstein*, set in motion just before World War I. He brought his wife Maria *geboren* Graus and their children Adolf, Hilde, Hedy, Sigi, and Rudi to Canada from Austria.

Like her parents before her, Mary Helen travelled to the very end of the earth on a westbound train.

"I want to visit Hilde in Calgary," Mary Helen said. Her older sister changed her Austrian name to an English-sounding one. She didn't want anyone to know that she had cousins fighting for the Germans. Hedy and Rudi changed theirs, too.

"It's only for a few days," she pleaded as she and her youngest sister Grace finished the washing-up one evening at the end of June.

Mary Helen knew that her mother would have refused her, had she known the whole plan. She told her just enough to get out the door and onto the railway station platform.

"I'll see you Monday, Mum!"

Hilde worked as a cook in a restaurant and thought she could get Mary Helen hired on as a dishwasher. If she proved herself, she'd eventually serve tables, but that wouldn't be for a while.

"Get your foot in the door," Hilde advised her younger sister. "Show Mr. Brown what you're made of. If we Gutraters know anything, it's how to work."

There'd be no telling what the future would hold for Mary Helen, with her well-turned ankles, red lips, clear singing voice, and confident laugh. She worked for a couple of weeks, washing dishes piled higher than she was tall in a sink deeper than a cast-iron, claw-footed bathtub fit for the Queen of England.

Then one day, Mr. Brown, a pencil behind his ear, asked Mary Helen to come in for the supper shift with a pretty dress on.

"You've served tables before, haven't you?"

Mary Helen demurred and hurried to tell Hilde the good news. For the rest of July, she learned the hard way how to waitress, taking orders and serving tables with armloads of plates. Appetizers, entrées, desserts, coffees, and drinks.

Always to the left, Mary Helen reminded herself as she served her customers. *Always to the left.*

Remembering who ordered what, serving which drink to whom, getting her orders to the cook, picking them up as soon as they were ready, and keeping track of her customers. Making sure they paid their bills before they left was the easy part.

Mary Helen was a quick study. Wearing the right shoes, dealing with men's beseeching eyes and hands, and still getting their tips took a little practice.

She enjoyed herself, mostly. This lark she had gone on turned into quite an adventure. Everything was going her way. The only upsetting thing was when she didn't return to Gleichen that Monday weeks ago. Mum phoned the house the very next day, and Hilde simply handed it to Mary Helen. No warning.

"Here, Sis. It's for you."

When the yelling and the swearing were over, Mary Helen hung up and hurried off to work. She didn't give her mother or her youngest sister, the green-eyed Grace, another thought. Her shifts at the restaurant transformed themselves into weeks. Her change purse soon bulged with coins. Luckily, she didn't make more than one or two mistakes a night.

Mr. Brown was eager and willing to cut her some slack. He liked the way she smelled and delighted in what he saw.

One evening, when her shift was over, Mr. Brown followed her out to the back stoop. As she tucked her pay in her pocket, he offered her a cigarette. They smoked and watched the shooting stars, the Perseids. It was early August.

"You know, Mary Helen," Mr. Brown confided. "You're a fine waitress. I've kept my eye on you, and I like your work."

Mary Helen had heard this sort of talk before. She knew exactly where it was heading. She took a long pull on her smoke and exhaled slowly into the night air.

"Mr. Brown? How are your kids? Is the Mrs. still feeling poorly?"

She then stubbed out her cigarette, tossed her apron into the laundry, and hurried home. The next day, she counted out her money and bought a one-way ticket to Vancouver. From there, it was a ferry ride to her destination: Victoria, where all the fellas were.

The war had been going on for a couple of years when Mary Helen stepped off the ferry and made her way downtown. Hedy signed up and was in Halifax. Johnny, Rudi, Sig, and all the other young men in Gleichen were overseas. They were training in England, eating enough mutton to last a lifetime, and waiting for the fighting in Europe to start.

Only old men were left in Gleichen. They made Mary Helen's skin crawl.

How could I have been so naive? I'll never know.

She vowed then and there never again to allow a man to touch her without her consent. If there was to be any messing around, it'd be because she started it, not him.

I may not have much money, but I can still decide who unzips my skirt.

A day or two after her arrival, Mary Helen knew she made the right decision. Victoria was a city filled with young men who welcomed young women like her. She found a job and a room near downtown. All she did was order a coffee at Terry's on Douglas and Fort. She sat at the counter and chatted briefly with the harried woman being run off her feet.

"Looking for experienced help?" Mary Helen asked. "I could start right now."

"Let's see how you do," the woman said. She handed Mary Helen an apron and a notepad with a pen.

"The pay's nothing to speak of, but the tips are yours."

When the noon hour rush was over, Mary Helen landed herself a job.

"By the way, I'm looking for a place to stay. Know of something?"

"As a matter of fact, I do."

Work, a clean bed to sleep in, and energy to burn—now all Mary Helen needed was to find the right man.

Then one day, he walked through the door, tall, slim, and handsome. Del looked mighty fine. He scanned the tables and moved to one that Mary Helen was serving. She liked his style when he asked for the bill and remembered him for the size of his tip. She made sure that she served him the next time he came in for the Soup and Sandwich Special.

"Just wondering if you'd like to come dancing with me tonight?" Del asked, smiling.

"Meet me here after my shift?" Mary Helen asked. "I'll have to go home first and freshen up." She wasn't letting him out of her sight after he had taken the bait.

He held her hand as they strolled along the harbour front. The Crystal Gardens was only a few blocks away.

Del looked smart in his dress uniform. Mary Helen was wearing a sensible pleated skirt and long-sleeved blouse that showed off her Rita Hayworth figure.

The band was already playing "Stardust" when they got there. By the time they took off their coats, everyone was on the floor dancing to "String of Pearls." When the band segued to "You Made Me Love You," the two young lovers were enjoying a little heaven on earth. They stayed on the dance floor all the livelong night.

The two didn't see one another again until Del's next leave. Mary Helen met him on the grounds at St Ann's Academy. They spent a Sunday afternoon strolling through Beacon Hill Park. Standing in the sun on Stone Bridge near Goodacre Lake, they watched the swans preside over their watery kingdom, in-state and imperial.

Mary Helen began to speak about her parents. Del smoked his cigarette and listened.

"They came to Canada from Austria in 1912 and found a place to live on Maggie Street in Calgary. It wasn't much compared to what they left behind in Graz, but was close to where Papa worked in the office for Pat Burns. Papa had more education than Mum, and his English was better than hers. He got on quite well, but Mum always had a foreign accent that embarrassed us kids.

"Joey and the twins Johnny and Margaret were born in that house. When the anti-German riots broke out in 1916, Mr. Burns was forced to let Papa go. His man Christian Bartsch knew of a place in Gleichen. It wasn't much more than a shack, but it would give the family a roof over their heads.

"Papa was rounded up with all the Germans and aliens from the Austro-Hungarian Empire and put in an Internment Camp until the war was over. When he was released, he came home and worked as a labourer until a returning vet was hired and replaced him.

"Papa took the train into Calgary, where he worked for Sink Lee Market Gardens. The pay was terrible, but his employers were good people, and didn't cheat him.

"By the time Grace and I came along, Mum and Papa knew not to give us German-sounding names. Bosch, Hun, Fritz, or Austrian, it didn't matter. We weren't welcome anywhere.

"Then Papa had a heart attack in November 1928 while he was chopping wood. He was 53 when he died. His death was a terrible tragedy for our family. My kid sister Grace had her first birthday the day after. It wasn't much of a celebration. I was a four-year-old at the time, but I sure have some big memories.

"Mum struggled to make ends meet, and we were dirt poor. Clean, don't get me wrong. Mum wouldn't let us out of the house if our threadbare dresses were at all smudged. Every square inch of them may have been darned, but they were spotless and newly-pressed. She was a proud woman and would never let us forget, no matter how hard we tried, that we were Gutraters, Austrians of noble descent.

"Mum called herself the daughter of a matchmaker, which sounded much more like a fairytale than a daughter of a prosperous businessman. Her family in Schwanberg south of Graz made safety matches with red phosphorous. They were good for catching fire, but not much for matching couples for marriage. Daughter of a matchmaker, indeed.

"What a row Papa and Mum had with his family when they told them that they wanted to get married. His sister Adrienne, who preferred the French spelling of her name, said rather dismissively that he was marrying a country girl.

"The Gutraters were high-ups with the railroad, and had little good to say about those who lived outside the city. They were too provincial for sophisticates from Vienna. However, they changed their tune when Maria kept the family together during the decades ahead.

"Where Mum learned to cook all those delicious Austrian meals, I'll never know. Homemade noodles, green beans fried in breadcrumbs, and plum dumplings coated with sugar—just the thought of them makes my mouth water.

"Can you imagine? We were living in a four-room house with ten kids, no electricity, running water, or indoor plumbing, just an outhouse, fully equipped with catalogues and newspapers. Only the Gleichen east-end snobs had toilet paper. We lived in that shack for years. Then the time came that my older brothers and sisters left home, Adolf first. He married Ina. Hilde married Alf and moved to Calgary. Then Sig met Vera.

"We were poor, but Mum managed to serve us goulash at supper, loaves of fresh-baked bread at lunch, and oatmeal or cornmeal for breakfast. I remember our old cow Bessie, but we kids never had milk. To buy flour, yeast, sugar, and coffee, Mum had to sell the milk and cream. We kept our own chickens. Every Sunday after Mass, we'd gather around our huge table. Mum served us platters of delicious fried eggs, golden yolks runny in the middle and sprinkled with paprika.

"As the years went by, we moved to a bigger house. I don't recall how many of us were home at the time, maybe six or seven. Of course, we still had oil lamps, a coal furnace, and a wood stove. Our water came from a pump in the backyard. It was my job to fill the bucket. Sure, we had running water, as long as I ran to get it.

"Then the war started. Three brothers signed up. My sister Hedy ended up as a WAC in Halifax. When I turned 18, I had to escape. It felt as if the whole world was on the move. Besides, I didn't want another old man trying to feel me up. I left as soon as I could."

When Mary Helen finally finished speaking, Del pulled her close. They walked towards the busy city. Neither would be left behind, if he had anything to do about it. He would have to survive this war first and get a job.

"What do you say, Mary Helen?" he asked as they strolled past the provincial legislature. "Shall we get married? There's got to be a JP around the corner."

For once in her life, Mary Helen hesitated—not out of reluctance, but to build some tension. Del had to think it was all his idea. Then she jumped in, feet first.

"Why certainly, sir. I thought you'd never ask."

4

Summer

1958

One of Antony's earliest memories is of hurrying down Centre Street in Calgary with Mary Helen clutching his hand and holding Izzy in the other. They were half-running towards Neil's car, which was parked down the block.

James George had been working on the rig for several weeks, and Mary Helen was stuck home alone and miserable. Tired of it all, she was waiting half-afraid for him to return. If anything wasn't to his liking, it'd set him off. He'd throw the aluminium tumblers at the wall and slam the Melmac dishes into the sink. He was as volatile a man as he was a fervent lover, which made being with him a living hell .

One time in a rage, James George broke Mary Helen's arm.

Then he found her in bed with Neil, the French-Canadian who'd been renting the basement suite.

James George's rig had shut down without notice and he had a couple days off. He drove his '58 Buick as fast as he could. He was desperate to see his kids. He was damn sure a roll in the sack with Mary Helen would do him a world of good.

Then his world collapsed.

"What the hell are you doing?" he hollered as he entered the bedroom and saw Neil struggling to put his pants on and Mary Helen trying to make herself decent.

"You better be goddamn gone when I come back," James George warned Neil. His temper flared like a gas well ready to explode.

"And you!" He pointed to Mary Helen. "We've got some talking to do."

He stormed out of the house, not daring to give Antony or Izzy a glance, lest he turn back to the bedroom and do something he'd regret. He had enough sense to keep going, because he was Christ mad enough to kill those two.

Mary Helen and Neil stuffed some things into a suitcase. Neil took the first load out to the car. Mary Helen grabbed the kids.

"We better get out of here before your Daddy returns."

Antony knew enough not to argue. There was no stopping his Dad once he blew his top. He and little Izzy were kids. Mummy needed loving, not hurting. Anyone could see that.

They ran bawling, scared, and afraid, down the street towards the car. Its doors were open, and Neil gunned the engine.

"She's full of gas. I have a place in Exshaw we can go to. It's not much, but it'll do until we find something better."

Mary Helen crawled into the backseat and held her son and daughter. She cried her heart out.

"That James George! The nerve!"

She didn't deserve to be treated like this. Yeah, he found her in bed with Neil, but so what? She knew he was cheating on her. What's good for the gander?

He should have found work close to home and stayed right where he belonged. Then she wouldn't have given Neil the time of day.

It's all his fault.

Neil nosed the old Ford out onto the street. When it was clear, he did a U-ey and headed up the hill toward the highway. He drove out to Cochrane and was about to turn on the 1A to Exshaw, a mining town with a limestone quarry nearby, when Antony said that he needed to pee.

They stopped at MacKay's for ice cream, and that helped to settle their nerves a bit. Antony strafed Germans while standing at the toilet, Neil used the urinal, and Mary Helen took Izzy to the Ladies'. When they were done, Antony washed his hands with soap and water. They went into the ice cream shop and Antony asked for Neapolitan. Izzy wanted strawberry. Mary Helen ordered rum-and-raisin and Neil got himself chocolate. They sat in the sun and enjoyed their treats. To passersby, they were a happy family on a drive out to the country.

The road to Exshaw passed through the Stoney Indian Reservation. Antony tried to imagine what it was like to live there in the olden days. Running buck-naked in the summer with a spear appealed to him. Hunting buffalo and deer and sleeping in teepees and never having to bathe fired his imagination. Taking scalps, going on scouting trips, being brave, wearing eagle feathers, burning sweetgrass, and passing the peace pipe thrilled him to no end. He should have been so lucky.

Antony wanted more than anything to own a pinto named Cheyenne. He dreamt about riding bareback in the foothills and looking across wide valleys to the mountains. He loved black-eyed susans and the smell of wild roses. He wished he could wear moccasins and leather leggings and eat with his hands. He would smell of woodsmoke and never be afraid again. He wanted to be brave, wear war paint, and face his enemies until they were the ones who backed away in fear.

There's no way any man would ever hurt Antony's mummy if he had his own knife and sheathe.

Neil pulled the car up to a little trailer nestled in the bush. Antony burst out the back door. He ran everywhere, exploring and running and laughing and jumping and stomping his feet. He had energy to burn and a lifetime of living ahead of him. He couldn't stay cooped up for a minute longer.

"I'm hungry," he yelled to his mum, and ran off, not waiting for an answer.

Mary Helen poked through the kitchen cupboards and opened the little fridge.

"It looks like we'll need some eggs and milk and cereal and bread for starters. We can get the rest after your first payday. I'll get this place cleaned up while you drive into town."

"The sign at the gate said they're hiring. I'll stop in and ask for a job. I bet I can start tomorrow."

Mary Helen hugged Neil.

"That's great, darling. The kids and I appreciate it."

Neil liked Mary Helen and loved her children. He thought he was the luckiest man in the world when he moved into their basement. He made sure he stayed out of the picture when James George was home. He kept himself busy until the coast was clear.

Except this last time, James George showed up a day early and caught him and Mary Helen in the sack.

It's a good thing he had an inkling about the job at Exshaw and already had this trailer lined up. He knew the clock was ticking and wanted to get out of the city before James George came after him with both barrels blasting.

Now Neil had a woman to come home to and a boy and a girl to father. He didn't mind that they weren't his own. They were fine kids. His life was turning out pretty good, after all.

Every day he went to work at the mine. On his way home, Antony would meet him. They'd walk together.

Antony wondered if Neil still had part of the cheese sandwich Mum packed in his lunch kit the night before. "Could I have a bite?"

Neil would look, and sure enough, there was a half left. It had a slice of Velveeta cheese and salt and pepper on white bread with butter. Antony would eat it all up and chatter nonstop until they got to the trailer.

That became one of life's rituals for them. Neil made sure he always had something leftover. Mary Helen always packed a little extra for their walk home.

How could you not help but love a kid like that? Neil wondered. The little boy, with his eager bright eyes and curious mind that wouldn't stop, was so gosh-darn adorable, he'd break your heart.

Antony was the finest boy around, and Neil couldn't be happier. Mary Helen made beautiful babies, and he could hardly wait to have a few of his own.

Neil wanted more than anything to take Mary Helen to Beaumont, the prettiest town in the province, and introduce her and the kids to his family and go to church at St. Vital's high on the hill.

"But isn't she a married woman?" Neil's mother asked when they made the trip in December just before the Blessed Birth.

"No," Neil answered. "She never got around to marrying James George. He seduced her, and before she knew it, they had a son together, and then a daughter. Soon he was beating the hell out of her. If she didn't get away, he'd start in on the kids."

That was just the kind of man James George was, like his father and grandfather before him: wife-beaters who ruined the lives of the people who mattered most to them.

You wouldn't believe that James George's grandmother on his mother's side, Elizabeth Beaumont from Galashiels, Scotland, was a captain in the Salvation Army. While her faith didn't take hold in her grandson's life, it skipped a generation, landing squarely in her great-grandson's.

It goes to show that prayers often get answered, but not always in a person's lifetime.

Or in ways people expect.

"No, Mary Helen wasn't married," Neil said. "But she needed unchaining, and I was there to help her. I rescued her from a terrible situation.

"Sure, she has kids, but have you seen them? You couldn't ask for nicer. That Antony is as fine a boy as you could ever imagine, and Izzy? She's a porcelain doll."

Against their misgivings, Neil's good Catholic family accepted Mary Helen as she was. They took her son and daughter in and treated them as their own.

"It's the least that we can do," they said when Mary Helen thanked them for their kindness.

Grace received and grace given is the way of faith. What goes around comes around. You try to be better than you are and trust that something good will come of it.

Antony felt safer than he had ever been under James George's roof. He was a happy little kid with smiles on his face and stars in his eyes. He believed in Santa Claus and the Tooth Fairy. He knew that Jesus from church would come again in the clouds. He was grateful that there was always more than enough food on the table for him to have seconds and a warm bed to sleep in when he was tired.

One spring day in Exshaw, the forest floor was covered with fallen leaves. King boletes were poking their dirt-covered heads out from the ground.

"It's time for a feast," Neil said.

They pulled up a few of the large, brownish-yellow capped mushrooms, cleaned them, fried them in butter and garlic, and ate a meal fit for the Queen. In the summer, they ate giant puffballs sliced and diced and of course sautéed in garlic and butter.

Antony fell in love with the taste of wild mushrooms. They reminded him of the best part of his childhood, when he lived in the mountains and learned to ride bicycle.

5

No Looking Back

In the fall, they moved from the little trailer in the woods below Exshaw Mountain to a roadside motel, north of the tracks in Canmore. It was a small, two-room cabin with a kitchenette, sitting area, and a black-and-white TV for cheering on the Habs and hating the Leafs on *Hockey Night in Canada*. There was a small bedroom where the kids could crash while the adults stayed up late and carried on.

Antony's hero was Maurice Richard, and nine was his lucky number, just like the Rocket's.

The snow reached the eaves of the cabin. In all his life, the drifting snow had never been as high. He spent sun-filled afternoons ploughing through chest-high drifts, making trails and paths and intersections in the snow. He, Izzy, and their friends played Fox and Geese in the trenches until they were rosy-cheeked, covered in snow, and ready for hot chocolate.

In the spring, Antony and his friends played Cowboys and Indians in the woods, except nobody wanted to be a cowboy. They ran barefoot up into the nearby hills, making rifles out of long sticks, and bows and arrows out of saplings. Pussy willows were the scalps they collected to show their bravery, peanut butter sandwiches their pemmican, and hockey cards their fur pelts.

During the summer, they picked bright orange tiger lilies in the forest, fragrant wild rose blossoms that grew in the sun, and bobbing yellow black-eyed susans. They crept along trails and climbed the high hills that reached toward the mountains.

Without an adult in sight, this small tribe of Stoneys ran naked in high meadows. They tried, to no avail, to light fires with pieces of stone.

Watching for marauding Blackfoot, they kept their eyes peeled for intruders. Not once did they leave their women and children unprotected.

On most Sundays, Antony would cross the train tracks and walk into town. He'd come late to the whitewashed church and sit at the back.

People would be kneeling and praying and saying AMEN. Then they'd kneel and pray and stand and sit and sing some more. Just when he thought he couldn't stand for a moment longer, they'd suddenly AMEN and sit and listen for a spell. Then they'd stand and cross themselves and kneel and pray for this, that, and some other thing. He didn't have a clue what was going on. But because he felt good being there, he wasn't going anyplace else.

Anything was better than going back home and smelling his mother's sour breath as she lay passed out on the couch.

Some adult would notice the little boy and show him to the room where he belonged. He'd colour and sing with the others. They'd read a story from the Book of the People and learn about Eema Mother, who cared for them, red, yellow, black, and white.

They were all precious in her sight.

Antony would go home happier than he'd been all week.

One afternoon, a helicopter was taking off and landing in the field beside their place. Neil sat on the porch with a cigarette in his mouth. Mary Helen had her pant legs rolled up to her knees, her feet free and easy, her nails painted red and luscious.

Izzy was dozing in the little bed that they found for her at the dump.

Neil jumped up.

"Antony! It's time you learned to ride."

While Antony was at church, Neil hauled a ratty old bike out of the junk heap. He straightened the forks and fixed the tires and tightened the spokes. He oiled the chain and lowered the seat as far as it could go, and plunked the little boy on it as quick as you please.

"Look where you want to go and the bike will follow," Neil said.

He pushed Antony down the long stretch of grass between the road and the field, where the pilot was practising his take-offs and landings.

Antony soon got the hang of it, and Neil picked up the pace.

"See that post at the far end?" he asked. "Whatever you do, keep your eye on it!"

Antony was pedaling as fast as he could go.

"Now steer the bike in that direction," Neil said. "Just don't look back."

Soon Antony was flying. Then Neil had to slow down to catch his breath.

When Neil stopped running, Antony was on his own. He looked back and was startled.

Swinging the handlebars in the direction he was looking, he tumbled to the grass. He started to cry, not because he was hurt, but because he didn't want to stop.

Neil got him back up on the bike.

"See your mum? Now aim for her. Whatever you do, don't look back. I'll be running alongside you."

Antony rode his bike straight to Mary Helen.

"Look at me!" he yelled. "Look at me!"

She looked at her son and beamed, and when he fell off his bike, she ran to him. They laughed and laughed.

Antony pleaded with Neil.

"Again, Uncle Neil? Again?"

"Of course, but first, I better teach you how to stop."

Antony pedaled as hard as he could and smiled and laughed and kept looking ahead. He didn't take his eyes off where he wanted to go, never again in his whole life. He rode as if his life depended on it, straight and true toward Eema Mother God. Mostly, that is. Except when he dillied and when he dallied, meandering in mazes, lost and alone.

The helicopter took off and landed and took off and landed again and again.

Antony looked back to his mother and Neil, who was standing beside her and smoking. He fell to the grass and hurt himself and started to bawl and got angry at himself. He jumped back on the bike and started pumping the pedals so fast Neil couldn't catch him.

"What a good boy you are! Everyone falls when learning something new. The only way to succeed is to get back on. Just pedal and look ahead until you want to stop, then pedal backwards. The brake will lock the wheel, and you'll skid to a stop."

Antony pedaled as hard as he could and stood on the back pedal. Sure enough, the wheel locked. He skidded to a stop on a patch of gravel right in front of Mary Helen.

He raised such a cloud of dust that she blew her top. Neil laughed so hard that Izzy woke from her nap. For once, all was good in the little boy's universe.

Then he suddenly had to pee.

When he came out of the bathroom and his hands were all wet and smelling of Ivory soap, Neil smiled at the boy.

"Since you've ridden all afternoon and had so much fun you don't know what else to do, I'll buy you a Coca-Cola and an Oh Henry bar."

"Please, Uncle Neil," Antony asked. "Could I have a Mountain Dew and a Mr. Big instead?"

Neil laughed and Mary Helen cried. They were a happy little family, and the helicopter pilot kept practising his take-offs and landings, and Antony burned to ask him for a ride.

Later, when the pilot refused, Antony was so disappointed he could cry. But Neil tried to comfort him.

"Don't be sad, Antony, you have your whole life ahead of you. There's lots of time for your dreams to come true."

While Neil wasn't completely right, he wasn't wrong, either. He was just a bit more optimistic than the situation warranted.

6

Christmas

Antony couldn't believe how lucky he was, sitting there in the front seat snuggled up against his mother, Izzy stretched out on the back seat sleeping, and Neil hunched forward driving through a blizzard back to Banff on the Trans-Canada.

They'd spent Christmas with Neil's family in Beaumont and attended Mass at St Vital's. Antony wondered for the whole trip. He had whispered to Santa Claus at The Hudson's Bay before they left Banff that he wanted a fire truck for Christmas, and now one actually showed up under the tree for him in Beaumont. *Santa must be real!*

He had his suspicions before, but now he believed. He would never doubt again.

Later, with his own children and grandchildren, Antony would say, it's perfectly fine not to believe if that's your choice, but all you'll get for Christmas will be socks and underwear. To this day, like him, they believe with a conviction that has not grown weary. A little faith is all it takes.

Before heading west into the mountains, Neil stopped at the auction on Blackfoot Trail in Calgary to see if there were any post-Christmas deals to be had. He picked up a blue girl's bike for next to nothing.

"You'll grow into it, Antony," he said. "This may be a girl's, but it'll take you places you've never dreamed. Trust me. We'll get you a boy's next time. Izzy can have this one when she's grown a bit."

Antony didn't mind. Honestly. He was happy to be going home. That fall they'd moved from Canmore into a small house on Marten Street in

Banff. He could hardly wait to see his friend Bobby Ray and show off his red fire truck and his bicycle.

Bobby Ray still needed training wheels, and Antony would soon be able to leave him in the dust when they raced down Banff Avenue on their way to the candy shop.

The whole way home and past the Park Gate, Antony whined and pleaded and wept and pouted and begged Neil to stop the car and let him ride his bike on the side of the road. Neil finally relented, because in spite of the snow, anything would be better than letting the little bugger carry on. There was no way he'd stop until he got what he wanted, and Neil eventually caved.

"There's no traffic, and what's this wall of snow to a born-and-bred Albertan?" he asked Mary Helen. "Besides, we're almost home. What's the harm?"

Mary Helen marveled at the fine man she had invited into her bed.

They rolled to a stop by the power station. Neil placed his hand on the window and asked Antony if he could feel the pane.

"No, not today, Uncle Neil," Antony said. "It still doesn't hurt."

"Must be an adult thing," Neil replied, and Mary Helen chuckled.

They got out of the car, and the snow swirled around him and the boy. The wind blew down from the mountain. He hoped this wouldn't take too long, because he didn't want the boy to get frostbite.

"You ride in front, in the headlights, so I can watch you. Stay on the side of the road in case another vehicle comes along."

Antony pedaled as hard as he could until the snow got deeper and deeper. His gears started to freeze, and he had to stop because he couldn't go any further.

Neil jumped out of the car, bundled the boy in with his mother, and put the bike in the trunk. They crept the rest of the way into Banff, the snow was heavy and deep.

Even with the bicycle, the days weren't all sunshine and jawbreakers for Antony. At least Mummy and Uncle Neil weren't drinking like they used to. On Sundays they'd sometimes go to Mass at St Mary's. Mary Helen went along because Neil insisted. In the evening, they'd watch the skaters at the rink and listen to Strauss waltzes over the loudspeakers. Couples like long-time lovers would glide in ¾ time, their arms linked, their legs in unison, graceful and languorous.

One winter's day, they were driving on the highway to Canmore and Neil hit an icy patch. The car tires cut into the ditch. The door popped open, and Mary Helen and the kids were thrown out. Izzy rolled into a snowball and came to a stop by a fence post, but she wasn't hurt.

Antony, however, was trapped under the car with a mouth full of snow. He was about to stop breathing when Neil grabbed him by the legs and pulled him out. He cleared his mouth and throat and pounded him on the back, and another Miracle of Miracles occurred.

Antony started to breathe again, all thanks be to Eema Mother, who knows the hairs on your head.

Mary Helen still hadn't learned her lesson or mended her ways. She was suddenly wracked with a pain that made her double over and start to bleed.

"That's twice," Eema Mother said from on high, but Mary Helen continued to live like there was no tomorrow.

An ambulance scooped her and Antony up and took them to the hospital, where Antony was examined and released into Neil's care. Mary Helen had to stay for a few days. She was pregnant with Neil's baby and had a miscarriage.

Neil was so heartbroken and devastated that he didn't know if he was coming or going. Mary Helen was so relieved that she didn't have to bear another child she could hardly look Neil in the eye.

In the summer Antony rode his bicycle up and down Banff Avenue. Neil worked at the mine and Mary Helen waitressed in the evenings.

The Stoney Nakodas from Morley set up camp outside of town.

They dressed in buckskin and beads and wore headdresses. They left their cars and trucks parked well out back, away from the grounds, and rode horses and ponies. They hauled their gear on travois and lived in teepees. Tourists took their photographs while they smoked peace pipes, danced, and beat drums.

Antony listened to their singing. Captivated by their free and easy lives, he could only imagine what it was like to live in the olden days when Daddies loved Mummies, and children played happily. Seldom was heard an angry swear, and mornings weren't clouded with cigarette smoke and smelling of beer.

He attended the rodeo and once even entered a teepee. He ate pemmican, watched the dances, and loved the smell of woodsmoke. Everything he knew about The People Who Cook with Stones, he learned at Indian Days and at The Trading Post, where he first dreamed of owning a buckskin jacket with beads and tassels and trim.

While the adult Antony still dreamt of owning such a coat, he wondered if the times had passed for such boyish dreams.

He hoped not.

Often, this broken down, about-to-be-scuttled wreck of a family would go to the Banff dump to watch the bears. Sometimes the family scavenged the treasures other people junked. After one of their trips, they came home with a wind-up phonograph and a box of old seventy-eights with the likes of such singers as Vera Lynn, The Andrews Sisters, and songs like "Deep in the Heart of Texas" and "San Fernando Valley."

Neil would put on a record, grab Mary Helen around the waist, and take her for a turn on the floor in their tiny cabin. Antony and Izzy would fight for space under the warm blanket on the sofa, their eyes on their grace-filled, happy mother.

One evening, they drove the long way home, stopping at the lookout over the Vermillion Lakes to watch the sun glance off Mount Rundle. There were some bears ambling by. Neil pulled his old Ford a little closer. One of the older cubs tried to stretch its neck into the car and take a swipe at Izzy's ice cream. Mary Helen, swearing at Neil, rolled the window up before the bear could get its head in.

"Let's get the hell out of here, before he crawls right in."

In September 1960, Antony and his friend Bobby Ray started school.

One day when they were coming home, little Bobby Ray asked the much-taller Antony if he knew what was in that red house on the telephone pole.

"No idea," Antony said. "Should we look? It's got a door."

"Boost me up?" Bobby Ray asked. Antony cupped his hands together and Bobby Ray stepped into them. Antony hoisted him up. Bobby Ray was about to pull open the little glass door to see what was inside when the old lady in the corner house came out on the porch, yelling her head off.

"What in God's name do you little shits think you're doing?"

"Just looking, lady," Antony replied.

"Well, that's no toy. You come and sit here while I call the police." She pointed to her step.

The two boys scattered like jackrabbits being chased by hungry coyotes. They ran home their separate ways and never walked by that house again, in case the old bird recognized them and called the cops. There was no way they were going to jail because of her, that miserable old snitch.

The next time Antony checked the inside of a call box on a telephone pole, he was better prepared and living in Calgary with Mary Helen's new boyfriend. He and his pal Matthew pulled on the lever and broke the glass. They hid in the bushes until the firetruck came barreling down the road and couldn't find a fire anywhere in the neighbourhood at all.

The boys were so chuffed and puffed they owned the city in that dark night. They couldn't wait until they got to school the next day to brag to their friends about what they did.

7

Calgary

While Antony thrived in Banff, the relationship between Mary Helen and Neil withered. He wanted children and she didn't. She had more than enough with Tom, Dick, and Harry. With Antony and Izzy now on a tear, that was that. Her child-bearing years were over. Then, before she knew it, Neil was gone, and Antony was heartbroken.

Once again Mary Helen waited tables and counted her pennies. She started cooking and they began moving, always before the rent was due. By the time Antony started Grade Two, they were back in Calgary.

Mary Helen skidded down the row. She dragged the kids out of one school and put them into another. She had more lovers than Antony cared to remember, but they always had room for her in their bed and a place on the couch for her children.

What else could she do? She couldn't afford to live on her own.

Money's tight, kids, needs must. When the Devil's in the driving seat, you've got to hang on. Once you start down a road, there's no stopping.

For a while they lived near the Crowfoot School on the west side of Calgary. One evening, some of Mary Helen's friends were over for a few drinks. She called Antony from his room and asked what he wanted to be when he grew up. He said, "A missionary to the Indians up north."

"What a kid! What planet did he come from?"

Everyone in the room laughed as they reached for another beer and lit another cigarette and told another story that didn't bear repeating.

39

Antony soon learned that the more people drink the stupider they become. One drink is fine, two borderline, but three? The joke's on them, and it's not worth the punchline.

One day, just for the hell of it, Mary Helen ordered a twelve-volume set of stories with red covers through the mail. They arrived shortly before they skipped the rent, and she lost the bill in the shuffle.

In retrospect, that was the best bit of thievery that could have ever happened to Antony. Throughout the rest of his boyhood, Antony read those illustrated stories about a brown-bearded, white-skinned teacher, blue-eyed mother, and faithful father; raging Samson, majestic Pharaoh, wiry David; regal Queen of Sheba, wise King Solomon; Manna and the Quail, Wandering for forty Years in the Desert, Moses holding back the Red Sea; evading the Egyptian army; Assyrians, Nebuchadnezzar; Ladder to Heaven, Elijah and his Cloak, and the Widow of Zarephath.

Those red volumes were full of stories about brutal lives lived on the edge of a sword. They gave him hope.

As he grew older and got a library card of his own, a Bookmobile would come to Quickfall once a week. He'd read and re-read *Call of the Wild, Curse of the Viking Grave, Lost in the Barrens, Grey Seas, Mutiny on the Bounty, Never Cry Wolf, Owls in the Family, People of the Deer, Swiss Family Robinson,* and *White Fang*; and all the Hardy Boys, Reader's Digests in the house; not to mention Alexandre Dumas, Zane Grey, Sir Walter Scott, Jules Verne, and anything else that the gorgeous librarian would show him; or the *Blue Lagoon* novels he'd find on his own. And the Pearl S. Bucks, Rachel Carsons, Robert Heinleins, Madeleine L'Engels that She Whom He Adored would allow him to sign out, age appropriate or not.

He was her most faithful reader, and she knew as well as he that any story between the covers was far better than the lives that they were both living.

Books were her livelihood and his salvation.

Of course, that was some years down the road when puberty hit, and books and breasts fired Antony's imagination.

In the meantime, girls were friends. There was nothing complicated about the relationships he had with them.

Before Antony finished Grade Two, they were on the move again. They lived for a time in a walk-up apartment, south of downtown. The streets were grimy. The people were desperately poor. There wasn't a blade of grass anywhere, just cigarette butts and shards of glass from broken beer bottles. Antony felt ashamed. He knew that they were in a bad situation and hoped better days were ahead.

Mary Helen brought in barely enough money to feed them and buy smokes. That year, Antony had chicken pox and also his first cigarette. It tasted so awful that he threw up in the toilet.

By the time he started Grade Three, they moved to a suite on the top floor of an old walk-up near Macleod Trail. Antony strolled down leafy avenues to school and often came home to an empty house.

One time, Antony was left alone for three days. He ate macaroni that he cooked with hot water running from the tap and slathered with butter. He kept the door locked and a chair jammed under the handle because he was afraid that Child Services would come and haul him away.

When *The Juliette Show* came on the television, he blew her a kiss and prayed that she would come and rescue him, but she never did.

One evening, the landlord tried to enter the suite and show it, but couldn't, because Antony stuck a knife in the casing and blocked it shut. The next morning, Mary Helen pulled him out of school and whisked him to another house in another neighbourhood. Uprooted again. Poor kids. Little Izzy was now in Grade One.

Antony's heart broke for her, but she was a care and a burden too great for him. He could barely keep his wits about him.

There was another boyfriend and another opportunity to make it through another month. Antony stayed in the bedroom he shared with Izzy while the adults drank beer in the living room. He crawled into bed and read another armload of stories. He fell in love with Cape Town and Table Mountain. The Black Beauty series. The Bobbsey Twins. Nancy

Drew. He read to escape and learned to relish happy endings. Reading gave him hope.

Then they had to move again. This time, Mary Helen had nowhere to turn, so she headed out to Gleichen, to Granny's, and all the bad memories that made her hate the place.

Antony loved his Granny because she smelled of freshly-risen bread dough and cigarettes. He loved the smell of the prairie sage and the sound of the meadowlark in the morning.

8

Meadowlarks and Sage

1964

Antony and Granny sat across from each other at a wooden table in a small house that burned to the ground many years later. He didn't know her name. To him, she was Granny, for that was all anyone ever called her. No one ever thought of her as Maria (*geboren* Graus) von Gutrater, Edler von Puchstein.

"Just out of curiosity," Antony asked. When she told him, he thought it was weird. She printed it on a piece of paper. The words on the page bore little resemblance to the sounds that Antony heard.

When he saw it for the first time, he laughed and laughed. He didn't see what she said. She read *"Graus, von Gutrater"* with her finger under each word, and he heard. "Grouch from Gut Rats." That was Granny when she blew her lid, which could be just about any time.

Then she read, *"Aid-Lure Fon Poochk-Shtine."*

He laughed. "Elder with Puke Stain!"

This boy! she thought. *He is just like all the others.*

They sat at the table and words stumbled out of her mouth. German and English tangled together. She could hardly speak her adopted tongue, had forgotten most of her mother tongue, and what was left, she stirred into a goulash of Canadian-grown vegetables—no meat, though. Only potatoes, turnips, onions, carrots, cabbage, and of course, paprika.

The sky rested lightly on the prairie outside Gleichen. Newcomers felt that they were on top of the world, at the outer edge of the universe, as far from the centre of human civilization as possible. They hated the

43

loneliness, the cosmic emptiness, and the isolation that the prairie imposed upon them.

People raised there embraced the freedom that the prairie offered, an open sky and an abundant land that easily bore the grace of getting to know it well.

Granny smoked a cigarette, while Antony devoured a bowl of Corn Flakes and hurried out to play. She sipped her coffee. Their breakfast was over.

Chairs with layers of paint stood at each end of the table and one to the side. The fourth waited in the corner. It was the company chair, used only when the table was pulled out from under the window and positioned in the centre of the room. The sun poured through the panes of glass and warmed the old woman in the early morning. By noon, it would be shaded, but at breakfast, the soft, lacy curtains played lightly in the sun.

A gentle morning breeze traversed the prairie, carrying with it a scent of sage and the distant song of the meadowlark—*wheet wheewoo widdlywoo*—perched on a fence post across the rise.

Antony noticed all this, for he was unaccustomed to the sights, sounds, and smells of the open country. Visiting Granny in Gleichen, a small village fifty miles east of Calgary, this city boy couldn't have been happier. He was safe and felt at home, not knowing that his mother, along with his younger sister, Izzy, had abandoned him. He didn't know where they were.

Neither did Granny. She suspected though and seethed inside. She tried not to take out her bitterness on the boy. He appreciated that. They said nothing about his mother and sister. Their worst fears filled the space between them. It was a chasm that drew them together.

The Beatle's "Hard Day's Night" played on the radio every half-hour. Antony was nine and Granny seventy-nine. When she cashed her pension cheque, she smoked Daily Mail cigarettes. When she ran out, she went back to hand-rolled Players tobacco and Vogue papers. She found hope in her cigarettes.

There is no point in going on if you can't have a smoke, she thought to herself.

For their lunch of buttered bread and jam, they sat at the small table. She looked at him when he talked. His happy chatter was almost non-stop, except for when his mouth was full of vanilla ice cream that he ate with his mouth closed and his temples throbbing with pain.

He may have been a little chatterer, but she loved him anyway, this old woman in her thin, cotton dress.

She will be dead before the next summer comes and he will burst into tears, his body heaving in sorrow. His mother will force him to swallow some whiskey. He will cry himself to sleep in the middle of the afternoon and will wake hours later with a headache. Granny's death will be the first of many losses that he experiences. Unlike the others, though, hers will cut channels deep into his heart.

He sat at the kitchen table with his grandmother. He split with joy. He smiled and listened. He finished his ice cream. It was his first bowl of the year. Chocolate would have been better, though.

Granny's linoleum floor was worn and clean. She shuffled in slippers from sink to water reservoir to pantry in a habitual trail of meal-making and meal-taking. The paths were nearly worn clear through to the floorboards.

Granny shook her head. Thoughts of the past clouded her mind. Antony was now over in the corner playing with his car.

"The cooking and cleaning I have done. What thanks do I get? Johnny is good but shot-up from the war. I see him but Marg is gone. He's emptied without his twin. Sig, too. Dead in Ortona. I can hardly believe it. They were so young. The only time I see Mary Helen is when she drops off her kids. Never any money for the food bill, but Granny's always here, picking up the pieces.

"I did get to Vancouver once to see Josephine, my first Canadian-born child, and Hilde. But Hedy, Rudi, Johnny, *und* Grace? *Ja*, they are struggling to get on with their lives."

In a domestic round, Granny cooked and cleaned and planned and prepared. She stayed in the kitchen and looked after her grandson.

He knew his own mother couldn't be with him right now. She had left him in Gleichen and would have left Izzy, but Granny refused.

"One child, not two. Antony, because he's older. The girl's too much work."

For weeks now, Mary Helen had been in Calgary, between jobs. Antony was confident that once she had better-paying work, she'd come back for him. In spite of everything, he still trusted her. She would eventually show up.

Cooped up during a thundering rainstorm in July, he spent a long day on his hands and knees, driving a red Matchbox car he stole from his school chum Franky. On Granny's floor, he drove from one end of the world to the other, Steve McQueen attempting to get away from the Nazis in *The Great Escape*, on a motorcycle negotiating curves, avoiding suddenly-appearing calves in brown-stockings and feet in slippers.

Flour dusted the floor when Granny kneaded dough for noodles and his car/motorcycle left tracks behind it, parallel lines, continents long. The kitchen evolved into roadways, alleyways, and raceways.

He crept up behind Granny, intently driving his car around a piece of wood and through some kindling for the morning fire. She didn't see him and stepped back. She stumbled, and he yelled.

"Granny!"

She stormed back.

"*Nervensäge*— nuisance!"

He didn't understand what she was saying, but scuttled quickly down the highway. The roadster's tires squealed as he gunned the engine. He raced out of her way before she started swearing.

Lightning and thunder rocked the clapboard house. Hailstones pummelled the fields of wheat, oats, and rye. The cattle sought shelter, turning their backs to the storm, lowering their heads against the wind, and huddling against their young.

That September, Antony started school. There was still no sign of his mother or Izzy.

Where are they? Surely, Mum must have a job now. Why am I still at Granny's? He fumed. He went to the Greyhound bus stop every Friday night at five P.M. to see if they were getting off. They never did. He'd been abandoned. He knew this to his very core, though he would never say it out loud. His mother was probably smoking lipstick-stained cigarettes, her blouse open at the neck. *Why is she so mean? Damn her!*

In spite of his mother's absence, these were, for the most part, happy days for Antony. He was safe. He had food to eat, a warm bed, and his nose was always in a book from the library. Granny yelled but he had no fear. She was good to him, and he slept through the night. He didn't pee his bed once.

That year in school, Antony was in Grade Four, and he flew on the playground swings without getting sick. When the recess bell rang, he'd run as fast as he could for the playground. If he was lucky, he'd get a swing and would throw himself into the sky. He ate his lunch in bits and bites and pieces on the fly.

If someone else got the last swing before he did, he'd hide in the bathroom, sitting on the toilet, eating his sandwich with the door locked, alone, and safe. He was an outsider. He hadn't a friend in the world. He couldn't talk to anyone. Where would he begin? No one would believe him.

His Granny, too, was an outsider. She'd lived in Gleichen forever. She used to be the town washerwoman, scrubbing people's floors or doing their laundry for 35¢ an hour. That was what his mother often said. People in small towns have long memories, and they didn't take to Granny Good Wrath. She was unlucky and she lived alone.

Antony was unlucky, too.

He didn't make any friends, not because he was a good-for-nothing Nazi-ratting Hun. He was just not at the Gleichen School long enough to work through the reserve small towns have for newcomers. He spent only a few months there.

One day, while eating his lunch in the bathroom, he overheard some of the older boys bragging about how they could pump so high on the swings that they could fly over the bar without getting hurt. He simply didn't believe them. He'd never seen anyone do it. One day, when no one was looking, he tried himself. When he reached the top, he became scared. He stopped pumping. He didn't want to get hurt.

He was smart that way.

Gleichen had a typical prairie school. The windows were large, the floors hard and scuffed and clean, the doors heavy, and the walls thick. Chalkboards and brushes, dust and varnish, lunches and glue, and the odour of fresh air, candy, and bodies that had played hard and sat too long filled the rooms and halls. Antony sat for hours on end, dopey-eyed, sleep-heavy, and bored to tears. He lived for swinging and his teacher lived for smoking.

Her pack of Black Cat cigarettes waited on the desk for her, and she for them. The haggard woman needed a break and a good smoke.

9

Strafing Nazis

One day Antony did not run home immediately after school. He stayed back with olive-skinned Franky Hunt from Grade Three. Franky had some pastel crayons, and he showed them to the strange new boy from the city. They drew some pictures on the east wall of the school. Then they dashed from one corner to the next, pulling out long lines shoulder-high on the wall as they ran flat out—red, black, yellow, green, orange anti-aircraft tracers that they dodged while bombing the Nazi bastards below them.

Franky's new oily pastel crayons had been a gift for his birthday. Loaded, straight out of the box and ready for firing, they were now spent artillery shells.

Red-haired Susie Gillespie, always in a dress, saw them in their play. They begged her not to tattle. She told the teacher the next day anyway, *the little snot*, and Antony and Franky had to spend a week of recesses and noon hours washing and erasing their war game—one knuckle-scraping inch at a time.

In class, Antony sat shame-faced. Everyone now knew he'd been playing with a Grade Three-er. His desk opened at the top. He lifted it to get out his book, scribbler, and blue ballpoint pen. Everyone teased him. He couldn't stand being there. He chewed his Double Bubble hard as he looked for his ruler.

The teacher spoke in a smudge of words that escaped him completely. They were blotted out of hearing as soon as she said them. He didn't even try to pay attention. At the break, the teacher bolted for the lounge, opening her Black Cats, and fumbling for her lighter. He bolted to the swings but spent the recess on the toilet. *Damn!*

That day, when the afternoon bell rang, Antony stuffed his things into the desk and raced to the coatroom to grab his jacket and run home. *The Three Stooges* started at four P.M. and he didn't want to miss it. The teacher stopped him dead.

"Young man! Aren't you forgetting something?"

He stood still, sullen, his head down.

"You and Franky are supposed to spend the next hour cleaning your mess."

"Yes, Mrs. Fraser," he replied. He slumped and shambled to the closet in the hall where the janitor kept his supplies, and filled a pail with soapy water. He grabbed a couple of brushes and headed outside. Franky joined him, and together they sulked, sworn enemies. The brick was hard and hurt the hands of the two POWs.

The crayon didn't come off easily, and they were morose. Parallel lines of red, blue, black, orange, and green, drawn at breakneck speed, must be worn off slowly, in the summer sun, autumn rains, the wind, and winter snow. The boys had begun their play as runners, sprinting out of the starters' blocks, breaking for the finish line. Then they became Allied pilots, shelling Germans, but were cut down by a traitor. They were now behind barbed wire, awaiting liberation, except there would be no great escape until they did their time.

At quarter-past four, Mrs. Fraser finally sent the boys home.

"I hope you gentlemen will never forget this lesson."

Franky and Antony ran away as fast as they could.

"Redheads!" Antony exclaimed. "I'll be more careful next time."

Franky reached his house first. Antony was jealous because his friend had a father who worked for the railroad and came home sober every night. Their house was full of kids. Each room was noisy and busy and cluttered. Laundry thrown in baskets, dishes in the sink. Patsy Cline's "Three Cigarettes in the Ashtray" blared on the radio.

Franky's mother seemed harried beyond reason. Antony knew that she could use a cigarette, but that she didn't smoke. Her world was as bleak as the open prairie in November before the snow came.

I just can't go on like this, she thought as she peeled another potato. *If only there was a way out.*

Antony ducked through the hedge at Franky's place and hurried on towards Granny's. He crossed the empty field alone. The older boys who chased him down the path were nowhere to be seen. They never were, until it was too late, and then, Antony would have to scram.

Shoulder-high grass, thistles, and weeds reached out for him on either side. He kicked a stone, crushed a rusty tin can with his heel, and heard a dog's warning bark.

He's in danger, he'll get beat up, he'd better hurry. His feet kicked dust behind him. He ran like crazy and burst through the screen door, yelling:

"The Three Stooges! Are they still on?"

Granny saw him and erupted like a volcano. She jumbled English and German. He didn't understand her. He didn't know what she was saying. The only German he'd ever heard was Hitler's on television, war shows when there were no cartoons. Granny's worry seared branding iron hot.

He was late. She didn't know. Crayons? What was he thinking? A phone call.

He burst into tears.

"Will I miss my show?"

She yelled, this time furiously:

"To hell *mit* you!"

Time didn't move. He hung his head and waited for her anger to pass. It would, eventually, he knew. His mother had the same temper. So did Eema Mother God. Even Izzy. *Probably him, too*. White-hot, short-fused, and short-lived—it ran in the family.

"I'm sorry, Granny. It was an accident. I didn't mean to."

She held her words back, angry, tense, and seething.

Her grandson trod very carefully. He set the table for supper. Fork, plate, knife-blade turned to the inside, spoon across the top, with the glass to the right. The birch trees on the plates—a seventieth birthday gift from Johnny in Calgary —turned properly. Antony was so very lonely. He was so very worried. *Where could his mother be?* He couldn't speak his love, so he ate like there was no tomorrow.

It was near the beginning of the month. They enjoyed pork chops, boiled potatoes, and vegetables from the garden. His favourite dish was green beans tossed in butter and fried with breadcrumbs, food so good that Antony would never forget it. Granny's cooking carried him through this valley of darkness.

He looked at her across the table from him. She was mighty, resilient, as vibrant as a sounding board, as tough as the land around her, and as vulnerable as an Alberta garden in the middle of May.

That Saturday, Antony was ready to crawl on his hands and knees to hell, just to get away from her. All he'd done was make a fort out of the woodpile. He restacked the wood and then collapsed from sunstroke. Granny sure went on the warpath. Soon she'd calm down. Right now, he needed a wet cloth on his forehead. She put him on the couch, in the dark, tiny, living room.

He didn't know that that was the spot where his grandfather died, from a heart attack, while chopping wood. She remembered, though, as if it were yesterday.

Pictures decorated the wall, and mementoes from the grandchildren cluttered the shelves. A couch, a chair, a coffee table, photographs, bits of lace here and there. From the ceiling hung a long roll of yellow sticky flypaper—dead, desiccated, blue black flies stuck to it from the top to the bottom. Soon Granny would have to take this one down and hang up another.

Antony dreamt about stalking Nazis in the huge field he had to walk through every day to and from school. He was Gregory Peck in uniform—Captain Keith Mallory—the young boy's magnifying glass a flame-thrower, and grasshoppers, Nazis to be killed without mercy. The young boy always completed his mission, and no girls ever betrayed him.

In his dream, he donned a uniform and fought bravely beside his uncles. When the war was over, he returned home unscathed. He wasn't wounded or shell-shocked, was never a patient needing care at the Colonel Belcher,[4] was never taken prisoner, and did not die under a wall of rubble.

Antony woke from his dream. He saw pictures of his uncles who fought in the war. Uncle Sig with his shirt off, Uncle Johnny with his pals, Uncle Rudi handsome and full of youth. Then he looked in a drawer and saw pictures of two German soldiers. Hidden.

He ran outside to ask Granny, but she was nowhere to be seen. She must have gone to the bar with Mrs. Spence for a drink and a smoke. He went out to the garden, picked a pocketful of peas for rations, grabbed the battered BB gun he found at the dump, and sneaked into the field behind the wood pile, looking for a Nazi patrol. He'll shoot those bastards if he ever catches them on Granny's property.

Antony saw her stroll down the path to the house. He knew better than to sneak up and surprise her. He stood and stepped onto the path where she would notice him.

"Granny!"

"Oh, son, what are you doing here?"

"Who are those German soldiers?"

"Was?"

"You know," he insisted. "The photos in the dresser."

"Oh, *ja*, the photos. *Mein Neffe aus Wien und der Mann meiner Nichte.*" (My nephew from Vienna and my niece's husband.)

"Did they fight against my uncles?"

---

[4] Veterans' hospital in Calgary

"Not really," she replied. "Karl who married Hertha spent most of the war defending the North Sea. The British captured him. Tiber, I mean Walther, fought mostly in Slovakia and Rumania. The Russians captured him and transported him to a Siberian labour camp. He didn't return home until 1957. They both hated the war.

"Walther's wife Mina served with an anti-aircraft unit in Vienna. She was a captain and he a private.

"The rest of their long-married life, she ordered him around, and he loved her with such gratitude he had to obey."

"'*Ja wohl, mein Schatz*!' he'd salute, click his heels, and bow from the waist."

"But weren't they Nazis, Granny?"

"Nazis? They were conscripted. If they didn't fight, they were shot. They had no choice. Not every Austrian wore a brown shirt, you know."

"Brown shirt?"

"A member of the Nazi Party. They joined to survive. They filled out the *Ahnenpaß*—a document going back four generations, detailing one's genealogy. After 1938, every Austrian had to fill one out. Officials looked through parish records back to 1815 to see if there was any Jewish blood in your family. If you didn't register, you lost your job, your house. Then you'd disappear in the night."

"Were there any Jews in our family?"

"Rumours only, Ashkenazi, but generations back. Nothing in the records. Your Great Aunt Adrienne married an assimilated Jew. He was wealthy and older than she. They met at a ball after his wife died. He liked her and proposed, not on the spot mind you, but after she met his children.

"They spent their honeymoon at St. Veit an der Glan in Carinthia. After a couple years, he grew tired and divorced her. His company made metal rims for carriage wheels. Even in the bad times, they sold their products for a lower price than anyone else. Now that family had money, let me tell you."

"But where are they now?"

"Auschwitz, probably."

"Granny?"

"Don't ask. Not yet, anyhow. You don't want to know."

10

Indian Summer

Gleichen residents had hoped for a few weeks more of Indian summer. Late September frosts had killed off the flies, mosquitoes, and wasps that found their way into people's homes, despite the window screens everyone put up as soon as the snow melted. The tree-lined streets—planted by Europeans who moved in when the CPR placed its railroad siding near the trail leading to the Siksika Blackfoot Nation— were covered with a heavy carpet of leaves. The trees had just begun to show their golden, yellow green-tinged colours when a strong southwest wind blew in.

With the temperature plunging, the trees were blown bare. The prairie grew dull and lifeless. Winter snows continued to hold back and Gleichen looked its worst. Her gardens were harvested and dug under, her flowerbeds put to rest. Only the hardiest marigolds held their orange blossoms high.

Granny's garden was filled with root vegetables. Antony helped grub the remaining beets, carrots, parsnips, and turnips, and carry them down into the root cellar. She could hardly dig her spade into the soil. She'd have to get one of the neighbours to rototill the garden for her.

Suddenly, one day, without warning and completely out of the blue, Mary Helen showed up. She was with a man Antony didn't know. As soon as he saw his mother, he ran to her and hugged her until his arms hurt. *This time, he wasn't going to let her go.* She introduced Antony to Steve who stayed back at the car and smoked a cigarette. The chrome hub caps on his '57 Chevy sparkled in the sun.

"We'll be taking Antony back to Calgary, Mum," Mary Helen said. "I finally found some work with enough hours to pay the rent and buy groceries."

Granny lit a Daily Mail and gave Antony a hug.

"Go, get your things, and don't forget your toy car."

He burst into tears, wanting to stay more than he needed to go.

It took him only a few minutes to gather his clothes and stuff them into a brown paper bag. He put the car into his pocket and held it tight.

He gave Granny one more hug. She smelled like dough and noodles, and he of fresh air and sunshine. It was the last time that the two of them would ever see each other again. She died a short time later. Then her house burned to the ground. Dust to dust. Ashes to ashes. All that remained was the foundation, a square of concrete on the corner of Gleichen Street and Second Avenue.

Antony jumped into the front seat of the car and snuggled as close to his mother as he could. She smelled of perfume, cigarettes, and everlasting love.

"Where's Izzy? Why isn't she with us?"

"She's playing with the neighbours. You'll see her soon."

Antony fell asleep as the car glided over the warp and wale of the heaving prairie between Gleichen and Calgary. He dozed in the warm sun and didn't waken until he felt the car slow down by Chestermere Lake. He looked out the window and saw kids swimming. He wished he were one of the guys on water skis. *It must really be something to be towed behind a motorboat.*

"Are we there soon? I have to pee," Antony said.

"We're almost there," Steve said. "Can you hold on a little longer?"

Steve drove down MacLeod Trail, just past the Stampeder Hotel. He turned right at the old church on the corner. He pulled up a hill and parked along Stanley Road.

Mary Helen opened the door and stepped out, and Antony followed after her. He had to pee, but he couldn't help it. He saw a steep cement embankment, rising from the sidewalk. He had to climb it. When he reached the top, he turned around and stood up.

"Look, Mum!"

She told him to be careful and to come down right away.

"Don't rip your pants or scuff your shoes. Let's go in. I'll show you where the bathroom is."

Antony remembered his bursting bladder and slid down the embankment as fast as he could. His mother took him to the bathroom downstairs. He shut the door behind him, unzipped his trousers, and peed into the middle of the toilet bowl. He liked the bubbles that rose to the surface and the sound of the pee hitting the water. He imagined he was shooting Krauts.

When he came out, Mary Helen introduced him to a boy his age.

"This is Mike. He lives here. You'll be sleeping in his room, until we move into the suite upstairs. Why don't you go out and play?"

The boys went into the backyard. They found a couple hammers and pounded nails until their wrists ached. Then they walked down the street, kicking stones.

"I bet I know something you don't know," said Mike.

"What's that?"

"I'll show you later, but we'll have to wait."

That Saturday afternoon, the adults drove to the Empire Hotel for a few beers while Mike and Antony stayed home to babysit Izzy. With only one station, they watched whatever was on television at the time. Sometimes it was *Bugs Bunny, Chez Hélène, Davy and Goliath, The Friendly Giant;* other times, it was *The Jetsons, Lassie, The Littlest Hobo, Mr. Dressup, Rocky and Bullwinkle, Romper Room,* and of course *Disney, Ed Sullivan,* and the *Three Stooges.*

Mike's older brother and his girlfriend showed up one afternoon, and went into the bedroom adjacent to the living room where the television was.

"Now I'll show you. Come here," Mike said as he crawled up on the sofa and peeked through a small hole in the wall. He moved aside and let

Antony have a turn. All he saw was Mike's older brother on top of his girlfriend. Her legs were wide apart.

Antony laughed because he had never seen such a huge, white ass before. Mike punched him in the gut and told him to shut up or they'd get into trouble. They sat in front of the television and finished their show. When Mike's brother and his girlfriend came out of the bedroom, the two boys started to giggle. They rolled around the floor punching and kicking each other.

After a couple of days at Mike's house, Antony, his mother, and Izzy moved into the suite on the main floor. They had to climb a steep flight of stairs at the back of the house to enter the kitchen, but the front was at street level. A laundry chute connected the upper and lower suites. The two boys would slide down it for fun. One time, however, Antony saw some electrical sparks from the wiring and never went down the chute again. *He knew better than to play with fire.*

Every Saturday afternoon, Antony and Izzy went to the matinees downtown while Mary Helen went drinking at the Empire Hotel. They watched Julie Andrews and Dick van Dyck in *Mary Poppins*, Audrey Hepburn and Rex Harrison in *My Fair Lady*, Sean Connery and Lenya Lotte in *From Russia with Love*, Omar Shariff and Julie Christie in *Doctor Zhivago*, Elvis Presley and Yvonne Craig in *Kissin' Cousins*, and Elizabeth Taylor and Richard Burton in *Cleopatra*. They sat through a single showing of that one. *Lawrence of Arabia, Bridge on the River Kwai, Cat Ballou, The Great Escape,* and *The Guns of Navarone.* They saw most movies at least twice, one showing immediately after the other, waiting for their mother to come and get them or to send them home in a taxi.

One day, they came home in a cab after being terrified by *The Birds*. The driver took them to Stanley Street instead of Stanley Road, but Antony was too afraid to give him directions. The driver eventually found the house and charged the kids the full fare on the meter. Antony couldn't say a thing, even though he knew the driver made a mistake. He and Izzy ate some cold macaroni and cheese and crawled into bed together. They left all the lights on.

11

Runaway

1913

Back in Gleichen, Granny sat alone at her small wooden table in the kitchen and rolled a cigarette. Pinching some tobacco onto a slip of gummed paper, she rolled it tight, and moistened the glue with the tip of her tongue.

She tamped it end-on-end and picked out the loose, sweet-smelling tobacco shreds that she put back in the pouch. Rather than strike a match, she decided that she'd far rather savour the smoke and a beer in the Gleichen bar than stay in this empty old house.

Sitting in the Ladies and Escorts would be better than being alone all afternoon. She walked the few short blocks in the blazing sun.

In the smoke-filled bar where Granny spent the hottest part of the day, there were no windows. But then, she didn't need to look out.

The bar was dark, beer-stained, and smoke-filled. Small round tables were covered with worn terry cloth. Circled with armchairs made for lounging, each table held an assemblage of pilsner glasses filled with draft to the line below the rim.

Farmers relaxed, their hats off, their foreheads white as dough, their long-sleeved shirts buttoned to the neck and to the cuffs. They sat back in their chairs and enjoyed themselves. The beer was 25¢ a glass.

Granny sat by herself.

Loud, brazen, pissed-off drunken talk echoed from the Men's side of the bar. Patrons staggered and leered, careening from the table to the bar to the reeking urinals and back again. Someone played "Love Me

Tender" on the jukebox. Bright red signs marked the doors and alerted the patrons to the exits, not that anyone ever left there of their own accord.

Granny bided her time. She didn't get drunk, though. She just sat and waited for someone to join her. No one did, though, not today. Not that she minded.

Her mind drifted back to her life before. She wasn't always lonely and feeling sick. She muttered to herself, to her dear long-dead husband Sigi, and to her niece Hertha back in Vienna.

"Where are all the letters we've written?" she wondered.

What an idiot I was to follow him here, she thought to herself, muddling the German she'd forgotten with the English she never really learned.

"Oh, we'll go back, Maria. It's only a few hundred crowns," she recalled him saying. What she'd do with that much money now, she wondered, the truth be known. All her friends and family back home were dead and gone.

"How were we to know a year later, the Archduke would get shot? That we'd be stranded here? Unable to get out, forced to spend the rest of our lives on this broken, unforgiving prairie?

"What did we know back then? Not very much, let me tell you. A match-maker's daughter and a fool. That's what we were.

"When God the Father shuts one door, He opens another. Just like a man, let me tell you. Fool's gold. You reach for the shiny under the rippling surface. What do you get in return? A kick in the ass."

"A Granny on High would do better," Eema Mother spoke out in the darkness. "She'd look out for you, not twist in the knife."

Granny stubbed out her butt end of a cigarette and took a sip of her beer.

"Sigi and I met in Schwanberg and made love in green valleys, beside pleasant waters. The days were full of flowers and every night was bright with stars. Sigi's looks, his fortune, his words, and finally his hands seduced me. Damn him! And this is what I get for those few moments of pleasure.

"Now I know why he left those Viennese women behind. *There was no one stupid enough to follow him to the end of the earth.*

"Then he up and died on me. We thought we hit bottom when we escaped the anti-German riots in Calgary and moved out here. We didn't know what bottom was.

"My sister-in-law and father-in-law disapproved of me. I wasn't good enough for the noble Gutrater name. Sigi should have listened to them. Then I wouldn't have had all this trouble.

"Be careful with your life. You never know what time will throw in your face. I wouldn't have made one step to the altar had I known I'd end up here.

"Why in God's name were my prayers answered? All I wanted was a man to love and to hold. But what did I get? A *Kronprinz Rudolf*[5] plucked from a tree, slightly tart, ideal for *Apfel Strudel*, but filled with the knowledge of good and evil.

"My opinion? God the Father gives and takes away. Woe to the people who are the apple of His eye.

"Alone, Sigi and I came together, our lives intertwined. His fingers played in my hair, and my legs pulled him into me. My womb was as fertile as the vineyards in the Schilcher Valley between Ligist and Eibiswald.

"Remember the wine? Remember our son Sigmund Joseph? He died the day he was born. Afterwards, our lives were never the same.

---

[5] An apple variety from Austria, first cultivated in the nineteenth century and named after Crown Prince Rudolf, who died in a murder-suicide pact with his mistress Baroness Mary Vetsera in 1889.

"We had three more and moved to Eggenberg. What an opportunity to start over. There was nothing for us in Schwanberg. We moved to Graz. Nothing seemed to fit.

"Sigi caught immigration fever. He thought the best way to solve his problems was to run away.

"The bloody CPR. They'll burn in hell for their lies.

"We left everything behind, even you, dear niece—Hertha and your brother. What was his name? Tiber? Walther?

"I forget.

"How did I make the voyage back then with all those children? We were so busy, we didn't even get a new portrait taken of us. The one with Hedwig as a baby had to do.

"First the train from Graz to Trieste. That was a holiday, just a summer vacation. Too bad we didn't return. Then the ship. The *Ruthenia*?

"And where was Sigi while I looked after the younger ones below-deck? Smoking cigars and strolling up top with Adolf and Hilde.

"We arrived in Montreal and were herded onto immigrant trains.

"I learned to make meals quickly, let me tell you. The maids Sissi and Dolly should have come to Canada with us. I sure needed their help. Where are they now? Enjoying the best Graz has to offer, I bet.

"I couldn't live without Sigi and had to follow him here. The Styrian sun warmed our bodies. The alpine winds refreshed our hearts. We rested in the meadows and smoked one delicious cigarette after another.

"Then we travelled to the end of the earth.

"Our year on Maggie Street? We named our first Canadian child after the emperor. What a happy beginning. Josefine!"

Then the anti-German riots in Calgary started. Even with his influence, Mr. Burns couldn't protect his employees any longer. The Gutraters moved out to Gleichen. He helped them the best he could.

"Sigi swung a sledgehammer on the section gang. He was so tired, I massaged his back, legs, and feet. He couldn't keep up the heavy work. The section boss fired him.

He found a job hoeing potatoes for Sink Lee. He was a good employer, but the pay was next to nothing. But the family ate; that was all that mattered; even though the kids never saw their father all summer.

Then that day in November, his heart stopped.

"Why did you leave me all alone with nothing?" Maria asked.

"If it weren't for the older children doing chores for other people, I don't know how we would have survived. We lived in disgrace. Poverty does that.

"One minute Sigi's out chopping wood for the winter. He feels faint and lies down on his bed for a bit. Within half an hour, he's dead.

"*Ich bin mit meinen Kindern nun verlassen*—I am with my children, completely abandoned.

"What could I do? Nothing, but feed my kids fried eggs after Mass on Sundays. We collected grain that spilled from the wagons on the roads on the way to the elevator. I washed floors, did laundry, and looked for pennies from heaven, except none ever came.

"I had to keep our family together, and now I have to look after my grandson.

"Antony, where are you? Why don't you come when I call? *Ach, Gott!*"

Maria (geboren Graus) von Gutrater, Edler von Puchstein shook her head. She stepped out of the bar and walked home. Her eyes squinted in the bright evening sun. She entered the house. The doors were unlocked. A few flies buzzed against the screen, trying to get out.

She sat down, impassive at her kitchen table. The still air in the kitchen was stifling. She didn't have the words to speak the words that roiled within her. They cried out from the pores of her skin.

All she could think about was the supper she would cook for Antony tomorrow. Egg noodles tossed in breadcrumbs that had been fried in butter.

She will feed him until he is bursting.

Part Two

12

East of Eden

1965

That spring, Mary Helen followed a pot-bellied man named Harry to Winnipeg, home of the north-facing Golden Boy. Harry had a big voice, a hearty laugh and liked to roughhouse with Antony, who loved and hated him.

This is the story of that move; a five-year interregnum when Eema Mother was removed from the throne in Antony's heart. He forgot about her. Knowing the end from the beginning, Eema Mother wasn't rankled by his inattention. She knew that if he didn't rebel against her as a young boy, he'd fight her as an adult. She cut him some slack; She set him free to follow his own devices in the hope that he'd return to her of his own accord.

This release allowed Antony the time he needed to develop into a teenager capable of making his own choices. It enabled him to become a man responsible for his own choosing, one who would take responsibility for the consequences of his actions.

He had to choose how he would then live. To be or not to be. That was the question.

On their last day in Calgary, Antony sensed something was up, but his mother and Harry were tight-lipped. They wouldn't tell him a thing, except to say that he should collect his toys and books and toss his clothes in a bag. They were going for a car ride. They wouldn't tell him where or for how long, and that made him fume.

Don't they know that's no way to treat a kid?

Later that morning with Harry swearing and Mary Helen hurrying the kids up, they packed the trunk of his 1960 Ford Fairlane and drove out of Calgary. They sped past Chestermere Lake, the whitecaps glinting in the bright sun, slowed up as they drove through Strathmore, waved at Granny buried in Gleichen, breezed through Bassano, and saw the concrete dinosaur off the road at Brooks. They stopped for lunch and gas at the top of Kin Coulee in Medicine Hat, and watched a herd of pronghorn antelope disappear over a bluff near Maple Creek. They pushed past Swift Current and Moose Jaw and had a bite to eat in Regina.

Harry drove into the night through Whitewood, Moosomin, Virden, Brandon, Portage La Prairie, and arrived in Winnipeg in the wee hours of the morning.

The sky darkened and clouded over, the further east they travelled. A headstrong wind buffeted their car as they pulled up their Alberta roots, and jackhammered them through southern Saskatchewan and into a new life in flood-prone Manitoba.

The Red River Valley loam is six feet deep. You can hear the plants thrusting their way through the soil to the surface, burgeoning into new and glorious life.

From Antony's perspective, however, not a single star shone in the gloom. This was the worst possible place in the world for a body to find itself.

He was to learn over the years that his exile in that far and distant land wasn't nearly as bad as he expected.

They weren't going west like the Three Wisemen. They weren't going north like George Carmack with Skookum Jim and Tagish Charley. They were going east, which was entirely in the wrong direction. It rankled Antony to the core that he had no say in the matter.

Having grown up reading stories from the Book of the People, he felt like Cain whom Eema Mother banished to a land east of Eden.

It just wasn't right, and he knew it in his bones.

Soon after they arrived on the banks of the north-flowing Red River, Harry disappeared, and Mary Helen took up with a man named Knut. While the two of them did not get along all that well, Knut had a steady job at a creamery and a big enough house for the kids to have rooms of their own. The periodic bout of sex seemed a small price to Mary Helen who had no other option available to her. She bit her lip and did what she had to for her children's sake.

She worked as a waitress at a nearby restaurant. Antony and Izzy ate their meals there whenever she had the supper shift. Antony's favourite was the lamb chops and Izzy's the boiled eggs and toast.

The adult Antony's memories of his childhood flood over the levees, dikes, and embankments of his mind. They jumble and tumble in order and out. They sometimes destroy his peace. Like river-born sediment, they settle down and roil up again. The good, the bad, and the ugly churn together. He cannot help but remember. He tries to let go. He wants a happy ending.

But first, he needs to forgive.

Notre Dame Avenue.

What a terrible place for a growing boy. Stop-and-go traffic. Cars with horns blaring at the slightest provocation, engines roaring at green lights, drivers punching their throttles at yellows, and tires screeching at reds.

Young Antony ignored them all. He went off to the store down the street and across the intersection. Not Notre Dame, thank goodness, but a busy one that demanded his care and attention. After all, he was on a mission of utmost importance, vital to domestic harmony and bliss.

He needed to buy smokes for his mother.

She was back at the house, drinking with her friends. Izzy was in her room, playing with the little puppy they just brought home. It was cute but not house-trained. Izzy didn't mind. She and the little dog were pals. They slept together now that Antony had his own room.

Antony volunteered to get the smokes. He was smart enough to know that there'd be a bit left over that he could spend on a handful of Mojos, little white gummy candies that burst bullets of flavour into his mouth, and that the half-corked adults would be too far down the necks of their beer bottles to ask for any change back.

The tiny store huddled on the dark street corner. It was gloomy. The windows were grimy from the slush that splashed up from the passing cars, buses, and delivery trucks. A long, wooden counter stood between the customers and the cigarettes they needed to buy.

Mr. Au, the owner of the store, sat in a low chair behind the counter. He operated the cash register without bothering to stand up. A hockey game was playing quietly on the radio near him.

"The Habs winning?" Antony asked. The television at his house was in the front room where the adults were drinking. He didn't want to be anywhere near them, even if it meant missing the game.

"Three to one for the Leafs," Mr. Au answered, but Antony could hardly understand him.

Mr. Au knew Antony—not his name, of course—but his face. Mr. Au's English was poor, but he understood enough. He could point to the item his customers were looking for and tell them its price. He had seen this boy several times in the past few weeks. He was new in the neighbourhood.

A tiny kid, and polite. He respects the elderly, Mr. Au thought. *Comes in most days of the week to buy a pack of Du Maurier cigarettes and a few Mojos*. Mr. Au watched him carefully.

He liked the boy but didn't trust him. The problem was, if you let your guard down for a minute even good kids will rob you blind, eventually.

They all thought he was a rich man because he owned the store. That was not the case. The books told it all. If he were rich, he'd have hired someone to mind the till. As it was, the only break he got was in the afternoon for a couple of hours when Mrs. Au took over so he could have a rest.

Money, money, money. Why was it so hard to scavenge the fewest of dollars? The margins were tight. Even on the most basic of staples, he could only charge a little extra. His customers were poorer than he. Their only luxury was a pack of cigarettes. But they drank too much booze to buy food for their kids, other than the Kraft Dinners that the little ones cooked for themselves.

Poverty bred a desperate sort of independence. Mr. Au and Antony had learned to fend for themselves. People disappointed them. They learned to expect only the worst.

Mr. Au watched Antony. He had some sympathy for the boy, but couldn't do anything to help, except to call the cops when the boy rushed in a few days later to say that his mother was being beaten up.

There was nothing Mr. Au could do. They were both outsiders, and powerless. He made the call, but the police never came.

Antony pocketed the cigarettes and kept the Mojos in his hand. With any luck, he'd have them finished before he got home. That way he wouldn't have to share with Izzy.

He stepped into the cold night air and made his way slowly toward the house. At a break in the traffic, he ran quickly across the side street and continued down Notre Dame, kicking ice clumps and frozen dog turds. He popped the last Mojo into his mouth and noticed a small group of people near his house. His sister was bawling, and Mary Helen was trying to console her.

One of the men from the party had picked up the body of the little puppy from the middle of the road. Honking their horns, the drivers were angry and impatient to get on their way.

Later, Antony learned that Izzy let the dog out to pee, but it broke away from her tiny grasp. She couldn't hold the leash. When the front door opened, it burst out and ran under the tires of a car speeding by. The driver didn't stop. Thought it was just another goddamn rut in the road.

Knut tossed the dog's body into the trash out back.

13

The Farm

When both Knut and Mary Helen had the weekends off, they visited Knut's mother, Saga. She lived on the farm outside Quickfall, twenty miles north of the city, near her oldest son Sverr and his family.

For an inner-city kid, sleeping upstairs in her old farmhouse and waking to bright sunshine and chattering birds was completely new. Antony'd get up with the sun and spend the whole day running around the yard and the bush. His imagination ran wild.

The farm abounded with places for him to explore. There were all sorts of old vehicles abandoned out back. Antony's favourite was a handmade snow machine. It was too old to be called a snowmobile, and it wasn't very mobile when Antony knew it. He had a blast pulling its levers and playing with its switches. He pretended he was riding it through blizzards along the shores of Great Bear Lake, travelling from one mission outpost to the next.

He was brave enough to venture out on the Barrens.

The Indians and trappers there needed to hear the comfortable words he had in his heart for them.

One day, Saga taught Antony how to milk a cow, but his hands weren't strong enough to squeeze the teat. She lived alone and kept a few dairy cows. He called her Granny even though his own Granny was dead. She showed him how to lean his head against the udder and pull down on the teat as he squeezed.

"Focus, *liten gut*—little boy. Pull harder and aim for the pail," she'd chide, then take over when the cow became impatient and began swatting its tail and shifting its legs.

When his hands grew stronger, he could fill the pail to the brim and squirt milk into the cat's mouth.

Saga was a thin and wiry eighty-year-old Norwegian widow. Her skin was burnished and coppery. Her long grey hair was tied back in a bun. She wore thin cotton dresses and saggy brown stockings, not tights, not leggings—certainly not nylons, just practical clothes that didn't have a stitch of nonsense about them.

She enjoyed having the boy around. He was respectful and decent in spite of that slut of a mother of his.

What was her dunderhead of a son thinking when he dragged her home? She shook her head in disgust.

As Antony helped with the chores, they spoke quietly about the necessaries of farm life. Milking, cleaning barns, throwing hay bales down from the loft, raising chickens, and candling eggs; calves that gambolled in the corral after being cooped up all winter; swallows swooping to and from the mud nests they built under the eaves; bees and the supers[6] on the edge of the hay fields; and hives in the pump house where they needed to be knocked down and cleared out.

"Now that's a crying shame!" Saga exclaimed. "All that honey going to waste."

Saga treated Antony well. He learned from her that if a person didn't work, he didn't eat. He helped her as much as he could. He never quit, and relished the second helpings she gladly offered him.

She introduced Antony to ethnic Norwegian cuisine. Her speciality was *Blodpølse*—blood pudding. Antony had only the smallest mouthful, yet it remains forever seared in his memory. Blood pudding is hell warmed up on a platter. That was the last time he'd knowingly try it again.

But *Rømme grøt*, the traditional Norwegian pudding made with milk and cream and thickened with flour? Slightly sweet and served with

---

[6] In beekeeping, supers are the boxes that beekeepers place on top of a beehive to store honey. They are set above the chamber where the queen lays her eggs.

melted butter, cinnamon, and nutmeg on top, he could eat that every day of the week.

The height of Norwegian cooking had to be the *Blod Klubb* that Saga made, and the family called crib. After peeling and grating a bag of potatoes, she would add a quart or so of pig's blood just for the colour and stir in enough flour and baking powder to make a thick, workable dough. As she brought a large canner of salted water to a boil, she would round the dough into goose-egg-sized dumplings. Into their centres she would squeeze cubes of pork fat that were dredged with salt and allspice. She would ladle them into the boiling water and let them simmer for about an hour. When they floated to the surface, she transferred the crib to everyone's plates. Like the homeless at a soup kitchen, Sverr's kids lined up one after the other for their daily ration.

The next day, Sverr's wife Flora would cut up the leftovers and fry them in a cream sauce for lunch.

Connoisseurs maintain that *Blod Klubb*, or *Palt*, as the Swedes call it, is best the day after.

It took Antony and Izzy quite a while to get used to the appearance and taste of crib. Huge and heavy, only a fool would try to eat more than one, lumpish grey and blood brown, with nary a vegetable to be seen. It is amazing how appetizing they become when that is all there is for supper and the only alternative is to go to bed hungry.

Pretty soon, Antony and Izzy clambered to the front of the line to get the biggest one in the pot. With this hearty food, the two strays from the city found safety with a family that was not their own.

They thrived on the kindness of strangers.

One day Antony had the worst toothache of his life, so Knut gave him a plug of chewing tobacco to kill the pain. Antony chewed down hard on the plug and passed out when the nicotine hit his system. That was his third near-death experience.

Knut carried Antony into the sitting room and laid him on the couch, and Mary Helen wiped his face with a cold cloth.

"He'll be all right, Mary Helen," Knut laughed. "Don't you worry. He just bit off more than he could chew."

In his delirium, Antony promised Eema Mother that he'd start going to church again and that he would devote his life to the mission field, if he ever made it out of this misery alive.

When Antony awoke, woozy, the pain was miraculously all gone. After a glass of water, he promptly forgot his vow to Eema Mother, who doesn't forget. While he ran outside to play, She bided her time.

One day near the middle of May, Knut brought Mary Helen and the kids back out to Saga's. Sverr and Flora and their children were also there.

Saga hung a Norwegian flag on her porch.

While Sverr and Knut sat in the shade, drinking Canadian Club and smoking cigarettes, Mary Helen and Flora helped Saga prepare the special dishes. The two sisters played with Izzy while Antony tried as hard as he could to keep up with the five brothers, who were kamikazeing from one end of the farmyard to the next.

They built forts in the hayloft and played with the forge in the shop, turning the bellows and raising as much coal dust as they could. They clambered over the old horse-drawn farming equipment that was rusting in the bush. They shinnied up trees and fired stones at the swallows swooping low.

The only time the adults noticed them was when they were playing around Saga's wood pile. She chopped her own wood by hand and piled it in cords for the long winter ahead of them. She was even on television—that old woman and her hundred-yard-long pile of wood.

"Better clean yourselves up," Sverr yelled. "Before Granny catches you!"

The boys pumped cold water for each other to wash their hands and faces, and they burst into the house.

"What's for lunch? We're starving." Saga swore a blue streak at them in Norwegian, and Knut and Sverr started laughing. Mary Helen and Flora stayed in the kitchen, their noses to the grindstone.

76

14

Twenty-Five Cents

All of a sudden, Knut and Mary Helen and the two kids had to leave their two-story dump on Notre Dame Avenue. The only place to go on such short notice was out to Saga's farm. Antony imagined that Mary Helen and Knut likely didn't bother to make that month's rent. They spent it all drinking.

It was early in the spring of 1965.

Antony and Izzy needed to go to school. Antony was in Grade Five and Izzy Grade Two. Waifs, really, and there they were, starting all over again, new kids in a new school and without a single friend.

Outsiders.

Antony and Izzy did not talk together.

They needed to fit in.

They didn't want others to know they were related.

On their own, they tried to make their own way, but Antony always felt it was easier for Izzy than him. People liked her. He rubbed everyone the wrong way.

Izzy was a cute little girl, and Antony was a head filled for trouble. Truth be known, he grew into a smartass who didn't know how to keep his bloody yap shut.

They walked down the long, dusty lane to the gravel road. They kicked stones and heads off dandelions. Grasshoppers spat brown juice on their hands when they captured them and held them for too long. Eventually, a long rooster tail of dust billowed down the road. It was the school bus, except it was more a ratty old panel van than a passenger vehicle. When it came to a stop, Antony and Izzy walked nervously toward it. The only door Antony saw was in the back. He tried to open it, but the door handle was too high. The driver rolled down his window.

"Not there, kids!" He yelled. "Up here, at the front."

Antony's face burnt red with shame. Humiliated, he led Izzy towards the door. They found their seats, and the driver shot off down the road. Rattling over the washboard and shimmying in the gravel, Mr. Easter had driven this road a thousand times before. He knew what to expect. It was a straight run for him, two miles more to town and then home again. He'd pick the kids up from school in the afternoon and deliver them one by one to their farmyards, just like clockwork.

Antony and Izzy didn't have a clue. For them, the road was long and unknown, a cliff on one side, a precipice on the other, a blind curve here, and the destination over the edge.

The early days on the farm had been great for Antony and Izzy, but they soon grew to be hell on earth for Mary Helen. At first, they stayed in the farmhouse with Saga, and then a very short time later, they were in the bunkhouse out back.

The two women couldn't stand each other. Mary Helen wouldn't spend another minute under the same roof with that cranky old bitch. Saga wasn't going to feed anybody who wasn't helping with the farm work.

Mary Helen may have been poor and desperate. She was stuck out in the middle of nowhere with nowhere to turn, but she was territorial and proud.

So was Saga.

Grown women with minds of their own shouldn't have to share the same kitchen on equal terms with anybody, unless they choose to, of course.

Saga and Mary Helen did not allow any accommodation to develop between them. Mary Helen had to leave. After all, this was Saga's place. She held the title to the lock, stock, and barrel. Trespassers would rather be shot than come face to face with her wrath.

The first step was into the bunkhouse, the second back to Winnipeg, but that wouldn't be for some time in the future. A lot of fat needed to be thrown onto the fire before that particular set of circumstances would flare out of control.

In the meantime, Antony and Izzy got used to farm life, riding the bus to school, and suffering through lunch hours and recesses until they could get back home again. At least in the city, Antony could cut class, shoplift, and smoke cigarettes. These were just a few tricks he picked up in his short time during Grade Five on Notre Dame Avenue.

You couldn't get away with anything in the two-bit town in which he now found himself.

Damn it all, anyway.

One hot, windless day in the summer, Mary Helen dropped Antony and Izzy off at Sverr and Flora's house in Quickfall. She had to go into the city to find a place. They'd be moving off the farm. She'd had enough of Saga and her ways.

Except Mary Helen never returned.

Sverr, Flora, and their seven children crowded in together to make room in their packed house with one bathroom for the abandoned city kids. They slid over and crunched in on the bench seat at their crowded supper table.

There was no way Flora would leave the kids with that fool Knut out at Saga's.

Antony's head didn't reach the light switch at the side of the front door. However, his elbows dug viciously into the ribs of the boys beside him. His tongue lashed out in anger when he didn't receive what he thought was his due. He had not learned to keep his mouth shut and to be grateful for what he was most generously given. Flora struggled to keep the peace in her family.

"These kids need us," she explained. "We can't kick them out," she said on more than one occasion.

In the fall, after several months of anxious waiting and no word from their mother, Antony and Izzy were made wards of the province. They became foster children without a home of their own.

During the five years Antony lived in Quickfall, he worked side-by-side with Flora and her boys. They each did their share of the chores, cleaning out the barns and carrying five gallon buckets of water to the cows in the winter. In the summer, they mowed lawns, repainted rusty equipment, and helped to unload boxcars of eighty-pound bags of fertilizer. Sverr operated the Esso bulk station in town and sold supplies to the farmers in the area.

Antony learned to drive the old, single-cylinder Lanz tractor and the Chev pickup truck that Flora used whenever she worked on the ranch, eight miles north and west of town.

That's when Antony fell in love with the librarian and her Bookmobile. Her curvy charms and thirst for knowledge fired his imagination. He could hardly wait for her to return each week, so that they could talk about the books he had just finished and find new ones for him to sign out. She treated him with kindness and respect. He never forgot her.

When his nose wasn't in a book, he took piano lessons from Mrs. Mann. He learned about Middle C, the treble and bass clefs, white and black keys, and the importance of learning the notes and the rhythm of a piece of music from back to front.

"Play the last few measures as slowly and as carefully as you can until you can perform them without error. Move forward a few more measures, learn them, and play the piece to the end. If you make a mistake, stop immediately and practise the notes and the rhythm until you have corrected the error. It takes discipline to play slowly.

"By moving from back to front and playing to the end, you will eventually play the ending a hundred times or more. That way you will get stronger and stronger as you move towards the final measure. What people remember in a performance is the ending, not the beginning. Play through to the finish and end with a flourish. That's how you get standing ovations."

Antony learned how to repair barbed-wire fences, a life skill he never forgot. He jabbed the six-foot crowbar into the hard, rocky soil. Raising a sledgehammer high, he pounded down on newly-sawn poplar posts from trees they just felled and stripped of their branches. Posts finding purchase, Antony sledged them into place.

He pulled the barbed wire tight, drawing staples out of rotten posts with the newly-oiled heavy fencing tool that fitted perfectly into his working man's groaning hand. Sixty years later, its heft is still familiar. The weight of its steel is still cold in his callous-free coffee-cup-holding hand.

One does not easily lose the sense in a hand of the right tool for the job. It empowers a person who has a good day's work to complete before he, or she, can go home to supper. Good work and aching muscles make a heart grateful for what has to be done before the setting of the sun.

Hard labour in turn gave Antony a love for working with his hands. Nothing beats a good night's sleep after a day of heavy labour. Meaningful, worthwhile work makes sense of the world and puts everything in order.

Separating her land from her neighbours, Flora built strong fences. They create good will between those who help each other when hard times come down as hail and pummel them into the earth.

Herds of cattle kept apart make farmers happy over coffee. In town, they chat about life's important everyday issues, the weather, the early frost, the bull two farms over, the upcoming curling season, the price of beef and a bushel of wheat, and the cost of fuel.

In the bush north of the Gilded Boy, between Lake Winnipeg and Lake Manitoba, those freshwater inland seas filled with Gold Eyes, autumn after the first frost is a beautiful time of year. The bright smell of decaying leaves filled Antony's nostrils. Heady, sharp, clean, it cut him to the quick. His heart was bitter and needed refreshing. All he needed was a deep winter cleansing, a rushing north wind, and a -35° deep-freeze.

In spite of his initial misgivings when he left Alberta, Antony grew into a sturdy young fellow in the land east of Eden.

He rode horses in the summer and herded cattle in the fall. In the winter before he ran away, he wrecked the family's new snowmobile, a blue 1970 Polaris with a twenty-horse engine. He shattered the windshield and cracked the fibreglass cowling. He lied about the details, saying he rolled it on the trail. There was no way he'd admit to that bunch of yahoos that he was spinning doughnuts on the ice by the church and hit a patch of rock. The Polaris flipped out of control and threw Antony into the snow.

He had not taken into account that nothing of interest remains hidden in a small town for long. There is always an eyewitness to whatever is unusual, like the time Abe Guenther rode his snowmobile down eight miles of gravel road from Gunview to Quickfall in the middle of July.

You should have heard the town gossips on the party line that day. Nothing remains secret.

Antony should have known that it's no use telling lies when the truth is plain for everyone to see. There is no place to hide when you act the fool. Once a year, the boys would go on a long bicycle expedition, riding for miles and skinny-dipping in the crystal clear gravel dugout west of town. They kept a lookout for the owners who didn't want anyone drowning on their property, and for which one of them had the smallest cock.

"You fat dickhead," one of the brothers called Antony after he cannonballed him and nearly drowned in the tidal surge.

"You shit face," Antony replied as he balled his fists and readied himself for another fight.

On their bike trips, they rode twenty hot, dusty miles on gravel roads with bald tires and a single, grease-starved gear. On long weekends, they would go fishing up north to Lake St. Andrew and St. George. The canvas tent they slept in was leaky, their air mattresses flat, sleeping bags thin, the eggs they ate for breakfast broken-yolked.

The pike they caught all day long were mammoth. They thought they had died and gone to heaven. Some of the fish they caught were for eating. Others were filleted, salted, and preserved in coolers that had no ice.

Of course, moving in permanently with this farming family in rural Manitoba meant getting used to a whole new kind of food: grass-fed beef fattened with chopped grains and forage, acres of potatoes, canned home-grown vegetables; gallon jars of milk that never ran out, an endless supply.

For breakfast, Antony learned to fry eggs to perfection. The yolks were dark yellow and runny. The whites were crispy on the edge. Four pieces of toast slathered with homemade butter, salted by the handful.

He couldn't get enough. He didn't feel full until he turned forty when his metabolism slowed down. Then the skinny boy with the bottomless pit packed the weight on.

They took turns churning cream into butter every Wednesday after supper. Antony learned that there was no play until the work that sometimes took all evening was finished. Churning went faster in summer when cows spent fat-rich hay-producing days in sun-filled pastures.

It went slower in winter when they ate hay that was cut, baled, and stacked outside for months. The cows languished day and night in barns dank with ammonia and manure-filled stench. They produced thin and watery cream that turned to butter slowly, butter lumps sloshing thinly in butter milk finally.

Wednesday nights were when public skating was at the ice rink. The shack was hot with wood fire and smoke. The metal stove in the centre cracked and popped with the chimney expanding and contracting. It warmed up red with dried pieces of wood and cooled to blue with embers dying. Clicking, snapping, and popping, another log flaring hot. At the start of another race to the top, the silver mercury in the thermometer climbed higher and higher.

Kids took off their mittens. Their cheeks red with cold. Their arches ached from the tightened laces. The first skate of the year was always the worst. But then it got easier, chasing the girls and buying Cokes, Pepsis, and Mountain Dews. The drinks cost 15¢, including deposit. Chocolate bars and potato chips cost ten.

A week's allowance, 25¢, could buy a night out for a teenager in that town of two hundred.

The Viet Cong offensive in South Vietnam and Neil Young arguing with Stephen Stills at Woodstock was the furthest thing from Antony's mind.

The world may have been in turmoil, but the butter still had to be churned on Wednesday nights when boys and girls flirted and skated and made out in parkas, mukluks, and toques pulled on tight.

It was indeed a good life for a golden boy exiled to the Land East of Eden.

Part Three

15

Broken Wings

In the summer of 1970, Antony and Izzy travelled west by train to see their uncles and aunts in Alberta and British Columbia. Antony didn't know how the family found out where they were. They hadn't heard from Mary Helen in years.

The rail journey took them to Vancouver. Not once did they sit in the seats they were assigned. Antony bolted as soon as the conductor turned his back. He spent the majority of his time up in the observation car smoking cigarettes he mooched from American tourists. When she could, Izzy sat with him.

They spent the first week with their Aunt Hedy and Uncle Orville, who took them on the ferry to Vancouver Island. Antony and Izzy stood in the front of the ship, the blast of the wind nearly blowing their jackets out of their hands. They peered down at the white caps far below them. The ferry came perilously close, or so it seemed to a land-locked lad like Antony, to the rocks along the shore of the islands in the Gulf. It was hard for them to believe that they were in the same country as back home in Quickfall. The ocean, the salt air, the luxury yachts sailing by, and killer whales cavorting in the ocean were all new and thrilling.

Uncle Orville took Antony to a BC Lions football game at Empire Stadium. Antony had never been to a CFL game before, though he watched countless ones on television. He cheered for the Calgary Stampeders in the house where the Winnipeg Blue Bombers reigned supreme.

Aunt Hedy took them to the horse races at Hastings Park. She gave them each a few dollars to bet, and while they didn't pocket any winnings that day, Antony sensed that he could easily get hooked with the excitement of the racetrack. Afterwards, they went out for Chinese food.

Antony and Izzy had never seen chopsticks before. This was a summer of firsts for them.

When their aunt and uncle invited them to come and live with them next summer, their eyes were opened to a life that could be. Antony's heart turned west.

They spent the second week of the trip with their Aunt Hilde and her daughter's family. One time over dinner, Antony silenced the whole family when the topic of conversation turned to circumcision. Antony hadn't a clue what it was, and when he asked, they were too embarrassed to say.

"Just pass him another glass of milk," his older cousin Dorie said, changing the topic and laughing.

While Izzy played with her second cousin Gail, Antony and Gail's brother Danny bicycled all over Vancouver. They rode to English Bay and swam in the salt-water pool right on the beach. It filled directly from the sea at high tide and changed regularly. They sat on the steps of The Sylvia Hotel and darted through traffic all the way down East Hastings.

Back then the East Side was tattered and torn, but not quite ripped to shreds. There was still some hope. When they went into a store to buy drinks and comics, they didn't lock their bicycles up. They simply leaned them against the window and went in.

That summer Antony fell in love with all that Vancouver offered— independence, freedom, and endless opportunity.

Antony and Izzy spent the third week of their trip with Aunt Joey and her two sons at Cultus Lake, fifty-five miles east of Vancouver. They swam every day and turned nut-brown in the sun. One morning, Antony squandered all of his pocket money, a whole $5 for the week, on pinball machines, while his cousins barely spent 50¢ each. Antony learned an important lesson about money: you can only spend it once, and you should never waste it on pinball. It's a lesson he's never forgotten.

One evening Aunt Joey told them about the first time she met her in-laws, who were living in Cranbrook at the time. She and Frank had married in Vancouver, but because of the distance and the cost, neither her mother nor his parents could attend the wedding.

In those days before paved roads and airplanes, travel through the mountains was almost impossible. The only way to get anywhere with relative ease and comfort was by rail, yet even that was difficult. Passenger trains competed with freight for the right of way. Sometimes, they would have to wait for hours at a time at a siding in the middle of nowhere for a steam engine hauling grain or coal cars to go by.

Joey and her new husband Frank, handsome and swarthy of Italian descent, were visiting his parents shortly after their wedding. It was a hot summer day. Frank was out with his father, haying. Joey was in the kitchen, trying to impress her mother-in-law, baking a cake. She mixed the ingredients, whisked the egg whites, and folded one into the other. She put the cake into the woodstove oven and washed up while the cake baked and filled the kitchen with the comfortable aroma of home. After forty-five minutes, she opened the oven door. To her surprise and horror, the cake was flatter than the tire on the 1928 Chrysler Imperial 80 out back. Mrs. Fare tried to comfort her young daughter-in-law.

"Joey, don't worry. It's only a cake. We'll feed it to the chickens, and no one will know."

Except, after eating the cake, the chickens rushed to the trough and gulped down water as fast as they could, stretching their necks and cackling piteously. To the women's horror, soon ten were dead.

"Joey?" Mrs. Fare asked. "What did you put in the cake?"

Joey showed her. It wasn't sugar she added to the flour as she thought, but salt. Enough to kill a coop full of chickens.

"We butchered those chickens before the men came back," Joey explained, keeping the secret of her failed cake from them. "At breakfast the next day, they did wonder why there were fewer eggs to go around."

"Must have been a weasel," Mrs. Fare offered as she passed a bowl of Red River Cereal to her perplexed husband.

Antony and Izzy took the Greyhound from Vancouver to Kamloops through the Fraser Canyon, spending the fourth week of their trip on Adams Lake, outside of Chase, BC, with their Uncle Adolf and Aunt Ina. Uncle Adolf was a short, bald man who always wore a hat. Aunt Ina was an artist who got up every morning well before dawn for her painting lesson. Out came the eyeliner, rouge, lipstick, and foundation. Even after forty years of marriage, Adolf never saw his wife without her makeup. She was dedicated to her art, and turned out the lights before she slipped into his bed.

Uncle Adolf managed a sawmill there, and he and Ina lived in a small house right on the lakeshore. You had to drive through the mill yard to get to their house, dodging forklifts carrying huge flats of sawn lumber.

Antony and Izzy slept in a small cabin beside the garden. There was no room in the main house for guests. Aunt Ina was such a pack rat that she even tied balls of yarn to the springs under the bed. She did not throw anything remotely useful away.

In the guest cabin during the evening, Antony smoked cigarillos and played Crib with Izzy. She beat him every time, Izzy with the dimple on her chin.

They took the bus to Calgary, where they spent the last week of their trip with Uncle Johnny, his Scottish-born war bride Marg, and their children. They went swimming every day and laughed under the hot Alberta sun. His eldest cousin had a complete collection of Beatles albums, and they listened to every track. Antony had never heard The Beatles' *White Album*. Before he left Calgary, though, he had memorized the lyrics to "Blackbird." They became his fight song.

When their week was up, Antony and Izzy were back on the train to Manitoba. They pulled into the station in downtown Winnipeg and saw Flora waiting in the crowd. She was by herself. Sverr and the kids were shopping at Polo Park, wanting to take advantage of this rare trip into the city. She called out to them as they stepped off the train, her laugh welcoming them back home.

For Antony, however, his heart was no longer there. He had been out west, and he had seen the life that could be his. His eyes had been opened to the outside world, and he was ready to fly away, a blackbird waiting for his moment to arise.

16

Run Away

In April 1971, Antony persuaded his friend Terry to hitchhike to Vancouver. Terry was a tall, affable kid who liked to smoke Player's plain cigarettes.

"They give me a kind of satisfaction no other cigarette does," he told Antony as they hung their thumbs out on the #7 south into Winnipeg. They were heading to the Perimeter Highway and then west on the Trans-Canada, which would take them to the coast over fourteen hundred miles away.

They ran away from school the day before the Easter holidays were to begin. Both boys were in the last months of Grade Ten. Antony was scheduled to have his driver's license road test the next Wednesday, but he hadn't given it a thought.

One of the more benign consequences of his decision to take off on that particular day was that he was unable to get his license until three years later.

The first time he took driving lessons, it was part of his Grade Ten school program at Clearwater Collegiate, and therefore free. The second time, it was on Tuesday nights with the British Columbia Automobile Association in Abbotsford the year he graduated from high school. He had to pay for that course from his own nearly empty wallet.

While at Clearwater, he took driver's lessons every Monday afternoon for a couple of hours. He learned to parallel park and drive the Perimeter, better known to locals as the Circle of Death, a four-lane divided expressway encircling most of Winnipeg. He navigated Portage and Main during rush hour and overtook cars on the two-lane highway thirty miles north to Sanders.

"Don't pass if you have to go over the speed limit!" the instructor exclaimed after one particularly harrowing judgement call that the pimply-faced Antony had unfortunately made.

Barely sixteen, Antony was ready for the open road, his learner's license folded safely in his wallet. He left a note for Flora. Abrupt, terse, and to the point, it wasn't much of a warning for her, or an apology. He was set to find his own destiny and wasn't looking back.

Without any forethought, planning, or preparation, he and Terry skipped out of school that Thursday before Good Friday and headed west.

The sun shone, the breeze blew gently on their backs, and they were as excited as larks. Honestly, nothing could go wrong.

Their thin-as-cotton-can-be blue jean jackets were too hot and heavy for them to wear, so they slung them over their shoulders.

"Oh, we're just going to Winnipeg for the day," Terry told the first driver who offered them a lift. He was heading east into the city and then north to Selkirk. They were going west toward Rosser and south to Headingley on the Trans-Canada.

Their plan not to tell anybody their final destination worked. Nobody's suspicions were raised. They were just a couple of young kids on the road to a friend's place for the weekend. Besides, hitchhiking wasn't all that unusual in the early 1970s. Nearly everyone under thirty was on the "Road to Enlightenment" and Haight-Ashbury, or off on an adventure to Scarborough Fair.

Both Antony and Terry had haircuts above their ears. They didn't know a joint of marijuana from a Cuban cigar, and they had no intention ever of eating, let alone wearing, sprigs of parsley, sage, rosemary, or thyme. They were two small-town teenagers in the throes of puberty and had adolescent crushes on girls who wouldn't give them the time of day.

"Ever been to Vancouver, Terry?"

"What did you say, Antony? Vancouver?"

" Sure did. Went there last year and had a blast. Got so drunk I puked on the sidewalk."

"Sounds good. Want to go again?"

"Why not tomorrow? It's the long weekend and I'll be stuck at home with nothing to do."

Then they disappeared. Without a trace.

At Grand Valley, just west of Brandon, they ate the lunches they packed for school that morning. They watched sea gulls whorl and wheel and swoop through the sky, following a tractor as it ploughed a field.

Antony bummed a smoke from Terry, promising to pay him back as soon as they stopped in a town with a store that was open. Terry gave him one.

"You'll have to use your own matches, though. I don't have any left."

Near Indian Head, east of Regina, Antony finally bought his own smokes and enough matches to last the trip. They grabbed a bite to eat at a restaurant near the highway.

"Remember that English class? With Mrs. Campbell?" Terry ribbed Antony, reminding him how his ass caught fire from the wooden matches he had in his pants pocket. First the pinpricks, then the stench of sulphur, and Antony jumping up and swearing and swatting his butt. The whole class was in an uproar.

"Shut up, idiot!"

"Gawd! What a smell!"

"Retard!"

"Hey! I'm outta here!"

"Prick!"

Mrs. Campbell had no choice but to stop teaching Macbeth and let Antony go out into the hall and try to regain his composure. Then she had to regain her control over her class on the first nice day of the year. Once she figured Antony wasn't intentionally trying to disrupt the class, for a change, she was quite sympathetic to him.

"Little dumb, don't you think? Wooden matches in your back pocket are certain to light."

Antony agreed. Sheepishly.

When he settled down, she resumed teaching. Then she burst out laughing. She reached the passage in Act Two when Banquo and Fleance are commenting on the darkness of the sky.

"There's husbandry in heaven. Their candles are all out."

Just like the matches in Antony's back pocket, words she daren't say, but split her gut.

Near Piapot in southern Saskatchewan, they watched a herd of Pronghorn antelope springing in waves through the open grassland. Once again, Antony smelled the familiar scent of sage. It reminded him of Gleichen. As they waited by the turnoff into the town for another ride to take them further along the Trans-Canada, he heard a Western Meadowlark. He followed its distinct and melodic up-and-down-the-scale song to a fence post. Sure enough, there it was perched, proclaiming to anyone who could hear that all was well within its kingdom and that intruders had better beware. Antony perked up his ears. There was no going back now, for him.

The further west they travelled, the closer they huddled in their insubstantial thin-as-cotton-can-be blue jean jackets, the air getting sharper, brighter, and colder. Snow covered the fields as they rolled past Bassano, Cluny, and Gleichen. They were in familiar territory now. Antony felt home in his bones.

This was where he belonged. His family's red blood drenched the ground here. Graves, births, living, and dying. This is the blood of my blood spilled for you. My body broken for you. Parents, grandparents, brothers, sisters, cousins. Aunts and uncles. Home of homes.

Eema Mother! I haven't forgotten! How good this feels! A deep yearning welled within Antony's heart. He hadn't felt it in years. A stranger in his own land, the familiar had become unfamiliar. Now he was reintroduced to his home and native land.

When they arrived in downtown Calgary, they were colder than they had ever been before. Terry and Antony huddled over a building ventilation grate near the Husky Tower, all concrete, shatterproof glass and taller than a grain elevator.

Where was the spring weather they enjoyed in Manitoba? This reality was too harsh and cruel for their taste. They pooled their money and hailed a cab. It dropped them off at five-thirty in the morning in front of Uncle Johnny's house.

"Marg! It's Antony! What are you doing here? Come on in. You guys must be freezing." Aunt Marg put on a pot of coffee and fed them some hot food.

"Johnny, let the boys get some rest." She spoke in her Scottish brogue. "We'll talk this through later in the morning."

Antony didn't have a clue what he and Terry were doing, even after his dreamless sleep on the couch in his aunt and uncle's basement. Uncle Johnny said that they would have to find jobs. They couldn't live with him. They needed to work.

"You only run away when you've got someplace better to go."

"That's the truth, Antony. Where are you going? What are you thinking?"

Antony couldn't give him an answer. All he knew was that he and Terry were heading west and that there was still a stretch of empty highway in front of them.

Aunt Marg packed them a lunch and Uncle Johnny slipped Antony a ten-dollar bill.

He gave them a lift from his wartime bungalow on Imperial Crescent down to the Trans-Canada past Bowness on the west side of Calgary. It would be easy for someone to stop and pick them up there. He wished them the very best. He knew that Antony was getting into trouble, and that there was nothing he could do about it.

"Antony, you better watch yourself," he cautioned. "This could turn out badly if you're not careful."

Their first ride took them to Banff. As they drove by the electric sub-station just inside the Park Gates, Antony put his hand to the window and pressed his palm against the pane.

Oh, that's what Mum was talking about, he said to himself. *It doesn't hurt at all.*

He was on a sudden trajectory to adulthood.

Another ride took them through the Rogers Pass. He had learned about hanging glaciers, erratics, and moraines in a geography book he'd just finished reading. All he had to do was crane his neck and look up and out the car window over the mountain valley. He could see what the writers had carefully described.

Just before Revelstoke, they ran out of gas. Antony hitched a ride into town, stopped at the nearest gas station, where he filled up a jerry can. He laid down a five-dollar deposit, and thumbed his way back to Terry and the driver, who were sleeping in the cold dark car.

The night was so black that they couldn't see their hands in front of their face, let alone pour gas into the tank. Then Antony lit one of the matches he bought back in Indian Head.

"Oh hell!" yelled Terry.

"What are you thinking, you stupid fuck?" the driver yelled.

The flames caught some of the gas vapour, pooled on the pavement, and long cow licks of fire jumped towards the car. Somehow, they managed to push it out of the way before it caught fire and exploded.

They jumped in, the driver floored the car out of danger, and they drove on fumes, fuming, the rest of the way into town.

Even in the height of his stupidity, Eema Mother wasn't about to forget Her young charge. She had plans for him, and they weren't all bad.

"Over there!" Antony motioned to the gas station where he left his deposit.

"Oh, you!" the attendant said, surprised and disappointed Antony returned.

Their ride said he needed to get some sleep. This was too much excitement for one day. He added as an afterthought that he'd pick them up if they were still on the highway when he got going again. He didn't offer to let them share the floor in his motel room, and they couldn't afford a room of their own.

Their only hope was to catch a long ride with a guy who'd have his heater on.

Cold and tired, they made it to Sicamous in the early hours of the morning. They huddled in a brightly-lit coin laundromat that was warm and open. If someone came in, they'd simply put a few coins in the dryer.

No one came, though, and they crashed stone-cold but warming with the dawn's slow arrival.

Salmon Arm, Sorrento, Adams Lake, Chase, and Monte Creek where their ride filled up with gas, Kamloops, Savona, and Cache Creek. From mountain forest to rolling hill and semi-desert, the landscape transformed itself with each progressive ride. In the heat of the day, they carried their thin-as-cotton-can-be blue jean jackets. In the cold, dark night, they wished they had their parkas on.

Their trip went mostly without a hitch. Two young, clean-cut kids with little baggage, it was easy to give them rides. They made good time as they travelled across-country. However, their westward momentum skidded to a dead stop at the junction on the Trans-Canada to Ashcroft, south of Cache Creek.

No matter what they did, they couldn't get a ride. Antony would try, then Terry on his own. They'd stand together. One would catch some sleep in the ditch. They'd get on their knees, and wave Uncle Johnny's ten-dollar bill. But all in vain, nobody stopped.

The sun set and they scrunched up and down the gravel shoulder in the pearl grey light of dusk. A guy in a turquoise-coloured, two-door Malibu finally picked them up around nine. He was driving from Prince George and needed someone to help keep him awake for the four hours remaining to Vancouver. Terry crawled into the backseat and promptly fell asleep. Antony sat up front and froze. The driver kept the car as cold as possible.

Antony thought his eyelids would freeze open. They made it through the Fraser Canyon, the driver honked his horn through each of the seven tunnels as they drove south: China Bar, Farabee, Hell's Gate, Alexandra, Sailor Bar, Saddle Rock, and Yale. The blare of the horn through the China Bar was loud enough to wake the dead, but that bloody Terry kept snoring away.

Asshole, Antony thought.

The Malibu cut through the heavy, humid, dairy-farm-filled air of the Fraser Valley. The smell of cow manure hit them like a wall as they drove past Chilliwack. The Trans-Canada closing in and claustrophobic, devil's claw, cedar trees and blackberry bushes filling the median and encroaching on the ditch's edge. They crossed the Port Mann Bridge arcing its way mystically over the Fraser River, and made their way through traffic down Broadway.

"I know a place where you can sleep for the night. It's a drop-in centre for kids like you, the Inner City Hostel. Tomorrow, you can get yourself set up," the driver said as he stopped to let them out before crossing the Cambie Street Bridge. "It's not too far from here," he added as Terry untangled himself, bones aching, from the back of the Malibu.

They asked what seemed to be a trip of hippies where to find the hostel, not that they'd ever seen a real-life hippie before, except on television. One of the bearded longhairs turned out to be a Jesus Freak. He gave Antony a Book of the People tract that had *Eema Mother Loves You!* emblazoned across the cover.

He pointed to a brightly-lit church down the street. Antony and Terry made their way there and found a couple of oak pews to rest on.

Rock of Ages cleft for me, Antony groaned as he fell into another bone-aching sleep. At least he was warm for the first time since he left Manitoba.

That morning after some breakfast and a couple hours of kitchen duty, they went out to do some exploring. They made it to The Bay downtown, their casual school friendship stretched taut after the rigours of four days on the road.

Terry decided he'd had enough. He wandered off to phone home and Antony stayed where he was, on the street with five dollars in his pocket. He wasn't ready to make any calls just yet.

He walked back to the Drop-In Centre alone and overheard someone say that he could get a bed to sleep in for four nights and $8.40 in meal tickets at the Catholic Charities Hostel. It seemed like a good idea. He remembered that he had a bit of money left in his bank account.

His new best friend Rob said he'd help him out. Over the next couple of days and nights, he and Antony hung out and sampled life on Vancouver's east side, seriously depleting Antony's meagre cash reserve. He smoked his first joint on Victory Square.

One night as Antony was walking alone, near Burrard and Fourth, a police officer stopped him and searched his pockets. When he found nothing illegal on Antony, he shook his head.

"This is how kids like you end up in the gutter," he said before driving away.

Antony knew then and there that it was now entirely up to him. He could continue in the direction that he had been heading, or he could turn around and run to safety. Nobody was telling him what to do or where to get off.

Yet.

Antony tramped across the Burrard Street Bridge and made his way to the Catholic Charities Hostel. By the time he arrived, he knew beyond a shadow of a doubt that he was in the wrong place at the wrong time.

While sitting on his bed and talking to Rob, a huge guy with a closely-shaved head came over to them.

"Hey, I'm Kane, your new best friend. I've had my eye on you since you arrived. That's a fine blue jean jacket you got there. Mind if I try it on?"

Antony gave it to him, seeing as he didn't have any choice. Kane had the letters L-O-V-E tattooed on the fingers of one hand and H-A-T-E on the other. He threw his green woollen army surplus jacket on Antony's bed.

"Let's trade," he said. "Me and Rob will get you some good shit to shoot up tomorrow night. What do you say?"

When the lights went out, Antony crawled into bed, his back to the wall. He knew he had to get out.

The next morning, he escaped the hostel as soon as the light of day broke in through the windows. He found his way to Social Services and told the black woman at the front counter that he was a runaway and that he wanted to talk to his aunt and uncle in Burnaby. They'd promised to take him in when school ended for the summer. He was just a little early.

"You've come to the right place, honey," the Eema Mother-like woman, dressed in a green and gold Kanga dress, said. "I'll help you."

Grateful, Antony sat in the chair while she filled out the paperwork.

She found him a place to stay in a safe house that was operated by some Jesus People, hippies disenchanted with the balls and chains and knives and needles that sidled up along young kids in the shadows. Their zeal kept them on the streets in Vancouver. They were there to save the lost, and Antony was in more trouble than he dared to imagine.

After lunch, while noodling on his brand-spanking new Norman guitar, a guy from Quebec named Larry suggested that Antony shouldn't be so ready to believe everything that other people told him.

"Among wolves, you need to be as wise as serpents and as innocent as doves."

That afternoon he and Antony went down to Stanley Park. They saw Pierre Trudeau giving a speech to a large crowd. They sat in the sun at the outer edge of the multitude and wondered what was going on. *It must be the dawning of the Age of Aquarius*, Antony hummed to himself. Then he realized how hungry he was. What he'd do for a piece of bread and some fish? That was anyone's guess.

"You ready to make the phone call?" Larry asked.

"Yeah," Antony replied.

17

Just One Bag

Social Services informed Flora in Manitoba that Antony turned himself in. They also called his aunt and uncle in Burnaby who agreed to come and get him, if that was what he wanted, but he'd have to behave. They wouldn't tolerate drugs or carrying on. He'd have to do his homework and chores without being told. He better know how to clean up after himself, make his bed, and put away his laundry.

"There'll be no staying out late," Orville said. "Or loud rock and roll music. You'd better toe the line or there'll be consequences. We won't tolerate any tomfoolery."

Orville supported Hedy. These were her relatives, after all. He knew she couldn't give them the cold shoulder. She was too good a person for that. She'd give the shirt off her back to help her loved ones. That's what he adored about her. Her generosity and kindness.

"Of course, Hedy," he said. "We'll give Antony a home, and Izzy, too. But if it gets too much, they're going back. I won't let them ruin your health. These kids need our help, but my first responsibility is to you."

Hedy lit another cigarette and smiled at her husband. He was a good and faithful man. He didn't know this, of course, nobody did. Just her sisters and they were sworn to secrecy. At eighteen, she had a one-night stand and got herself pregnant. Twenty-seven-year-old Asa Morris slipped out of her life as quickly as he slipped in. He gave her a son, whom she had to give up for adoption. As a teenager with a child born out of wedlock, she didn't have a choice. She didn't have a chance. He had no intention of marrying her. His eyes were on someone else, his wife whom he had no intention of leaving.

Giving Antony and Izzy a safe place to live seemed the right thing for Hedy to do. It might make up for all that she had lost, her boy raised in northern Alberta, and his son, born in Fort Smith, and raised in Inuvik. There is little grace in this world for lost mothers, unknown fathers, and castaway children. These left behinds have the heart of Eema Mother God. They are Her flock, the ones She tries to shelter in Her fold.

"Oh, Mother God, why can't you do more to help us in our distress?" Antony prayed on more than one occasion. *"I am doing all that I can,"* She replied. Something he had a hard time believing, shaking his head at her inability to alleviate human suffering in the here and now. *The crux of faith is a hard one to bear. Just ask Simon of Cyrene.*

At the end of the school year, Hedy and Orville drove to Quickfall in a brand new Nordic-blue hardtop 1972 Oldsmobile Supreme.

"This is a good opportunity," he said. "The engine needs breaking in. We'll take all the time we need. Visit Johnny and Marg in Calgary, make a stop at the grave in Gleichen. See Hilde's daughter at the ranch outside Hussar. Maybe Vera in Bassano."

They drove and took their time. They were in no rush to get back to Vancouver. What had they been thinking? Taking in a sixteen-year-old? That Antony was a troubled boy. He had a chip on his shoulder.

"Izzy would be a delight. A fine little girl. She'd be no trouble at all," Hedy was certain.

Orville agreed.

They spent the night in Winnipeg before driving out to Quickfall. That way, they could get an early start and maybe reach Regina the first day.

Izzy collected her things and bade a tearful goodbye to Flora, who had rescued her, mothered her, and raised her as one of her own. Flora was the only mother Izzy remembered. Antony had run away without saying a word. With Izzy now leaving, Flora's heart was breaking a second time. She feared for this girl soon turning into a woman.

But reuniting kids with their relatives is the right thing to do, Flora assumed, *the family thing. Blood after all is thicker than water. Or is it?*

Only time would tell.

Izzy was going where she belonged. At least that's what everyone told her.

But she didn't have a choice; her opinion didn't matter.

Hedy and Orville did what they could for Izzy and Antony.

They moved into an apartment in Middlegate in South Burnaby, near New Westminster on Kingsway Avenue. Izzy spent time with Aunt Hedy while Uncle Orville was out of town at his job. Antony worked at The Red Barn, a fast-food restaurant. He got to work on time, completed the tasks he was given, and banked most of the money he earned.

After a month, he bought a Peugeot ten-speed bicycle with his savings and spent as much of his free time as possible with his cousins Alex and Michael. They rode bikes everywhere and walked to every rock concert that came to Hastings Park: Jethro Tull, The Moody Blues, John Lee Hooker, Yes, Leon Redbone, and Chilliwack.

They spent hours in the basement listening to Bruce Cockburn, Leonard Cohen, Joni Mitchell, Bob Dylan, and Savoy Brown. With LPs playing as loudly on the sound system as the speakers could handle, they scoured album covers. While Antony experimented with weed and got stoned out of his mind, Alex and Michael practised on their guitars and dreamed of playing in a rock and roll band.

It never occurred to Antony that he, too, could plan for his own future.

Late that August, the house Aunt Hedy and Uncle Orville were building on Timms Crescent in Clearbrook was finished. They packed up the apartment and moved out to the Valley. Over the coming year, their dream of becoming a happy family fell completely apart.

Izzy was inconsolable. She missed Flora, who had become her mother in the five years since Mary Helen abandoned them. Antony's thin skin and cocky self-absorption didn't help him fit in with his aunt and uncle's Lawrence Welk music and out-of-fashion attitudes. They were older than thirty, after all.

They despised each other.

In the winter semester of Grade Eleven, Antony ran for President of the Student Council. It was 1972, and Bruce, the only one in their gang with a job and a car, a green 1957 Chevy Nomad station wagon, was his campaign manager. They promised cold beer machines in the student cafeteria, red carpets, and chandeliers in the dining room.

Bruce and he were on a tear. Mr. Keis the Principal called Antony into his office one day.

"Antony, your grades aren't very good. You aren't taking this seriously."

Antony vowed to clean up his campaign immediately and said he would fight for something real, legitimate. The school needed new bleachers for the soccer fields, not that anyone, as far as he could tell, ever went to the games. That would bring in the votes.

The candidate who eventually won pork-barrelled the voters. He brought in a truckload of watermelons to bolster his campaign. His posters proclaimed, "Mellon For President!"

That's when Antony learned that you needed money and good looks if you wanted to win elections. Planks and platforms were only part of the equation. You needed promise, and he came up short.

In response, Antony upped the ante with a plank that the Rhinoceros Party later adopted. He promised to resign immediately if he won. He and Bruce came in third out of a field of six.

After the election, Mr. Keis, in his worn thin at the elbows Harris Tweed jacket, started smoking again.

That Easter, still pumped from his near-electoral win, Antony lied to his aunt and uncle, saying that he and Alex were going camping for the week, and thumbed a ride to Vancouver. They crossed the border at Blaine, Washington, and hitchhiked down the I-5 to San Francisco.

It may not have been a particularly numinous trip for Antony, but it made him see life on a much broader canvas. The world did not revolve at all around his good feelings and sense of well-being. He smoked some weed with one driver. Another pulled out his handgun and put it on the dash.

"I don't mind giving you two a ride," he said. "But I don't want any trouble."

That sobered Antony up.

They made it to an off-ramp somewhere in the Bay area, bought a bottle of red wine with Canadian dollars, took a couple of swigs, and gave it to a guy on the street. Then they walked back to the on-ramp and thumbed their way north, back to where they belonged.

The trip was a blur in his memory. What exactly did he remember? Getting fingerprinted at the border before crossing back into Canada. And Alex saying,

"Antony, next time, take just one bag, not two."

Antony had a story to tell, and all he needed was an audience. Who would listen? Would anybody care?

Outwardly, his life was a sham. Inside, it was spiralling downward. He would have clutched at anything, anyone who would have paid attention, given him real meaning, affection, and love.

He was a lonely soul crying out for help, using the only language he knew, swearing and smart-ass replies.

He honed his sense of humour to a sharp edge and cut people who came too close.

One day, a blonde-haired girl named Chris strolled into his ken and became the focus of his earthly delight. How Antony wanted to tell her his story and explore this New-found-land! But that was never to be. She listened but never went any further. He was not allowed to plant his flag on her virgin soil.

She walked him straight through the front door into her church, and hurried out the back before he could tell her about his encounter with the police officer on the Burrard Street Bridge.

It was time to get his act together.

Antony barely finished Grade Eleven. If he wasn't arguing with his new church friends, he was cutting class and making plans for the weekend. Doing his homework was never a priority.

One night after crawling home from a party, all the lies he had told his aunt and uncle so that he could go out, came crashing down on him. It was now or never. Eema Mother had finally had enough.

"Tell the truth!" she told him. "Stop the lying."

That morning, he tried to make amends, but his aunt and uncle weren't having any of it. This latest drop in the bucket of Antony's misdemeanors set the whole thing to overflowing and there was no stopping once it started.

After breakfast, Antony helped to level the pile of topsoil that had been dumped on the front yard.

"You know, Antony," his uncle said as he shovelled dirt in the wheelbarrow that Antony was manhandling. "This just isn't what we expected. It's not working out. Your aunt is sick and tired. I am out of town with my work. Your attitude hasn't made this any easier."

Antony apologized and promised things would be different, but his uncle stopped him.

"It's too late for words, son."

18

Talking Tree

At the end of June, Izzy returned to Quickfall, and Eema Mother put the squeeze on Antony.

He couldn't stop attending Book of the People Studies and Youth Group activities. He wrangled with anyone who'd spar with him about Jesus, sin, and suffering. He accused them of being hypocrites, all the while attending their campfires, potlucks, wiener roasts, and baseball games. He squabbled with each and every one of them, all the time enjoying their kindness and hospitality.

He nailed them with every sin he could imagine. Their narrow-mindedness, intolerance, and bigotry. Their pride, anger, lewdness, and lust. These were his sins, too, and he was just as guilty as they were. He just wouldn't admit it.

"Where do you get your so-called authority? The Book of the People? What if I don't accept your premise? I don't believe it's the word of Eema Mother. I don't…What if…."

And they kept inviting him to their ballgames, fondues, summer patios, and car washes. They made room for him in their kitchens and living rooms. While he rankled them to no end, they nudged and loved him closer into the Kingdom of Eema Mother.

From what he could see from the outside of the church looking in was that he preferred their stable lives and marriages, double-car garages and carports, baseball games, corn roasts, and sing-a-longs to the overflowing ashtrays and emptied beer bottles of the life that he knew all too well.

There was something in the words they spoke that were filled with hope. He wasn't sure what. Something about living in the light, telling the truth, and being charitable. That struck a resonant chord within his heart.

He was seventeen and boarding with an older couple who rented rooms out to Social Services.

The words of the police officer who stopped him on the Burrard Street Bridge made him pause. How did he want to live, and what did he want to do?

Antony decided to make a change.

Without a home and all alone, Antony volunteered to spend a week as an Assistant Counsellor at a camp close to the foot of Squeah Mountain near Yale, at the start of the Fraser Canyon. Ron's clean cut, good-natured, hardworking, "The-More-Stoned-You-Get-The-Boulder-You-Become" attitude towards drugs and living showed Antony that there was another direction that he could follow.

Antony knelt before a talking tree.

"Eema Mother, have mercy upon me," Antony prayed. "Forgive my sin and grant me thy grace that I may live for you and honour you with my thoughts, words, and deeds."

That September, when school resumed, Antony was on his own. He wore an "Eema Mother Loves You" button on the lapel of the suit jacket that he picked up at a thrift store, and lost all the popularity he had garnered during his presidential campaign. He was too religious to party and too new and fervent for the church crowd at school to be accepted into their clique.

What he found thrilling and exciting, they found lame and boring. He wanted in and they wanted out. They had not yet tasted the bitterness that Antony lived his entire life.

"Antony, you've changed too much, it can't be real," the beatific Luella said to him. "I no longer trust you."

None of his friends from church attended his school, and he didn't want to hang out with his drinking buddies. He stumbled from class to class in his journey of faith. At a Halloween party, he sat on a sofa with Heather, a babe from Dr. Pastro's Biology class.

"Antony," she said. "You aren't the same guy I used to know. What happened?"

"I don't know, little bird," he replied. He smelled the fresh scent of shampoo in her hair, held her hand, and loved the delicious taste of tobacco on her tongue.

"Hmm," she sighed as she put her hand on his leg. "Perhaps you haven't changed as much as I thought."

While Antony wanted to go all the way, he was not ready to have a one-night stand. Somehow, he resisted her feminine wonder that hallowed evening when all was not as it appeared.

She went home a woman scorned, and he carried on in his noble quest for a happy ending.

In English class the next day, Mr. Wittenberg was explicating the ribald Miller's tale from Chaucer's *Canterbury Tales*. Antony could not believe his eyes when he read the passage about the foolish parish clerk Absolon who kissed the lovely Alison through her bedroom window:

This Absolon began to wipe his mouth so dry.

Dark was the night as pitch or as a piece of coal

And out of the window she put her ass's hole.

And Absolon he felt no better nor any worse

But with his mouth he kissed her on her naked arse

Full savourly, before he was aware of this.

Aback he started and thought something was amiss

For well he knew no woman had a beard.

The thing he felt was rough, all long haired.

He said—Fie! Alas! What have I just done?

Teehee!—said she and closed the window to.

"Look. Earle, did you read this?" Antony whispered to one of his dope-smoking rowdy friends who lived on Mount Lehman Road.

They laughed.

"People in the Middle Ages swore. They played jokes on each other. They had SEX!"

When Antony read how Absolon got his revenge, he decided then and there to become an English major. If only Eema Mother would help him get a place to sleep at night. The landlords where he was staying were fed up with his religious zeal.

He was always reading his Book of the People, spending hours on the phone talking to girls, and not staying in his room. They gave him until the end of the month to find somewhere else to stay.

"Almost eighteen?" the social worker mused. "You're too old to be placed in a foster home. You'll have to find something on your own."

At the Inter-Varsity club meeting over the lunch hour that week, Antony asked for prayer.

"I need a place to stay. Do you know anyone with a room to spare?"

The faculty sponsor Mr. Wiebe, the German and Music teacher with hair like Herbert von Karajan, invited Antony into his home to meet his wife and children.

"You should have been at the school's Inter-Varsity meeting," Henry explained to Marge. "He asked for prayer. Did someone know of a family who'd take him in until he finished school? I couldn't ignore him. Eema Mother's call is clear. This kid needs our help."

Just before Christmas, Antony moved in.

Henry, however, left it to Marge to figure out exactly where to bed Antony, what to feed him three times a day, and where he should sit at the family dinner table.

Mr. Wiebe spoke to Antony about the importance of balance. "Faith is important, yes! But so is life in this world. A body needs to be spiritual, but you also need to fit in."

Mrs. Wiebe taught him to wash behind his ears and not glob ketchup on everything she cooked.

Some things Antony caught immediately. Others he learned the hard way. Once he was bucking up a tree that Mr. Wiebe had just chopped down.

"You can't just say you're a follower of Eema Mother," Mr. Wiebe said. "You have to live it. Remember what Eema Mother said was the greatest commandment? Love your neighbour as yourself."

Mrs. Wiebe showed him how to iron his shirts and to wash his pots after cooking in her kitchen.

"Antony, you'll find Eema Mother in the small things, but you have to look. And whatever you do, don't leave your dirty dishes in the sink again for someone else, namely me, to scrub up and put away."

They introduced him to chamomile tea, home cooking, sit-down family meals, daily Book of the People readings, Andrés Segovia, Fritz Kreisler, German, music lessons, and the secret to a happy life—the way of the Cross.

Antony had been tossed out on his ear, but the Wiebes took up the challenge.

At school, it soon became apparent that two were better than one. Antony and Earle found refuge in each other. They ate their lunches together and attended the House of James Coffee House on Friday nights. The proprietor Lando would book bands from all over the Lower Mainland, fill the coffee urn when it was empty, and make lost souls feel welcome.

Over the next year, they put hundreds of miles on Earle's little Isuzu Berette, driving from one church to another and one coffee house to the next, enjoying the potluck dinners and checking out all the chicks. Coffee, Eema Mother, girls, and singing. What a smorgasbord of faith! A fertile ground for new belief. How they flourished, one Faithful and the other Hopeful, two stalwart pilgrims on their way to the Celestial City.

19

Due North

In 1973, Antony graduated from Grade Twelve near the bottom of his class, but the new direction that he had set for himself was clear. His grades may have spiralled ever downward, but he wasn't heading into the drain of downtown Vancouver's east side. He spent the first summer out of high school working as a counsellor at the camp where he secured his faith the year before.

As he told everyone who fell into the trap his groan-inducing sense of humour had set, he found Eema Mother beyond Hope, but before Hell's Gate.

Some of the best jokes were the ones he had to wait ages for until the right set-up formed. When he'd let out the punch line, it seemed light and spontaneous. He appeared to have a quick mind. In reality, he was a careful planner who waited patiently for the circumstances to align properly before he set his jokes free.

Antony was full of puns and the bane of all literalists.

That autumn, he travelled to Sebastopol, California, an hour or so north of San Francisco, to attend a three-month-long boot camp that provided basic training in the fundamentals of living for Eema Mother.

"Hit the sack, sinners!" the Sergeant bellowed as his raw recruits fell asleep, exhausted from their first day.

"Sleepers awake!" he roared after their heads had just hit the pillows. "It's almost dawn! You need a three-mile run to get you up and at it." He rousted them and they stumbled slack-jawed from their beds.

"Eema Mother's mercy may be boundless," he warned. "But mine is finite. Now get your rear ends out that door and start pounding the pavement! You got some running to do before breakfast."

In this rugged, John the Baptist, wear-wool-and-eat locusts, pay-your-tuition-and-shut-your-mouth kind of school that Antony enrolled in, the thought of going AWOL and heading back to Canada just never entered his mind. He ran the good race every morning, the Sarge barking and yapping at their heels.

He read his Book of the People like it was the only tome on earth. Most of it, he discovered, especially the first part, was decidedly written for a mature audience. Stories of judgement, adultery, murder, back-sniping, and being cruel to your neighbour were its usual fare.

The Book of the People, he decided, was not something a guy could read to get all comfortable and settled in a middle class and pay your mortgage sort of way. It was a thistle and a burr that irritated and rubbed him raw and pushed him over the limit. There was no prosperity gospel in the pages he read. Just serve others, wash their feet, and feed them loaves of bread and baskets of fish when they're hungry.

It was all about being poor in spirit and rich in service.

As September metamorphosed into October and October stripped down to the winter minimalism of November, Antony wrestled with tumult in his heart.

He was angry with Mary Helen, disappointed in James George, ashamed that he had not cherished the generosity that his aunt and uncle had offered him, and guilt-ridden over abandoning Izzy.

In December, he presented his body and soul full of regret and woe to Eema Mother as a living sacrifice. He weathered the training he received. His faith became a matter of choice and discipline, not whim and circumstance.

He took control of his life but needed to find direction.

He returned to Abbotsford on Christmas Day, which was not the best of days to walk in on somebody unannounced, even if they are as devout, hospitable, and kind-hearted as the Wiebes.

On Boxing Day, having collapsed in their basement after his one-day ride in a car with five others, he scrambled to find work, a place to live, and a roadworthy car. His old friend Bruce knew a guy who knew a guy who needed a day labourer to strip forms from newly-poured foundations of some houses he was building on spec in Richmond. He'd pick Antony up at six the next morning.

"You got rubber boots?" lean and lanky Billmer asked. "It's wet out there."

As soon as they got to the job site, Antony set to work, slicker on, rain coming down, just above zero, not cold enough to be sleet or snow, but mighty inhospitable.

"Why am I so broke?" he moaned. "Shouldn't life be a little easier now that I am walking down the Queen's Highway?"

He hammered his pry bar between the new concrete and the oiled plywood, and nearly lost his boot in the heavy, river-bottom mud that covered most of the Fraser Valley, east of Vancouver.

"Hey, nitwit! You gotta remove the metal form tie before you pry off the plywood," Billmer yelled. "Greenhorn," he muttered as he heaved another sheet up onto the wooden pallet.

By the end of the day, all Antony could do was chatter from the damp and cold, a Lower Mainland Baptism for the Newly Employed. He spent that night at Billmer's place, so they could get an early start the next morning. They ate breakfast at Albert's Restaurant.

"Order a big one," Billmer advised. "We ain't stopping until this job is done. Make sure you pick up the pace a little. You were kind of slow yesterday."

Antony, who had been reading Romans for devotions, nodded.

"My old man is going to drown in rain, blood, sweat, and tears before this day is over."

As much as he needed the money, Antony decided that he wasn't going to strip forms for the rest of his life. He figured that he'd work there until he earned enough to pay for driver's lessons and buy a car. It was too hard, living in Abbotsford and working in Richmond. Besides, he couldn't bunk at Billmer's place forever. Their relationship was getting a little strained.

Antony had never done this sort of piecework before, getting paid a flat rate for each job. The faster you work, the more you get paid. Billmer was an old hand at stripping forms. He knew what he was doing and didn't like to be held back by Antony's inexperience.

"We work as a team," Billmer warned, "or I find a new helper who can do his share. I'm no social service agency for dimwits and retards."

Near the end of January, Antony found work in Abbotsford, doing odd jobs for seniors. He'd bicycle to the shop, get his work order, and catch a ride to the job, his tools, bike, and supplies thrown in the back. More often than not, he'd be painting a kitchen or staining a fence for an old widow who'd feed him lunch and serve him coffee, plain glad to have some company in her home. One time, however, he spread an old bachelor's ten-year-old pile of compost over his garden. It was riper than a pig barn, Antony decided, as he shovelled and hoed and raked the garden over.

"That corner is a bit low," the old man said, pointing his finger over Antony's shoulder, sipping his coffee and supervising.

Antony now understood Mary Helen's antipathy towards grumpy, old men.

They make believing in a Father God difficult.

When Antony finally had enough money to pay for his driving lessons, he signed up for the course. After seven two-hour, in-car driving lessons and eighteen hours of classroom instruction, Antony passed the test, and found a 1962 Chevrolet Biscayne for $118. He and Mr. Wiebe went to the dealer one Saturday afternoon to buy it. Antony tried to dicker, but the salesman, all huffy, rose to leave.

"This is a good deal," he asserted. "You won't find a better car for cheaper."

Antony had no choice but to lay his money down.

"You'll have to get insurance before you can put a plate on this thing," the salesman added as he plumbed the depth for Antony's cash.

"Insurance?" Antony's heart sank when he realized his wallet was as empty as a water well in the dust bowl of the 1930s. He needed to wring a little more from the rocks at the bottom to get through the demands that this day was making on him.

"Don't worry, son," Mr. Wiebe said. "I'll cover this for you until you get paid." He knew that the only way to get Antony out on his own was to help him with the car insurance. He didn't mind. Antony seemed to be paying his own way, for the most part. He was being faithful in the things that were set in front of him.

He's turning out to be a good kid, Henry mused as he wrote out the cheque. He'd get Marge to balance the account when he got home.

Antony's new car had a straight six oil-burner of an engine with a three-on-the-tree standard transmission. The shifter was on the steering column, first gear down and close to Antony's belt buckle, second over and up and close to the dash, third straight down from second. Reverse was back over and up and close to his excited-and-bursting-at-the-seams chest. Kind of like the letter H, two legs up, two down, and a catwalk in the middle.

That car was his lifeline. With it, he could go to work in the morning, go out on dates on Saturday, and attend church on Sunday. Soon he was renting a basement suite of his own and learning to cook, one scorcher after another.

At least I know how to wash my pots, Antony reflected, after burning another meal. "Eema Mother! Are you in there?" he asked as he rinsed off the suds and peered deep into the reflection in the pan's newly-scoured surface.

Not as far as I can see.

At Easter he had a few days off, so he drove his little Chevy down the I-5 to visit Lee and his wife Mary, a couple he met in Sebastopol where he went for Basic Training in faith and service. This time he phoned ahead. They lived on an acreage on the outskirts of Santa Rosa in the Sonoma Valley.

For some reason, Antony didn't know why, his battery wasn't keeping its charge, though the generator seemed to be working fine. He'd turn on the key, the solenoid would click, but the starter wouldn't engage. He'd have to give the car a push to get the engine started, which was a little problematic on his trip down the I-5. He learned to park it on a hill.

One time, though, he needed to buy gas in Olympia. The gas station he stopped at was as level as the Utah salt flats after a rainstorm. For some reason, the attendant wouldn't let him keep the engine running as he filled the tank. He said something about volatile gas fumes and a spark from the distributor cap on old cars like this one.

Antony thought the guy was a bit of a turd, but turned the engine off only after he agreed to help him push the car to get it started.

Antony was always a little nervous about filling up the gas tank. The Revelstoke episode was still fresh in his memory. Now with the battery problem, he was even more on edge. When he paid up, he nodded to the attendant.

"You ready?"

"What do you mean?" the kid replied. "Weren't you joking?"

"Uh-uh," Antony motioned. As soon as the car was rolling, he put the tranny into second, popped the clutch, and was off down the road, puffing blue and going seventy-five in the middle lane and getting passed on both sides, as if he were standing still.

Those Americans and their 55 speed limit, he said to himself. Later in his life, he'd reflect that was the only Freedom Fifty-Five he'd ever get to experience.

The rest of the trip, buying gas, Cokes, and chocolate bars went by without a hitch. Because the engine was hot, Antony only rarely needed help with the pushing. Besides, people were always ready to give him a hand when they heard his story.

"You're going where? How far have you come? You better get that thing fixed," they said. Concern was evident on their faces.

"Good country folk, these people are," Antony said, wondering if he had any American cousins.

He was making good time, checking the map, and seeing where he was on the I-5 and where Santa Rosa was on the US 101 N. He wondered how he was going to get from where he was to where he wanted to be, and which exit to take and what lane to be in.

Somehow, he managed to turn off the I-5 onto the 505 to Winters and make the 80 going west. Unfortunately, he was in the wrong lane and missed merging onto the 37 over to San Rafael and the simple north to the 101 that would have taken him right into Santa Rosa.

Within the blink of an eye, the 80 was hauling his sorry white ass straight into the heart of downtown San Francisco, which was something he formerly might have enjoyed to the fullest, had the circumstances of his life gone other than they did. But they didn't, and he was completely lost. His car was nearly out of gas. The battery was as dead as an ex-girlfriend's stone-cold heart. He was a little more than agitated.

"Officer," Antony called to the state trooper when he pulled his car over to the shoulder, just before the gridlock he was in inched its way imperceptibly west across the Bay Bridge. "Did I miss the turn off to Santa Rosa somehow?"

"No, son," the State trooper chuckled, checking the safety on his gun. "You didn't miss it completely, but you sure got yourself out of the way. You from Canada, eh?" he said, eying the BC plate and confirming his suspicions.

"Yeah, how can you tell? What do you suggest I do about the mess I'm in? How do I get back on track?" Antony didn't go into the details of the condition of his car. He was sure the officer didn't want to hear any State of the Union on the old Chevy Biscayne.

"If I were you, I'd stay on the 80 until you see the turn off to 101 North, the Central Freeway. Take the Mission Street off-ramp, which should be Exit 434 A. Go north and turn left on 11th Street. Turn left again on Market, and right almost immediately on Van Ness. Follow Van Ness until you come to Lombard Street. It'll take you west and lead you automatically to the 101 N, which you'll follow until you come to Santa Rosa in about fifty miles. This route will take you over the Golden Gate Bridge. You got all that?"

Antony nodded numbly and somehow, miracles of miracles, Eema Mother God made good on Her promise to lead him out of the wilderness and into the Promised Land, made all the turns the officer told him to make. He bought gas at a station on an incline and made it to Lee and Mary's, overlooking a vineyard outside the town.

He saw their old Italian neighbour behind his horse and plow, gently working the rocky soil between the grape vines.

When Antony first visited Lee and Mary's for last year's Thanksgiving dinner, sun-ripened Marco spent the entire meal toasting Mary's prowess in the kitchen and lecturing Antony on the virtues of slow-growth farming.

"People these days are too interested in production to be concerned about quality," he advised.

"Get rid of the tractors. Horses are better, slower. Lighter. You don't get the soil compaction you get from heavy machinery. You can watch your vines as you till the soil. You're right there, not sitting up high in some air-conditioned rig listening to Pavarotti. My God, you should have heard him sing 'Donizetti' at the Met."

He filled Antony's glass with a shimmering Cab Sauv he brought over from his cellar.

"Hold the stem so you don't warm the wine," Marco advised.

Antony backed his Chevy up Lee and Mary's steep lane and parked it under an oak tree. He stepped out of the car and waved to Marco, who looked up to see who was visiting.

Marco immediately recognized Antony. His darkly tanned face broke into a broad smile.

"*Mona!*" he yelled to Antony, who didn't have a clue what he was going on about. Mary watched Antony park his car from her west-facing picture window, the sun slipping below the dark horizon.

Over supper that night, they talked about life and work and vocations and callings. Antony wanted to teach, but he didn't know how he could ever do that or if and when it would come about. But he was certain that he wanted to do something that would make his life count. He didn't want to end up passed out like some drunk on the street. He needed some direction.

Mary passed him the plate of Pad Thai, a dish she learned to make when she was teaching English in Bangkok.

"Antony, there are different kinds of success. Some people are front and centre. They make all the money, and they get all the attention. Other people work the back rooms. They travel down by-ways and alleys and help those who live in the shadows. They work the fields and harvest the grain by the bushel. You know Eema Mother spent nearly all of her life in a Roman backwater. Her success was quiet and lowkey."

Just then, Antony bit down on a red-hot Thai chilli pepper and his throat filled with hellfire. The pepper scorched his mouth while Mary's words tore at his heart. He wanted some water and Pepto-Bismol, but Lee gave him a spoonful of sugar.

"Eat this and drink some jasmine tea. That'll take the burn away."

It did, and Antony never forgot what Mary said to him. He knew that he had to head north to make his fortune. He had to go home to escape the heat.

20

The Ethics of Potlucks

With his characteristic poor sense of direction, Antony headed off the wrong way when he left for Abbotsford the next morning. He drove due south from Santa Rosa instead of due north. He saw a sign, however, so he did not get completely lost. At the last minute he merged onto the US 101 to San Francisco. By exiting on the 37 toward Vallejo, he barely escaped a repeat of his worst stuck-in-traffic nightmare, a stall on the Golden Gate during rush hour.

The compass needle on the dash of his car finally pointing towards the Klondike, every Gold Digger's Dream, he motored up the 505 towards Redding. He merged onto the I-5 and mainlined it all the way to Sumas, Washington, push-starting his Biscayne at gas stations, parking it on the incline at restaurants, and arriving home fifteen hours after he started.

The next day, he took his smoking blue-jet-streaming Biscayne into the garage to get the battery checked.

"Battery?" the mechanic asked while poking his mulletted head here and cocking his freckled ear there. "Why would I replace that when it's your starter that's hooped? The battery's fine."

"Really?" Antony asked. "I just got back from California and the engine's burning a lot of oil. It blows so much blue at stoplights that I need to turn the engine off while I am waiting for the green. It's down a couple quarts every time I fill up. Do you think it's worth rebuilding, or should I fix the starter and sell it?"

"Depends how much you like the car." The mechanic looked under the hood. "I have a fine 283, a little V-8 that'd fit in here nicely. If you

122

want, I could slip it in for you. The price, you ask? Because you're a regular, $400, or so. You'd be amazed. This baby'd really move."

"Sounds expensive," Antony said, already making up his mind and wondering what his bank balance was. He was determined beyond any shadow of a doubt that all he ever wanted in life was for that 283 to be under his hood. He decided that, yes, he could pay the bill, and wondered exactly when would the work get started?

There was, after all, a big slow pitch tournament on Saturday night and a hot dog roast after. He could really use his hopped-up car then. That was for sure.

The mechanic smiled.

"Tomorrow morning. Bring her in for eight and I'll be finished on Friday," he said, cinching the deal with a firm handshake.

He then put an Oakland A's ball cap on his head. *All the way to the World Series,* he thought to himself, feeling flush as flush could be.

Antony left the dark, cool shop and walked into the sunshine towards his soon-to-be-transformed Biscayne.

That Saturday, Antony picked up his car with its new engine. Though it wasn't a small block Rocket, it was pure gold to Antony, and he loved every one of its husky-voiced decibels. Antony wrote out a check for $537.52.

The mechanic explained that his original estimate hadn't included replacing the whole exhaust system. Petrified, Antony hoped he'd get to the bank first to transfer another $137.52 into his account before the cheque bounced.

"How'd you lose the tip of your finger?" Antony asked.

"This?" The mechanic stretched his right hand palm upward toward Antony, a fallen Jesus preaching a sermon in the Lower Fraser Valley. "It happened when I was a first-year apprentice, before I learned not to stick my finger in any place I wouldn't poke my dick."

At church that Sunday, Antony idled into the parking lot, his window rolled down, his white stallion of a four-door Chevy Biscayne with vinyl bench seats, in his opinion, sounding and looking just as good as any souped-up GTO.

None of the girls he was trying to impress with their heavenly miniskirts, faith-inspiring blouses (Yes! There is a God!) and divine necklines gave him the time of day.

They were too busy sniffing around Jaz, who memorized the *Book of Insults* and delivered them with unerring accuracy to notice Antony, the hippest tomcat who just strutted onto their block.

Jaz was Antony's sparring partner at the Thursday Night Book of the People Study. They'd go for each other's throats. Antony would attack Jaz's university-educated cynicism and Jaz would dismantle Antony's home-spun zeal and blind faith.

"I just don't know, Antony," Jaz would posit thoughtfully. "The world is much more complicated than you make it out to be."

And Antony would scoff that someone as smart as Jaz could be so stupid.

"Jaz, you just gotta believe. Act it out until your faith grows. It'll just happen, brother. Eema Mother is good."

And Jaz would wonder for how long Antony would waste his life as a labourer and construction worker. He had so much to offer if he would just stop being so idiotic.

Like a whetstone to a knife, they sharpened each other to a razor-thin steel edge until they were ready to slit each other's throats.

Hostile interrogators, they brooked each other no quarter.

"Hey, Jaz, how's it going?" Antony asked as he bounded up the stairs, fought his way through the perfume and the hairspray, and barged into the middle of exactly what, he didn't have a clue. This circle of she-cats in heat had more than love in their eyes.

Jaz disengaged himself from the intense discussion he was having with a hot little number Antony wished he had known a whole lot better.

Jaz's eyes went from her to Antony and then to the lovely Biscayne.

"That's a mighty fine piece of transportation you have there, Antony. Interested in selling it?"

"No way, man," Antony replied. "I just invested all my life's savings into her. Want to go for a little spin after church? She's faithful and good and doesn't cause a bit of trouble."

"Why, sure, Antony," Jaz said. "My clunker died on the road back from Squamish. The mechanic said the engine seized and I'd have to spend another $500 to get it repaired. There's no way I'm wasting my hard-earned cash on an old hulk that only cost me a hundred when I bought it."

Antony kept silent about the new engine job his sweeter-than-honey had just received. He looked around him and suddenly noticed the tidal surge of femininity that was now encompassing Jaz and him.

By sidling up to Jaz, he had trod where angels fear to tread, into the path of a storming woman and her closest friends.

"Hey!" Jaz exclaimed, all spontaneous-like and companionable, putting his arm around Antony, turning on his heel and walking into the church, more than a little eager to hear the forty-five-minute sermon the Preacher spent a week preparing. "You want to give me a ride tomorrow? It's only a couple hours. You could stay over a few days and help me with some painting I need to get done by Thursday."

Antony mulled over Jaz's proposition during the preacher's arcane explication of the Second Coming. He had quit his dead-end job because of the pay and now he needed to work and get some cash into the bank before the rent was due.

Jaz had work, but needed a car. It looked to be a match made in heaven. He'd help Jaz and Jaz would help him. Seemed a pretty good deal all round. They'd just have to overlook a few of the differences of opinion that they had developed during the past few years.

While they agreed that Eema Mother was indeed resurrected, they diverged over matters of faith that didn't involve death or taxes, like whether or not Adult Baptism by immersion should be with the person's head upstream or down, and even more critical, what the etiquette at church potlucks should be.

Do you take two helpings on your first pass down the table and grab a dessert on the way back, or do you risk, for charity's sake, there not being enough left of Mrs. Penner's cherry pie by making a separate trip to the dessert and coffee table?

It was a thorny and divisive issue for the single young men who loved Mrs. Dyck's home cooking better than gawping at the divine Belinda, standing there aloof in the sun, ignoring her worshippers.

Those of the latter persuasion, of whom Antony happily counted himself as one, had gone without more times than he cared to remember. He preferred a present earthly delight, that of gazing with his eye down a long and languid form. He adopted a more heavenly strategy, in the hope of winning the heart of the one he loved, by being kind and generous to those further down the line.

Those of the former persuasion, of whom Jaz was numbered, took their cherry pie along with their vertiginous entrées, laying waste to the Groaning Board behind them.

They left not a single crumb of Mrs. Rempel's second-best matrimonial cake for the picking by those silly boys who chose goodwill and love over predatory self-interest.

Antony's thoughts towards those selfish SOBs who cleared the table before him were less than charitable. He may have been a follower of Eema Mother indeed, but his lacking in the actual act of the transgression was just as telling as his omission of the good.

He was guilty no matter which way you cut it.

To add more heat to the chilli pot, Antony dated Jaz's younger sister for a bit, which caused no end of concern for the young girl's family. Antony wasn't yet what any young woman with a head on her shoulders would call marriageable, and Jaz was dating that gal whom Antony once had his eye on but still didn't know he existed.

"Antony who?" she asked, her blue eyes narrowing to a pinprick, when Jaz told her he finally found someone who'd take him up to Squamish that week. They'd been having a little dispute about their future when Antony unknowingly and characteristically barged up the stairs straight into the heartbeat of their un-conjugal dust up.

The next morning, he and Jaz packed their things into the car and left by nine. They drove with all the windows rolled down. Antony had one hand on the wheel. The tires dug into the pavement as he passed one car after another, trying not to hit the crystal fog markers down the centre of the driving lanes. He and Jaz were on their own.

There were no women around to complicate their lives. They could just work and make money and savour the sweet gifts Eema Mother was pouring down their throats.

Jaz with his tiresome Heldentenor and Antony with his mellifluous Bel Canto baritone sang that old spiritual—"Free at last, Free at Last! Thank God almighty, we're free at last."

Except they weren't. Jaz and his sweetie were engaged but going through a rough patch, and Antony was pulled over by the RCMP.

"The posted speed limit is there so you can keep time with the other drivers," the tall female officer explained in her dusky voice. "If you don't follow the beat, everything falls apart, like singing in a duet," she added as she filled out his speeding ticket, not paying him any heed or giving him any allowance for his boyish charm, sunny disposition, and gorgeous smile.

She is one lucky woman to have stopped me, Antony initially thought. Then he read with a start the astronomical sum she had written out for him to pay.

"Do Not Pass Go!"

"Go Directly to Jail!"

"Work in Servitude for Twenty Years!"

Antony saw the finger of Eema Mother in the lovely hand of this woman, writing his immediate destiny on a bank of storm clouds, on the way past Horseshoe Bay.

"Make some money and pay your bills."

21

As It Happens

S quamish is a busy little town, up Howe Sound, north of Vancouver on the 99. On the other side of the water is a pulp mill. It takes a little discipline when the wind is blowing the wrong way to remember that the smell of pulp is the scent of money. Profits flow from the company's bank accounts into the portfolios of its investors. Cash trickles down into the registers of every gas station, grocery store, service provider, and bar in town.

Prince Charles had an innovative way of addressing the problem of the odour when he visited there a few years back.

"Put a sock on it," he suggested.

The townspeople preferred to view the smell as part of the solution to their economic woes than as a problem that needed fixing.

"It would be devastating if this mill were ever to close," Jaz pontificated with his characteristic self-promoting, authoritative stance on every subject in every conversation that took place in his vicinity.

That was just the kind of man he was, the (un)welcome centre of everyone else's attention. Antony loved and hated the man.

As soon as they arrived at the new subdivision north of town, Jaz hauled out his brushes, rollers, and rags, and set Antony to staining a deck. He'd come back every half-hour or so to check on Antony's progress and make a few suggestions for how to speed the work up and do a better job.

Antony seemed to have an excuse for why he was doing what he was doing and the way he was doing it. By the end of the day, Jaz was ready to send Antony packing, but he kept thinking of the handy little Biscayne with the new engine that just wouldn't quit. He needed Antony for his car and kept his mouth shut.

Sometimes the price for success cuts to the bone, he thought as he hurried back to the job he was completing, his teeth on edge.

That evening, they stopped for a supper that they cooked on a Coleman camping stove in the basement of an unfinished house where they had rolled out their sleeping bags. They became master chefs cooking with gas, Kraft Dinner, gourmet pork and beans, and eggs and toast. They heated up Lipton soup and Idaho instant potatoes and tins of salmon. Del Monte stewed tomatoes and sliced up all-beef hot dogs over rice were a special treat they savoured every other day or so. While they warmed up their hash, ate their meals, and washed their dishes, they listened to *As it Happens* on CBC radio. Barbara Frum and Alan Maitland explored mercury poisoning in Grassy Narrows northeast of Kenora, Ontario, and discussed amnesty for draft dodgers. The kidnapping of Patty Hearst filled the radio waves.

They drank protein supplements so they could paint from eight in the morning until after midnight, four days a week. On Fridays, they'd clean up the basement they had stayed in and would drive down to Abbotsford for the weekend.

Before long, Antony had made enough money to pay $1700 cash for a 1964 Volvo PV 544 B18 Sport. Then women stood up and noticed him whenever he drove his fine piece of Swedish engineering down the two-lane, bumper-to-bumper South Fraser Way.

"No, it's not a Ford," he'd sigh on numerous occasions to inquiring minds with lovely legs. And "Yes, I will! Yes, indeedy. I will give you a ride on Friday night to the corn roast up Sumas Mountain." He replied with a gracious sincerity and eagerness to please those young women. They were more than willing to drape their gorgeous figures over his car's fine Hunter Green fenders with a pearlized finish. They knelt down in adoration to double-check their mascara in the glossy reflection of its chromed solid steel Baby Moon hub caps.

Antony's Canadian dream had come true. He had the car and got the girl! Loads of them! As many as he could fit into the front and backseat.

One time he suggested that Peggy Sue sitting in the passenger seat should take the stick in her hands and shift the gears for him. For some reason, Antony didn't know why, but Peggy Sue slapped his face so hard, he couldn't see next Tuesday on the calendar.

When he stopped the car, she got out and never talked to him again.

"Jaz," Antony said the Monday they were driving to Squamish. "Women just don't seem to understand men. Our lives are so simple and straightforward. Theirs are so complicated. We want to live and be and they, well, to be frank, I don't know what they want. But it sure hurts, let me tell you, when I get it wrong."

In September, much to Jaz's delight, Antony drove to Winnipeg to see Izzy. Jaz now drove Antony's Biscayne on a permanent loan, and no longer had to pay the price of Antony's irritating insecurities. He finished their painting contracts and fast-tracked his way to medical school.

On the way to Manitoba, Antony slept in the back of his car, huddling up against the dark green leather upholstery. He kept himself warm with the sleeping bag he was delivering to a friend in Caronport outside Moose Jaw. What he'd do after he dropped off the sleeping bag, he didn't have a clue. Stay in a motel? The thought never entered his mind. He had forgotten how cold southern Alberta could get in the fall.

Once again, he was on familiar territory, back on the Trans-Canada across the prairies, having hitchhiked this road three times, the first out west when he ran away three years before, and the second and third a round-trip from Abbotsford to Quickfall in his Grade Twelve year to visit Izzy. He also did a return trip for Christmas one year on the Greyhound, drinking dandelion wine at the back.

Of course, the very first trip he took was nine years before with Mary Helen and Izzy. This trip, however, was his first time solo, in his own car with hitchhikers he picked up as payback. There was no way he was suffering any bad karma for being selfish. He trusted the guys he gave rides to and let them drive when he needed to sleep.

On the turnoff at the Perimeter north towards Quickfall, the hitchhiker, who was driving at the time, had to wake Antony up when he pulled over, so they could continue their separate ways.

The purpose of his trip was to see Izzy. She was finishing Grade Twelve and living in the city. When she came back from her year in BC, she was no longer satisfied with what her life had been. Her next years were rough.

Unknown to Antony, she was living on her own, just north of downtown, which was certainly no uptown. She had to make a special trip out to Quickfall to see him. He hadn't phoned ahead to make arrangements. He just showed up.

It didn't occur to him that she was as broke as broke could be and that she could have used some of the reserve that he had left in his storehouse.

My, how blind that boy was! He couldn't see what he needed to see. It was staring him straight, straight in the eye. His sister couldn't count on him. She had to make her own way, working and saving and making her days count, one penny at a time.

In his haste, Antony left her behind, so intent he was on his survival. The survival of the fittest.

He had barely enough gas money to get back home.

Driving west on the Trans-Canada, he stopped in Calgary to see Uncle Johnny and Aunt Marg.

"You know, Antony," Uncle Johnny said, passing him a slice of roast beef, "your dad James George called the other day. We didn't have your number, so we couldn't help him, but he told us to give you his, the next time we saw you. It's sure something you're here now, not even two weeks later."

Antony hadn't seen James George since Mary Helen dragged him and Izzy down Centre Street in 1959. That was fifteen years ago. Antony didn't know what to say. He took the paper, folded it carefully, and put it in his wallet. He'd travelled many a mile down the highway since then and was unsure how meeting his father again would fit in with the life he was presently trying to live.

He remembered nothing of James George, just the photographs that were taken back then of Izzy and him. Antony was wearing a cowboy shirt with snap-down buttons and a bolo tie and Izzy a cute little gathered skirt, a pudgy baby doll.

When Antony arrived back in Abbotsford, he made the call. A woman answered the phone.

"Hello?"

He replied, uncertain how to continue. "Is James George there? I'm his son, Antony."

"Antony! Oh, James George, come to the phone quick. It's Antony. He finally phoned."

James George picked up the extension.

"Antony?"

"Yes?"

"We should meet."

22

Sins of the Fathers

In the late autumn of 1974, Antony drove his 1964 Volvo with summer tires through the Fraser Canyon, honking his horn through all seven of its tunnels. The bright lights, tight curves, and his echoing horn filled him with joy unspeakable. He loved the thrill of driving fast in the mountains.

He was a happy young man on his way to visit his father, whom he hadn't seen in decades. He had high hopes and enough faith in Eema Mother to recognize that She obviously had a hand in this reunion. He would not be disappointed.

The long, cool day grew chilly in the evening and frosty at night. He bought food in Kamloops, paid a dollar a gallon for gas in Blue River, turned the heater on high in Jasper, and filled up in Edson. He continued east on the 16 to Carrot Creek, then north on the 32 along the frozen McLeod River to Whitecourt, where James George ran a fleet of water trucks serving the oil fields up towards Valleyview. It was a tough business where he spent $500,000 a year to make 400,000.

They gave each other the gruffest of hugs when they met at the door of James George's mobile home. Antony hung up his coat, slipped off his shoes, and settled down at the kitchen table.

To ease the tension between them, James George offered his long-lost son a rye and ginger and a White Owl cigar with a sweet grape flavour and an easy peel-off wrapper.

But Antony declined.

"I don't do that anymore. My body's a temple."

What the hell? James George wondered. *Got me here a son who doesn't drink? Won't share a twenty-minute smoke with his father? What is he? Some kind of freak?*

"I must be the white sheep of the family, eh?" Antony said. "I've had it with booze and smoking and drugs. I've become a pilgrim on Eema Mother's highway. Straight and narrow is the path."

"Then I guess we better drive into town," James George said. "The old lady's out and I'm not sure when she's coming back. There's a Chinaman Buffet that has a good spread. That is, if you're hungry?"

"I don't normally do Chinese because of the MSG, but sure. This once? It's an occasion worth celebrating."

James George shook his head.

They jumped into a hot-as-blazes 3/4-ton 4x4 Dodge pickup with the Cummins engine so durable that when the body fell apart, the dealer would pull the old good-as-new engine out of the beat-up hulk of a chassis and drop it into a new one ordered straight from the factory. The owner wouldn't lose a day of work.

James George's life was drinking and smoking and swearing up a storm. He worked 24/7 and was away from home most of the time. When he wasn't out in the field, he was balancing the books, sending out invoices, and waiting months to get paid. Securing contracts, finding drivers, picking up parts, repairing equipment, or getting stuck out on a lease waiting for a tow was all part of a day's work.

Latching on to James George was like riding a Brahma Bull at the Calgary Stampede. You had three seconds before he exploded out of the chute. He was a hard man to live with for long.

His second wife and kids up and left him. His third was out on a limb.

Now he had a long-haired son to call his own.

Jesus! Who wouldn't want a drink after all that? he asked himself.

"This is no way to live or raise a family," Antony decided as he looked his father up and down. He wanted none of it. "The oil patch ruins lives."

"The last time I saw you kids, I caught your mother with that bastard Neil. I was so mad, I told her I was going out, and that she'd better be gone before I returned. I deeply regret kicking her out and losing you and Izzy. Sorry, son."

And that was that—the closest James George ever came to reconciling himself with his boy.

Antony wished to Eema Mother that James George had been man enough to curb his temper and treat his wives and children with love and respect.

"The sins of fathers and their fathers do not have to be carried on in the lives of their children," Eema Mother whispered to Antony in the depth of his disappointment. "The cycle of abuse can be broken."

The next day, they drove to Vermillion to visit Antony's grandfather Grady. He was a thin old man whose face was a mask of red-hot anger. He had a shock of thick, white hair in a brush cut, and rheumy, red-rimmed eyes.

As a young man, he had been strong and wiry and wore cowboy shirts with snap buttons. His was a surly disposition and easily riled. When he spoke, people knew he was from Leicester, North Carolina.

Antony later learned that Grady's grandfather Marcus Quintilian Roberts resided in Buncombe County. He enlisted with the North Carolina Troops on September 11, 1861. Mustered as a private when he was seventeen, he was later promoted to corporal.

On August 1, 1864, he surrendered to the Bluebellies and was confined at Chattanooga, Tennessee. On August 5, he was transferred to Louisville, Kentucky. After taking the Oath of Allegiance, he was released on August 10 and walked home.

By that time, the family's help was gone. The Roberts offspring never recovered from being on the losing side. They headed west to Idaho and north to Alberta, looking for the cheapest land available.

Antony noticed that Grady kept a case of unsweetened grapefruit juice under his bed. He liked to take long drinks straight from the can. When he finished, he'd wipe his mouth dry and put the opened can back where the attendants couldn't see it. Sometimes it'd last three to four days.

It's a wonder he didn't die of poisoning. He was probably too pickled from all the bourbon he had drunk over his lifetime to notice the tin infiltrating and annexing his musculature, one cell at a time.

After Grady died, Antony inherited two of his Philishave razors. Decades later, he was still using them. They're plain and simple, well-engineered, and effective. Intended to last forever and give a man the closest shave.

Grady was a drinker. He wasn't particular if the alcohol he consumed was store-bought or from a still behind somebody's barn.

When his family crossed the line in 1912, they saw the advertisement *Drink Canada Dry*. Grady and his brother Wayne vowed right then and there to do exactly that. They settled on the wrong side of the tracks in Kitscoty, Alberta and drove the goodhearted church people who lived on the neighbouring farm to get down on their knees.

Decades later, they were heartened to see the faith that grew in Antony's heart. Their intercessions were answered.

Grady set about farming and drinking and wiving and fathering forth in vicious abandon. Wayne never married, just pined for a woman he could never have—his brother's wife.

As soon as he could, Grady's father set himself back to North Carolina where he belonged.

"Nearly killed me, working from sunrise to sunset," he told his friends in Greensboro. "I had to get me back home so I could rest a spell."

His wife Allie Lorraine followed her other children to Wenatchee, Washington, The Apple Capital of the World, where she spent the winters. She'd had more than enough of her husband and couldn't stand his temper for a minute longer.

"The liquor is all," Grady declared on more than one occasion. He often told the story of how his family back in Asheville would put money on a stump at night. They'd return in the morning for the corn in the jar that the hillbillies left for them. There was no such thing as Prohibition for Mountain Folk, just for Methodists in brick houses with fancy cars and fat bank accounts.

"What good is all the money in the world," Grady asked. "When a man can't have a drink whenever he damn well pleases?"

What was far worse than Grady's drinking, though, was his temper. He was a mean drunk when liquored up.

Shortly after James George was born, his mother Isabel escaped her husband's hand. She returned to her parents' farm. When her mother Elizabeth (*née* Beaumont) Pogue died in 1941, Grady somehow persuaded Isabel to return home. She soon gave birth to a daughter and two more sons in rapid succession. The youngest one died a day or two later.

No doubt, Grady promised to lay off the bottle and never hit her again. That lasted until he suspected his brother of being young James George's father. Then he went berserk, hammering Isabel until she was completely emptied out and as fragile as Irish crystal.

When Antony met her, she was little more than a throwaway. He would often visit her in the Jubilee Nursing Lodge in Edmonton. It was a beautiful building on the side of a hill with a slope of grass that reached down to the road and high up over the crest. He and Isabel would stare out the window at the sea gulls as they swooped in close and flew away on a whim. There wasn't anybody holding them back from doing whatever they pleased.

"You know, Antony," Isabel said, in a soft, befuddled, moment-of-clarity sort of way. "Most times, life isn't any fun. You have to endure what's thrown at you."

After her youngest died, Isabel broke down and spent twenty years in the hospital at Ponoka. She hadn't ever had much, this spare slip of a woman.

Grady vowed before Eema Mother to take Isabel to be his lawfully wedded wife, to have and to hold from this day forward, for better for worse, for richer or poorer, in sickness and in health, to love and to cherish, 'til death do them part.

Isabel took him at his word and paid the price.

Bitterness was her gall.

23

Broken Dreams

While attending the Montreal Olympics in July 1976, Antony met a Norwegian woman named Synnøve. She was a spiritual doula.

He was there to evangelize, preach good news, and make disciples of all nations. She was there to sit with him on a lawn in a park.

"If you want your life to count, you need to forgive those who have hurt you. Bitterness will ruin you if you let it. No woman will ever trust you enough to let you love her."

In the bright sunshine of that hot humid afternoon, world records were broken. Some realized their hopes and dreams for winning gold, silver, or bronze. Most went home to try and try again.

Synnøve led Antony through prayers of forgiveness.

She laid hands upon him and asked Eema Mother to cleanse this boy, not yet a man, of the wounding that others had inflicted upon his heart, and to heal him of its effect upon his body and spirit.

"This is not a once and only," she said. "It is a spiritual discipline that you must adopt and practise daily. Beg Eema Mother's forgiveness for the ill that you have done to others. Accept Her Grace and forgive yourself.

"Repent of what you know you should not be doing.

"Do good and make restitution.

"Forgive those who hurt you. The burden is on you to take the first step. Do not wait for them. This is all on you."

In that busy park, kids played with their friends. Parents kept watch. Young couples flirted. Old men played chess. Women sat on benches with the sun warming their aching bones.

Antony bowed his head and closed his eyes.

Synnøve placed her hand on his back.

"Visualize the people who hurt you. Say their names out loud and speak the pain that they caused you."

As the faces of the men his mother lived with when he was a boy came to mind, Antony did what Synnøve told him.

"I forgive you, Neil, for having sex with my mother and abandoning me when I gave you my heart.

"I forgive you, Harry and Steve and Knut, for taking advantage of Mum when she had nowhere to turn.

"I forgive you, Dad, for destroying our family.

"I am sorry, Izzy, for abandoning you."

"Mum, I …" Antony hesitated.

"Pour these words out," Synnøve counselled.

He mumbled and stumbled. The words he needed to say were stuck in his craw.

"Imagine a clear flood of water from Heaven washing over you, flushing the dirt, filth, and anger from your heart. Let it flow through your body. Allow it to sluice the hurt that is in you until you are washed clean. Watch the water pool black at your feet and drain away. The water of this baptism will set you free."

The bondage of Antony's childhood fell from his shoulders. Its overburden shifted and was swept away. He stood up to receive Eema Mother's blessing. Synnøve hugged him close. She would not let him go until he drank in fully of Eema Mother's release.

"Now, my child," she said. "Do not wait for your mother to apologise. There is so much pain in her heart, she will only disappoint you.

"Yours is a higher calling, the way of forgiveness without expectation. As you forgive those who have sinned against you, you will be healed.

"Precious one, you are golden. The world is yours. Go and make the best of the life you have been given."

And so, he did. One day at a time.

Antony received his marching orders from Synnøve in Montreal. He discovered that the Eema Mother, whom he thought he knew from his childhood, did not automatically rain Hellfire down from the Heavens upon those who transgressed against Her good and proper injunctions.

She did not have to. They brought judgement upon themselves for the lives they ruined.

While She ruled on high, Eema Mother was not responsible for the pain and suffering that principalities and powers brought upon the innocent and the vulnerable. They could not blame Her completely for the trouble they had seen.

They could only look to Her for the strength to endure and the courage to persevere.

In this generation or the next, light will eventually overcome darkness. It is geologic in its pace and inevitable. Over the course of lifetimes, the light will prevail.

The life of faith demands that a person takes the long view.

Unlike Antony's volatile and unpredictable mother, who wore silk and expensive perfume, Eema Mother wears homespun. She bears the pain of the world in Her body. She was and remains a good and faithful friend. Her Yes is a sturdy Yes and Her No emphatic and full of portent.

One does not ignore Eema Mother God's injunctions.

She is a woman whom a sensible man learns to love and fear.

She may be a hurricane in high dudgeon, but She speaks in a still small voice that can barely be heard on the leeward side of a sheltering rock. She proclaims in the quietest of whisperings Her will for the world.

"Pure and undefiled religion is to forgive those who have sinned against you. Helping abandoned children and desperate mothers is a good and proper thing. The secret to a happy life is to act justly, love mercy, live humbly, and show compassion to others.

"Not throw your weight around.

"Not sit in judgement."

The heavy hand is not the way of Eema Mother who spoke Creation into existence. With the slightest breath, She put chaos into order. With a whisper, She filled the universe with life.

Not a Big Bang, not a lightning bolt, not even a shrug of Her shoulders, but a tear of joy dropping from Her eye was all that took to set the force of life into motion. Spontaneous creation, life will fill the outermost reaches of the universe.

Eema Mother continues, inhaling and exhaling existence into being. Her breath—ripe and redolent, full, and lush, as fertile as dung, river bottom and delta loam—is pregnant and teeming.

It reeks like an aged French cheese. Umami, Ur-Mami, Ur-Mother, Eema Mother. Foul-feeted, fêted, and foetid, hell-YA-toe-sis. One whiff could knock you over, it is so ripe.

Eema Mother, not Abba Father.

Not after James George. One quick to anger, slow to forgive, and never sorry. A man you could love until his fists drove you away.

Not after Mary Helen. Her children made it in spite of her.

They found refuge in the nurture of other women. All praise be to grannies and aunties who see the world not as we see it but as it could be. They welcome the little children who come their way.

Creative, loving, and full of grace, Eema Mother took Antony as he was. He flourished in her world made craftily.

Redemption is possible. Forgiveness can be given, and it can be received.

Three little words freely given bring light to a world betrayed by endless night.

"I am sorry."

And then three more.

"I forgive you."

In this way, the world is turned upside down.

On the seventh day, Eema Mother was well-pleased with the breath she had breathed and the words she had spoken. She rested.

Antony learned that the life of faith is delicate yet robust. A seed scatters on stony ground, sprouts with spring rains, grows tall under the summer sun, and bears fruit in the autumn. It engages in a struggle that is easily lost, a tilling of the soil, a weeding of rows, and a separating of the wheat from tares.

Faith is found in the sowing, the ripening, and the harvest. It is in the nurturing and the raising-up, not the tearing-down. A life of faith builds, walks slowly, and notices things. It grinds the grain, kneads the dough, and tends the ovens.

Give us this day our daily bread. Loaves upon loaves, golden and delicious.

Golden Boy.

Eema Mother of small means, good and kind, gentle and trusting, true and faithful. She is mighty and kind and has your back when you are flat-out and shattered.

She prefers a broken and contrite heart to a grand gesture. An insignificant deed, hidden and done with compassion, has more effect than a sacrifice made public. True devotion is revealed in darkened corners, desert storms, and by-ways that seem to lead nowhere.

What Eema Mother wants more than anything from those who call upon Her in times of trouble are lives lived with poise and aplomb, not only in the best of times, but also in the worst. When things do not go as planned.

She has a special place in Her bosom for quiet-hearted people who find their way along this thoroughfare of broken dreams.

Part Four

24

Women of the Moor

Eema Mother was with Antony on the day of his First Epiphany. He had travelled to Europe looking for love in all the right places. He found himself, instead, staring in mute disbelief at the rusted undercarriage of a Citroën *Deux Chevaux* in Eindhoven, Netherlands.

In retrospect, he wished that he had visited the Van Gogh Museum in Amsterdam. *But why?* he thought. He'd never been to a museum before. *It'd be boring.*

The family of his Dutch girlfriend were having serious second thoughts. They loaned him their car and told him in no uncertain terms to wear his seatbelt whenever he drove it.

It had a 16 hp engine, top speed of ninety km/h, and extremely low fuel consumption. An umbrella on four wheels with a gear shift that came out of the dash, the 2CV was a fine French-made car built for Everywoman. It transported mothers and children from here to there as cheaply as possible.

"The only way you'd survive an accident is to be thrown from the car," everyone other than his soon-to-be-ex's family said.

Antony was in Europe, overseas and lost, and trying to find his way.

The car he was driving needed some work done, but he couldn't afford a mechanic. He had to do it himself. The nuts were seized, frozen in time and place. He had no blowtorch to heat them, no WD-40 to free them, just a long-handled breaker bar, a six-point socket, not to mention an immoderate amount of brute force and grim determination.

Of course, the socket slipped and skinned his knuckles. He cursed the heavens. He was unlucky with women and cars. He had no one to blame, just himself for the trouble he was in.

The arms of Eema Mother that day in Eindhoven, eight kilometres from Nuenen where Van Gogh lived and worked and had his being as a young artist, were strong and mighty.

Like the *Two Women in the Moor* (1883), Eema Mother was used to the hard labour of loving. Her body was thick and Her clothing coarse and heavy. She was a peasant of a woman who hefted Antony's burden from his shoulders and carried it upon Her back.

"I have you, my son. Don't worry about tomorrow. Sufficient unto the day is the evil thereof. Life may be a Dutch Treat, but no one, least of all me, is keeping a tally of your mistakes and failures. You need to forgive yourself as you have forgiven others, again and again, seventy times seven. With me at your side, you need not live in a perpetual cycle of loathing and self-recrimination."

She loved this lad with his skinned and bleeding knuckles, and did not judge him in his misery.

She was there. Her feet were in the mud and muck of his life. She did not turn away.

Antony heard Her call. He was ready to do Her will. He listened for Her still small voice to whisper in his ear the way that he should go.

"Return to the land of your birth," She whispered. "There you will find a wife, a Rebecca watering camels at the well. She will be there for you, a good and faithful friend who will not leave you nor forsake you. She will be a sign of the love that I have for you."

Antony vowed to Eema Mother that he would be a true friend in return. He would father their children the best he could.

He would be a man they could count on, depend upon. He would lay down his life for them. He would love them as Eema Mother loved the church.

She heard him and smiled.

"This is a fellow in whom I am well pleased."

The next thing Antony knows, he's back home, sitting in Dr. MacLaren's English class, reading Franz Kafka's "Metamorphosis", and attending Dr. Clark's European History lessons. He's discovered Churchill's penchant for drinking single malts in bed before getting up in the morning and smoking up to ten *Romeo y Julieta* and *La Aroma de Cuba* cigars a day. He's learning German, studying Modern Art History, and taking typing classes at night.

He's thrown out his Josh McDowel, John Warwick Montgomery, Winkie Pratney, and Francis Schaeffer. He's kept his Dietrich Bonhoeffer, Viktor Frankl, C.S. Lewis, and Henri Nouwen. He reads Robert Alter, Harold Bloom, Harold Goddard, and falls in love with Milton and Shakespeare.

He feels that this is exactly where he belongs. His college instructors introduce him to Frantz Fanon, Karl Marx, Bertrand Russell, and Virginia Woolf. He spends a guilty weekend reading *Lolita* when he should have been reading John Kenneth Galbraith, Christopher Hill, and Gerard Manly Hopkins.

He gets to know Annie Dillard, Doris Lessing, Flannery O'Connor, Ann Patchett, and Susan Sontag.

His brain becomes muscular, fit, fitter, and fittest. He asks open-ended questions. They are not easy to answer. His instructors are dodgy. Their answers are cagey. He explores the liminal space between black and white, certainty and uncertainty, and absolutes and relativity. His yeas become maybes and his nays possiblys.

"It all depends," he says, looking below the surface.

He comes to class with unanswered questions and his instructors humour him. They encourage him to explore the unknown. He becomes comfortable with ambiguity, the mark of an inquiring mind.

"So many books and so little time," Antony said. "My soul needs fattening. I've read so little in the last years, I'm starving. I didn't realize how hungry I've become. This is a smörgåsbord I'll never leave."

After reading *Lucky Jim* by Kingsley Amis, he starts wearing a Harris Tweed and wire-rim glasses. He has a pipe in his pocket and sports a goatee. This learning is as intoxicating as whisky in a jar. He downs one drink after another. His head is about to explode.

He's broke, crashing with friends who've given him room and board, and loving the student life. He's living his dream and grateful to Eema Mother, although he's uncertain about how to integrate his faith with his studies. The Universe has opened Her arms wide to him, and he is enthralled.

Then he receives a letter from Holland, and he's been dumped, set free, allowed to chart his own course. Not returning to Europe anytime soon, he's at a loss, directionless, and broken-hearted.

His grades are meteoric. In his first semester, they flash high in the night sky, but in the second, they fizzle as they plummet earthward.

His friends try to help. They say he's more durable than fourteen Karat Canadian gold, but she wanted someone closer to home. A twenty-four Karat Dutch boy. In retrospect years later, Antony couldn't blame her or her family. *They were wise beyond his years.*

"You may be just 58%," Eema Mother said but "it's the alloy of copper, silver, nickel, and zinc that has made you the Golden Boy you are, and the writer you will eventually become. She is just a temporary setback. You need to keep going. Don't allow a broken heart to ruin your life."

His friends concurred. "We didn't think she was much of a catch. The two of you weren't a good fit, in our opinion, anyway. But we kept our mouths shut. You needed to figure that out for yourself."

His life turned in a direction he hadn't anticipated.

Later he would say he dodged a bullet. Got out in the nick of time. Was saved by a grace founded on someone else's good sense. He thanked Eema Mother for looking out for him.

Antony had a good heart, a good head, a stubborn streak, and a persistence that wouldn't quit. He had a temper, was impatient, shot his mouth off at exactly the wrong time, made inappropriate jokes, and often acted the fool.

"An idiot," his closest friends would sometimes say.

In Eema Mother's opinion, he was a young man in need of a good woman to set him straight. But he had to be brought down a notch or two before he would truly achieve his majority. That, however, would only occur over the course of a long life. Eema Mother knew this.

"I love me a late bloomer," She said. "If he's lucky, and lives into his sixties and beyond, he might get over his insecurity."

She liked him as he was, an immature man about to make a fool of himself.

"Try to do the smallest measure of good in this world of evil. That is all I ask of you, dear child," She said in a downpour of tears.

Antony made Her laugh. She enjoyed his company. She liked to see him squirm and wriggle out of trouble.

He made Her chuckle.

25

Tempest and a Teapot

Antony scraped through the first year of college, but needed a summer job.

There's no life like it. Working construction to pay for tuition. Or joining the Canadian military and learning the hard way. Going on missions and coming home scathed.

"I just need to make a pot of money for the coming year."

On the phone, he talked to his father.

"You being in Abbotsford is like living in a foreign country," James George said. "Why don't you come to Alberta? You can drive water truck for me. I have lots of work, servicing gas wells in the Suffield Block."[7]

Except, by the time Antony gathered his kit and kaboodle, James George hired another operator. Which, in the grand scheme of things, was a good thing, given James George's fiery temper and Antony's complete lack of trucking experience.

While painting houses a few years back with Jaz in Squamish, Antony met a couple of stone masons. He loved the artistry of their work. In September when Jaz returned to university, Antony found a job as a bricklayer's labourer. The deal was that if he kept up his labouring duties, he could do some trowel work and become a skilled tradesman. He worked quickly and spent half an hour a day learning how to lay bricks and blocks. If he stayed on past a year, he could register as an apprentice. Once he became a journeyman, the sky was his limit.

---

[7] A 2,700 square kilometre military training base in southern Alberta.

"There's no life like it," his boss said, echoing the military's call for young men and women to join their ranks.

But Antony had other things on his mind. He learned to work quickly, to lay bricks, and build fireplaces. He learned enough of the trade to take on side jobs but had post-secondary aspirations. He just didn't know how he'd achieve them.

In the meantime, he soldiered on, shovelling sand, mixing mortar, pointing joints, and handling a trowel when he had spare time.

Before he left for Alberta, he built a fireplace for his friends. They had stood by him when he was down and out. While he mixed mortar and built up the facing, golden-haired Elin and ruddy-bearded Meriwether wore sack cloth and ashes, praying they wouldn't have to tear out his work as soon as he vacated their premises and crossed over the mountains to the Land of No Return.

They were as surprised as he when it was done.

"Not bad," Elin said, relieved, as she brought a kettle of water to boil. She warmed the tea pot and lid.

Meri, obedient and well-trained, eager for the tiniest treat she might have for him, matched her move for move in a long-practised and choreographed tea-making ritual.

"Could have been a lot worse," he tittered, lapping up Elin's affection.

She emptied the now-scalded teapot. Meri spooned in three scoops of rich, strong, and malty Indian Assam, smoky, musky, and umamic, as savoury as Eema Mother Herself, perfect with milk and sugar, not honey.

Elin filled the pot with fresh, boiling water, still fully oxygenated, and gave it a quick stir. Meri put on the lid. Elin fitted on the cozy. Meri set the timer. They fandangoed as only tea-makers could. The stereo blasting, the crescendo of Ravel's *Bolero* building steadily, rhythmically with well-practised intensity toward its climatic ending.

"Is it ready?" Antony asked, prematurely reaching for the cream in the fridge. In red, Elin cast a scornful glance in his direction. "Foolish boy!"

She tore herself away from Meri, his Suit of Lights all lit up and glistening, ready for some action in the arena upstairs but penned up and strained in the kitchen below.

"We use slightly warmed room-temperature milk in our tea, not ice-cold cream," Elin said, her blue eyes coolly assessing this foolhardy boy's vulnerabilities.

"*Olé*!" Meri barked, stamping his feet in perfect three-quarters time.

Elin leapt forward, blocking Antony's assault on the tea. The brave woman put herself in harm's way and saved the pot.

"You've got to wait a full four minutes," snarled Meri.

"Five!" Elin corrected her wayward husband, giving him a piece of chocolate.

Confounded, Antony opened himself to another of their counterattacks.

"But it's only tea," he said.

"Only tea?" Elin repeated. "I would gladly give my life to save this holy grail from your untimely foray."

She plighted her troth once more to the sanctity of a properly made cuppa.

Eema Mother, sipping a divine Oolong, set her *Limoges* cup of China Blue down. She looked with smiling grace upon this Viking warrior. "At last, a woman after my own heart."

"Only tea? Struth!" Meri swore, once again coming late to the game, his hackles raised.

He gnashed his teeth, and Elin joined him in a plaintive cry, a painfilled *flamenco cante* that lifted heavenward.

"Oh dear," Eema Mother said. "There's trouble brewing."

She peered over her towering parapet and saw shiny-pated Meriwether and Elin in uncivil dudgeon.

"You Philistine," Meri bayed.

"You scoundrel," Elin wept. "Only tea? Indeed!"

Meri thrust a copy of George Orwell's *Essays* into Antony's hands.

"Read the one about making tea before you darken our door again. It is the minimum standard. Only tea? Indeed!"

With that, he pushed Antony out the front door.

"Don't forget your bag," Elin said as she tossed it out the window. "The bus stop is just down the road."

Antony gathered his things and made his way to the land of his birth. *BC's good*, he thought, *but Alberta is divine.*

"Meri, you old dog," Elin said. "There's got to be some Grieg we can listen to now that we finally have the house to ourselves."

26

Alberta Bound

"Was it something I said?" Antony wondered, grabbing his bag, and walking down the long and lonely road to the Greyhound station. He caught the next one heading east.

On a stopover in Calgary, a brown-eyed girl and her mother in a loose-fitting summer frock climbed the stairs ahead of him. The little girl dropped her red-covered, illustrated Book of the People as she struggled up the stairs in front of her mother. Antony picked up the familiar children's book and handed it back to her. Her mother settled into a seat as near the front as possible, out of the smoking section.

He sat across the aisle from them.

"I'm Antony."

Madeleine introduced herself.

"My name's Sara without an H," the little girl said.

"Sara, please," Madeleine said. "Why don't you read your stories?"

She liked how Antony looked and how he treated her daughter, but experience taught her to be wary. "We'll be home soon."

Antony waved to Granny as they passed Gleichen, smelled the sage when they stopped in Brooks, and exchanged phone numbers with Madeleine before they said goodbye at the bus depot in downtown Medicine Hat. Antony promised to meet them at church on Sunday.

James George picked him up and they drove out to Seven (short for Seven Persons) where he had a trailer on Mildred Street and a couple of water trucks parked in the back. Antony could stay in the second bedroom and use the spare half ton until he got settled.

The job James George had for him was long gone. He'd have to scramble for another, but hard-working labourers with a clean driver's licence were few and far between.

He phoned Moritz's Masonry and showed up the next day at 6:50 for a seven A.M. start. His employers thought they won the jackpot.

"You've done this before?"

"For longer than I care to admit," Antony replied. He kept the bricklayers well supplied as they built their walls, course by course and ever higher.

"What I learned the hard way?" James George said when Antony finally showed up home after his first day of work. "You let greenhorns burn through a couple of clutches with another company before you hire them yourself. Once they get the hang of the gears, you take them on. Good employees are hard to find but you sure as hell don't ever want to train them."

That reluctance to throw his money away saved his relationship with Antony. As rocky as it was, the two of them stayed on speaking terms for the rest of their lives.

Upon reflection, Antony didn't want to work for his father. The man was too volatile. He wouldn't last a week before all hell would break loose. That's why he dillied and dallied and put off his move. He had to make sure James George hired someone else.

That Sunday, Antony drove into town to church, hoping to see Madeleine and Sara. But they weren't there. Nobody knew who he was talking about. "Must have been angels," Antony surmised. "They were heavenly."

A tall, lean fellow with curly black hair and an olive complexion stepped right out of the Book of the People. He had a glorious, Roman beak of a nose.

Keel-like, mariners could use it to navigate the waters off the Cape of Good Hope. It was hooked and eaglelike.

His proboscis prominent and stately, Laverne stopped Antony before he could make a hasty exit.

"You new here? Never seen you before. My name's Laverne, after the goddess of minor criminals. You can only please her with drinks you've poured from your left hand. Everyone calls me B.S. It's short for my favourite motorcycle, the BSA Spitfire. Outta the box, it's supposed to go 120 mph."

"I'm Antony, named after St. Anthony of Lisbon, famous for his preaching, knowledge of scripture, and humility. He's the patron saint of lost things."

They shook hands.

"What's the fastest you've ever ridden?" Antony asked.

"One hundred and nineteen," B.S. confided. "But that's our secret, okay?"

"Absolutely."

Antony was well acquainted with the Male Code of Silence. There are some things you never share with women: speeding tickets and the price you actually paid for whatever it is you just bought.

"Hate to have your Mum find out, eh?"

"Dad, though!" B.S. said. "He checked the timing, adjusted the carbs, and put some air in the tires.

"'Added up,' he told me. It's the little things that keep you from going top speed. Get them in order and you're off and flying."

"You always want to go a little faster," Antony said. "I understand that."

As they walked in the blazing sun towards B.S.'s partially restored, just up-and-running 1961 Morris Mini Woody Wagon, they agreed to go for lunch.

"You better bring your own vehicle, though. Mine might break down and I'll need a tow."

They met at the Shell Restaurant near the Trans-Canada for a plate of the best perogies south of Vegreville.

"Those Ukrainians up north may know their stuff," B.S. said. "But Pyotr here? His swim in butter. Got the recipe from his Baba, handmade. Not those frozen factory Cheemos. My treat. You can catch me next week."

With an invite like that, Antony couldn't refuse. Soon he was attending a Book of the People study on Tuesdays, Prayer Meetings on Wednesdays, as well as morning and evening services on Sundays. On Fridays, he was checking out the girls at the church socials, potlucks, and ball games.

They had their eye on him, too. Sending out signals, but cautious, testing the waters. He was a bit of an odd duck. Intriguing, but slightly off-putting.

"Driving his daddy's truck and living in his daddy's trailer?" they all asked. They had every right to be suspicious.

On the surface, he didn't seem much of a catch. They'd wait and see how he panned out.

The Preacher took Antony out for coffee and asked him what he wanted to do with his life.

Antony, who had never articulated the words before, suddenly felt a calling, a deep inner yearning. He wanted to expound the Word.

The Preacher took Antony under his wing and taught him this and showed him that. Soon Antony was working flat out, volunteering four days a week at the church and labouring three days a week to buy groceries, gas money, and pay the rent.

Needless to say, by September, he didn't have two bits saved for tuition. He took a gap year, having barely finished his first.

"We'll know in six months if you're cut out for the job. No use going to seminary for four years only to find out you don't have what it takes. This year will be good for you if you use it wisely. But you should buy yourself some new threads. If you want to be a man of the cloth, you better dress for it."

One sunny day, the Preacher drove Antony up to Calgary. He wanted the District Superintendent, Reverend Ardrey, to catechise the lad and see if he'd qualify for a Local Preacher's licence.

"You want to spread the good news," Reverend Ardrey said. "This is a worthy first step, getting mentored and testing the water. But you'll need more education. One year isn't enough. Next September you better return to college."

Reverend Ardrey gave Antony his blessing and sent him back to the Hat, cap in hand, to do the work that Eema Mother had for him.

Then Antony met Eleanor and lost all perspective. A gorgeous brunette with Swedish blue eyes. Small and delicate, her feet did not touch the ground when she walked. She smelled of spring and was as smart as a whip.

She thought Antony was odd. His worn-out clothes and that ridiculous goatee.

What was he thinking? She didn't have a clue.

And him labouring. He wasn't much of a catch. She certainly wasn't bringing him home to meet her parents anytime soon.

"Just look what the cat dragged in," her father would be sure to say. Her mother would chuckle. She'd hold back to see what would happen next. She trusted her daughter, but the boy? *This could be highly entertaining.*

Eleanor just couldn't and wouldn't bring him anywhere near her parents' doorstep. Not yet anyway. She didn't encourage the boy in any way, shape, or form. *It's just that the blasted fool wouldn't take a hint.*

He kept smiling at her, and being nice and kind and cheeky, too.

In September, he had the nerve to ask if she wanted to go to Vancouver with him. He needed to collect the last of his things.

Her immediate response was a resounding, *Not in your life*!

Then she remembered that she'd never been to Vancouver.

They could stay at her parents' in Fernie the first night and make a long day of it on the Crowsnest to Abbotsford the next. They wouldn't overnight it, and he wouldn't try to slip under the covers with her.

He promised.

When they arrived, they'd have separate bedrooms. She wouldn't have to worry about him trying to sleep with her.

She finally said, "Yes."

Meeting the parents didn't go too badly. At least Antony didn't embarrass her by telling an off-colour joke or using the wrong fork for his salad.

The closer they got to Vancouver, the more excited and relaxed and happy he became. His friends weren't half-bad either. Except them and their tea, though.

They were decent and kind, and smart and intelligent and cultured. They had a good opinion of this boy who was trying to worm his way into her heart.

She suddenly didn't mind.

A few years down the road, after Eleanor said her, "Yes, I will be your lawful wedded wife" and Antony plighted his troth and unflagging obedience to her, he had his Second Epiphany. He tried to tune his bright orange 1973 Volvo 145 station wagon with a high-compression B20 engine and the Bosch D-Jetronic electronic fuel injection. That was before he knew how to use a timing light.

He didn't know which of the cylinders was No.1, or if it was in fact the one that was used in the timing procedure. He didn't know about Top Dead Centre. He didn't know that the specific number of degrees of crankshaft rotation before TDC was critical for determining when the spark plug should fire.

In short, he trod mechanically where experienced journeymen were loath to tread. He had skimmed the manual and thought that was enough. He had the tool, he had the means, but he was a fool.

He hadn't learned the basics.

His spiritual quest for oneness with the universe evolved into a swift and agonizing epiphany of mistaken exclamations. "OMG! What the f***! What'll I tell Eleanor?"

The engine wouldn't start.

He had to call a tow truck and haul the car to the garage.

He handed the distributor cap to the driver.

"Have them fix it," Antony said. "No questions asked, please."

The driver smiled sympathetically. He understood Antony's dilemma.

Birthday boys getting tools for presents that young wives buy them from Canadian Tire and trying them out before they know how to use them. It's a marketing ploy aimed at DIY-ers.

Some guys have beginner's luck. Others learn the hard way.

Anthony's spiritual development happened through trial by error. Greenhorn revelation. One mistake after another in rapid succession.

His foray into engine tuning led him directly to the brink of his incompetence. It led him straight to a sudden overturning.

To stumble and fall is sometimes a good thing. It makes you wary. For Antony, it emptied his wallet.

Timing a Volvo takes preparation and care. Woe to the fool who rushes in. The best learning he will ever receive comes from the mistakes he is about to make. In his slow, haphazard way, Antony learned that in the universe of small matters, there is an interconnection between this and that that is both delicate and symbiotic.

Sometimes the tightness of a bolt is of crucial importance and requires the lightest touch. That's why John H. Sharp of Chicago invented the torque wrench in 1931. It kept greenhorns more astute than Antony from twisting the head off a bolt. More importantly, it ensured the proper tension of the threads in the fastening of a given application. Wheel nuts, for example, need to be torqued to a precise measurement. If they aren't, tires fly off vehicles at highway speeds and tragedies occur.

Except Antony didn't stop in time, and paid the price. Not a stiff one, as it turns out, but enough to make him bow his head in contrition.

Eema Mother, who smiled benevolently from above, knew that there is a spirituality in having the right tool for the job and knowing how and when to use it.

There is a wisdom that comes with the learning of a lesson the hard way.

In the world of small things, the right tension is a spiritual matter that makes a difference.

The itty-bitty parts are important.

27

Petra

There was the time Antony had his Third Epiphany.

He traded the six-by-twelve snooker table he received from Orel, Mary Helen's third husband, for a 1973 Yamaha XS650 motorcycle. Although Mary Helen's love life was as flirtatious and as on-again and off-again as Elizabeth Taylor's with Frank Sinatra, Orel was Mary Helen's last and best. While he looked out for his parents, and made sure Mary Helen had more than she could ask or imagine, he had his share of losing, and did what he had to do. His way.

When Eleanor heard about the back-room deal Antony worked out with B.S. , she took out a life insurance policy on her one and only.

"If you're gonna go," she said. "Make sure it's in an accident."

She had a no-nonsense way about her that Antony came to terms with early in their marriage. She was a woman to listen to, a woman whose loving made demands that could not be ignored.

He loved and feared her. He didn't want to disappoint her.

To be honest, Antony didn't know the half of what he was getting himself into the day he took possession from Orel of that Art Deco-style snooker table. It was the sum total of the inheritance he received after Mary Helen shuffled off her mortal coil.

He named it Petra for her rock-solid beauty. Players would fall to their knees and cry "Uncle!" the first time they saw her. To the unlucky one who got to play her every day, she was a rock. A dark force in slate, black and immovable. Petra, Dominatrix of the Pool Hall. She expected much from her submissives who knew exactly what they were in for.

Shortly after acquiring her, Antony realized that he had to be stone-cold sober to have any hope of ever potting a shot in one of her six pockets. The two sides were the hardest, while the four in the corners weren't any less challenging. The table was a stern taskmistress who exacted her due.

She expected the players who brushed their thighs against her apron to pay her homage. In her taxonomy, the player was made for the snooker table, not the table for the player.

She had been in the family for years. Orel bought it so his father Dido and friends could get some exercise. They spent hours in the basement, laughing and drinking rye-and-water. They shepherded the balls from one end of the table to the other. They had no illusions about their skill or their chance of ever getting lucky again. They certainly weren't going to give up their liquor.

The old guys stepped back from the table, enjoyed their drinks, told ribald jokes, and laughed from the heart. They had their exercise, and didn't go powerwalking with their wives at the mall. It was a win-win situation for everyone concerned.

Dido and his friends refused to succumb to Petra's demands and were content to walk for miles around her perimeter. She glowered in her den, an ominous, unmotherly, ungodly presence. Her hunger for acolytes could not be easily satisfied. She waited patiently for young men who could still be taught the way they should go, not old ones who had lost their capacity.

Like Mary Helen, She preferred men who didn't fall asleep as soon as the game became interesting.

Snooker tables, much to Antony's everlasting chagrin, are unbelievably hard to play. It takes time and commitment to master a table that is six feet wide and twelve feet long. Angled shots from corner to corner must be thirteen feet.

The pockets have narrow mouths that are 3½ inches at their widest point and seem to slam shut when a ball comes near.

Their jaw cushions are angled in such a way that if a ball hits them too hard, it bounces straight back out. The striker's shot must be deft and bewitching, the momentum of the white cue ball as light and as deft as a lover's kiss in the cool of the evening.

Gentle is as gentle does.

Snooker tables do not suffer drinkers lightly. They are not the kind of table a bar owner wants in his establishment. Little four-by-eights are the bartender's delight. Wide-mouthed 4½ inch pockets whisper, "Come to Momma, baby." They are as wide as a barn door and as easy to score into as an open net.

Impaired, beer-drinking ball-bangers love these tables. Their cues shiver with excitement and splinter from one end to the other. The leather tips splay like mushrooms from relentless showmanship. The striker pulls the trigger. The white rifles to the end of the table. The balls ka-thunk and scatter. Their report echoes over the pastel oilskin that covers the tables.

Four-by-eight surfaces are as durable as bulletproof vests. The striker quaffs his beer and bang, bang, bang, another frame goes down.

"Another round, boys? How about another jug?"

The bartender smiles. His patrons enjoy themselves and spend their money. He'll take home a fistful of dollars in tips, that's for sure.

One sad, cold day in November, Dido's heart stops dead.

As one thing usually leads to another, Antony suddenly found himself the proud owner of a snooker table of his own. He hadn't yet learned that it is sometimes best to say no to once-in-a-lifetime, golden opportunities that come your way.

The only catch was that he had to haul it out of Dido's basement and set it up in his.

"That's a job best left to the professionals," Mary Helen said as she slipped him five hundred dollars.

It had black plastic rails and brushed metal aprons that ran down the sides. The orange support structures were heavy enough to hold the timber bridging and six 450-pound slabs of 1½-inch slate.

A snooker table like this is not lithe and nubile. She's as sturdy as the Rock of Gibraltar. She requires a good eye, a steady hand, and patience from those players who dare run their hands across her smooth, green baize.

Of course, Antony had to do some renovating. Nobody could acquire a table that size without making some accommodation. Out came the wet bar that Antony and Eleanor didn't use. It was a huge thing made of 2x4s and deck screws and covered with cedar siding.

"Uglier than that old, battered K-car up on blocks in the neighbour's front yard," Eleanor complained.

Antony refitted his basement. He managed most of the plumbing and had Jimmy Dean do the electrical. Antony finished the boarding and sanding, and Eleanor chose the paint colours.

Initially, she wasn't all that enthralled with the idea, but then she began to see the table as a possible surface for her quilts. She'd better bide her time, though.

Antony would have to get through the initial protective and possessive stage of ownership before she could stake her claim.

Once the lustre wore off, the table would be hers. This would take a while, she admitted, but she was a patient, kind-hearted woman who knew how to get her way. She played her man any which way she chose.

Their two daughters born fifteen months apart were excited, right from the get-go. They wanted to build a fort under the table. "No parents allowed!"

Nicola piled blankets and pillows between the orange supports. Rosalita set their stuffed animals as guards at the entrance. They had fun under there, by themselves, doing what little girls do. They carved their initials on the timbers, painted their nails, decapitated their Barbies, and scrutinized their Kens.

On their sleepovers with friends under the slate-heavy sky, they dreamt about boys.

Crouched over the snooker cue, his head canted, peering through progressive lenses while focussing on the ball at the other end, Antony wished he had a spotter's scope with a laser.

He needed the white to touch the red, so it would curve toward the open pocket and drop in. With a spot of English, the white would roll toward the coloured in the centre.

"Nobody knows the shape I'm in," Antony hummed. The hymn of all snooker players.

Of course, he mis-shot. The white followed the red into the pocket and he was down another four points. That was the story of his life with this table.

The only way he could win was if he minimized the number of scratches he made. Take a safety shot, leave the white so that it is nearly impossible for the next player to make, and not worry about potting or finishing a run on his own.

This way, Antony could rack up points from the mistakes his friends made.

He hooked them, made a feeble attempt at making his shot, all the while driving the white to the furthest rail. It was a nasty maneuver, but the only way he could keep from completely embarrassing himself.

Antony soon recognized the true cost of owning a snooker table. If a guy had one in his basement, he had a burden and a responsibility to play it well. But that took hours a day, and Antony did not have the time or that kind of commitment.

He was an unworthy man who owned a table but would never play it well.

As Antony's affection for the table flagged, Eleanor decided to make her move. It started when the girls carved their initials in the table's oaken timbers. Then came springtime, grow lights, protective tarps, and a self-watering system. Eleanor transformed unmaternal Petra into a nursery for bedding plants.

The final insult occurred when Eleanor had Anthony heave a queen-sized mattress up onto the table. They needed a guest bed for James Eadie and Red Molly, who were riding two and a half hours north up Highway 2 on their '52 Vincent Black Lightning at speeds approaching 140 km/h, their Walkmans blasting Richard Thompson over the engine's roar.

That Saturday night, James and Red Molly were feeling a little frisky in the northern City of Lovers. Climbing a small ladder to get into the feather bed that floated on the green baize, they decided to take advantage of that once-in-a-lifetime tabletop mountain of an experience.

Turning to one another, they enjoyed a long game of one-on-one.

Theirs was an act of joy and celebration. Left-handed, James scored one hundred and twenty-seven, and Red Molly once again wrapped her man around her little finger. The slate didn't give that moment in time, but the earth shifted on its axis.

Red Molly rang in another century and James was a happy man.

Petra, however, was not amused.

"Screw you," she swore after the defilers rode back down Highway 2 and Antony dismantled their love nest. He pulled off the mattress, folded the blankets, and put the sheets in the washing machine.

He brushed off the baize. On a whim, he decided to play a game. It had been quite a while.

He racked the red balls, placed the pink at the top of the pyramid, set the black on the dot behind the frame, and the blue in the middle. The green, brown, and yellow on the baulk line, and the white in the D.

He chalked his cue and aimed for the red second from the corner at the base of the pyramid. He hoped to tap two reds free from the pack, with the white bouncing off the rail at the foot of the table, hitting the side, and angling back across the table to the opposite end.

Banking from the head rail, it should come to rest innocently behind the green or the brown.

Of course, that didn't happen.

Antony hit the third red from the front and the white rolled straight into the corner pocket.

Not only did he scratch, he sewered. The white followed the red into the pocket like a fool jumping to the wrong conclusion. "Never again will your Golden Boy ever make a safety break," Petra vowed, which suited Eema Mother fine.

She wanted Antony on the strait and narrow, not hanging out in pool halls with gamblers, hustlers, and other such like troublemakers. That was her domain. Hers were the lost and hurting. Hers were the ones who needed a helping hand.

Truants were Her speciality. Drifters were Her people.

Runaways Her hope.

28

Cordelia

When Antony and Eleanor sold their home, they were as reluctant as the new owners to include the snooker table in the sale.

It was, after all, the only tangible connection that Antony had with Mary Helen. He told his friends about the dilemma he was currently facing.

His Risk-playing opponent B.S. began to experience acute back pain and reached for his half-empty bottle of Ibuprofen.

"I am all ears, Antony. What is your problem?"

B.S. was ready to writhe in pain as soon as Antony mentioned moving, crew, and help all in the same sentence.

Antony, however, knew that he had asked B.S. to help one time too many, and had no intention of hitting him up again. There is only so much furniture moving you can ask of a friend. Besides, Antony'd been cultivating a whole new set of acquaintances for his next move. A man has to plan ahead, which helps to explain why Antony had so few male friends left in his later years. He had milked them for all their worth.

"As you know, B.S. , Eleanor and I are moving soon. Now don't get all hot and lathered. I have enough help. We're gonna get Eager Beaver to do the heavy work. I've lined up a crew to help with the boxes and the like.

"The problem that I have is with Petra. I don't want to sell her, and I certainly don't want to leave her in the house for those 'Since I'll be paying cash, will you give me a deal?' vultures to gloat over.

"Do you know anybody who'd have the room and would be willing to part with a few coins?"

"Hmm," B.S. said. "I reckon I know just the guy who'd care for that table better than you. He'd take it off your hands real quick, but he doesn't have any money."

"Who would that be?" Antony asked, as if he were reading the words straight off a teleprompter.

"Well, me, of course," B.S. piped in. "I don't have any money to complete this transaction in a way that'd fill up your pocketbook. I do have an idea though that'd bless you to kingdom come, but the lovely Eleanor less so."

"What's that?" Antony intoned, growing curiouser and curiouser.

"How about I trade a 650 Yamaha for that table of yours? Let's make it an even swap."

Antony thought for a minute and decided that this was an offer he couldn't refuse.

"Why sure, B.S., I think that this is a fine arrangement. I just don't know how I'll break it to Eleanor, though."

"Tell her it isn't running."

That gave Antony reason to pause, but he shrugged off any misgivings that grew in his heart. He'd seen Jack Nicholson wearing a football helmet on the back of Dennis Hopper's Harley too many times to let a little hiccup like this keep him from the open road.

"*Easy Rider*, an empty highway, and life everlasting," Antony envisioned his dreams coming true. "When are you coming over with your pickup truck to haul that table outta here?"

"This weekend?"

Antony grinned a grin that went from ear to ear and B.S. smiled all the way home.

On a groaning spring morning, B.S. arrived with a 1978 Ford ¾-ton truck. It had a smoking diesel, and a transmission geared so low it could walk a bull to market.

"This'll handle your little snooker table. No problem."

Antony wasn't so sure, but he was prepared to give B.S. the benefit of the doubt.

They went down the stairs with pliers, wrenches, and screwdrivers and dismantled the bumpers around the table. Laying them to the side, they took out the staples that anchored the felt to wooden strips, which were bolted into the slate. They rolled the woollen cloth and treated it the way one of Antony's American cousins would handle his flag at the funeral of a fallen comrade—with awe, respect, and a sorrow as wide as the Mississippi.

You see, Antony had already forgotten what a curse that table was. It would let you play with her in the evening. It would tease you until late at night. In an early morning hour, it would tantalize you with worldly delight.

Then, at the last minute, just when a guy was ready, prepared, and poised, and a little more than willing to pot that longest of shots, with all the anticipation of a man about to get lucky, she'd get frisky and coy and leave him hung out to dry.

With the felt rolled and folded and secured in the cab of the truck, Antony, B.S. , Jimmy Dean, Darwyn (Eleanor's Swedish cousin from up Lund's way), and an English professor named Chuck looked the slate up and they looked it down.

The quickest bet would be for them to hoist each slab up over their heads and out the high basement window. Given that none of them actually laboured for a living, they decided to go for the long haul, four men, each holding a corner, the fifth in the middle at the bottom and hauling it heavy assed up the stairs.

The first slab wasn't bad. Antony had given each of the guys a brand new pair of work gloves so they wouldn't mash their fingers. He told them to lift from the knees and go slow.

The last thing he wanted was to see that quarter ton of dead weight drop from their hands, crushing their arms and feet as it avalanched to the stair and thundered to the floor below.

Everything went smoothly until the last piece. It was the heartbreaker; they were so tired.

Darwyn stumbled at the top of the stairs and broke through the drywall at the back of the closet. The others braced themselves, and somehow, somehow, held on to the slate. It didn't fall. It didn't crack and nobody was hurt.

The only collateral damage was in the closet. With Antony's promise of a feed of Norwegian Klub, Darwyn volunteered against his better judgement to repair it with some drywall, mud, and wallpaper. He just knew Antony's wouldn't compare to the Swedish Palt he had grown to love.

After they loaded the table into the back of the truck and covered it with a tarp, they went out for a celebratory feast of Vietnamese soup and coffee.

"The #36 is my favourite," Antony suggested, thinly-sliced beef and noodles with fire in the pan. Chuck, a guy so smart he earned two doctorates, went with a #86 lemon-grass rice, cashews, and the like.

B.S. sniffed the air. His was the nose of a gourmand.

"I'll order the Beef Satay Phở if I have to, I guess. It won't be as good as King's Wonton in Calgary, but it'll do. I suppose."

He was discriminating. If you couldn't grow it or raise it within a hundred kilometres of Seven, he wasn't really interested. Unless he was hungry, then he'd eat about anything, complaining the whole time.

Pinto beans from Bow Island, sugar buns, corn from Medicine Hat, Taber's second-rate peaches and cream was all marketing and hype, peppers from Red Cliff, sausage from Erb's, and russets from Bassano, along with Hutterite chickens, beef, and pork. He'd go as far as eating Wonderbread baked in Calgary but no further. They were his staples. Anything else was foreign, eaten under duress, and most often regretted.

The closest thing to exotic in his diet was mild Gouda cheese and Black Forest cake.

But he was there whenever Antony needed help, and that was all that really mattered.

"You know, Antony," Chuck started in, "when you have a little time on your hands, you should watch those Joseph Campbell videos with Bill Moyer about the hero's journey. You'll find them mighty interesting."

Antony appreciated having Chuck around. He was not only an intellectual, but also a likeable guy with a booming voice and a strong back. He was the only person Antony knew who had read Shelby Foote's monumental three-volume *The Civil War: A Narrative* in its entirety.

Moving the snooker table was the first opportunity Antony had to plumb the depths of his friendship with Chuck, so he paid his dues and listened to what the doctordoctor had to say.

"The hero receives a calling to leave his normal surroundings and follow some dream. Along the way, he meets various guides and faces numerous challenges. After a period of time, he returns home and imparts his newfound wisdom to the members of his community."

"If you say so, Chuck," Antony replied. "I'll mosey on down to Rogers, ASAP. I'd much rather listen to Joseph Campbell than watch another Jackie Chan movie. You like Merchant Ivory?"

Antony had a finely-honed sense of irony, so that he rarely said what he meant. This was precisely one of those times. There was no way he was gonna watch something that aired on PBS. Chuck may be his friend, but this was going too far.

Watch public television? You gotta be crazy, he thought as he bit into a red-hot Thai chilli pepper and nearly blew his head off. He grabbed a spoonful of sugar and reached for his cup of green tea.

Man does not live by bread alone. He needs a daily hit of capsaicin. Food that hurts is good for the soul.

Trading Petra for B.S.'s 650 Yammy seemed like a win-win situation to Antony, but he was mistaken.

Flat-tired, headlight askew, wires tangled worse than the line in a child's fishing reel, it had spent ten long years abandoned in B.S.'s shed.

When Antony popped the hinged gas cap of the tank open, the smell of stale petrol filled his nostrils. Petra's evil twin Petro settled in the reservoir. He fed himself white-hot as naphtha while Antony readied the bike for the road.

Antony sanded and buffed the dull tank and prepared it for painting. He used Nevr-Dull on the chrome, an Aladdin rubbing the lamp, except in his case a turbaned genie with three curses emerged.

He worked on the wiring, soldered the connections, and re-taped the shorts. The engine fired on the first kick. Antony roared off down the street in a puff of blue. He could taste the freedom of the open road, and the distant horizon never looked sweeter.

On his first trip out, the mirrors rattled off.

On his second, the front tire went flat.

On the third, Antony finally got the hint.

"This bike isn't made for riding. It's meant for pushing home."

The day Antony had his Fourth Epiphany was as sweet and as bitter a day as anyone could imagine.

How something that ended so badly could have started so wonderfully, Antony didn't know.

Just the day before, he commented to a friend that in his next life, he'd rather have wealth than wisdom.

He was about to find out why the wisest among us are usually the poorest.

His bike had an engine that had not run in ten long years. It had a polished brass headlight from a British military firetruck, a black handmade seat that fitted no one's bum in particular, a bright yellow hand-spray-painted gas tank, and gorgeous red NGK sparkplug wires. Antony named her Cordelia in *King Lear* for the daughter he never had, hoping Nicola and Rosalita would eventually read the play and get his joke.

On one of those special days in the late Canadian autumn, the sun shone brightly in the sky. Although the frost was heavy in the morning, it was warm enough in the afternoon to go for a twenty-kilometre ride without becoming hypothermic.

Oh, he had his long johns on, scarf to cover his neck, full-face helmet, boots, and heavy leather gloves, but he still felt the precursor of winter cut him to the bone.

The road he travelled went south from Edmonton through Beaumont—a little French village in the heart of Anglophone Alberta— to Rolly View, a tiny hamlet where he stopped to buy gas. He luxuriated in the sun while the station attendant chatted it up with one of her twenty-something customers. Locals get prompt service while day-trippers from the city have to wait until she's good and ready.

With a full tank, he turned the bike around and rode back through the undulating landscape and up the rise that gives the town its name. The sun shone low over his left shoulder. The wind bore down on him from the north. The engine ran hot and smelly with burning oil. Gas seeped through the gaskets and rubber hoses.

Antony couldn't have been happier.

One of the challenges of riding a motorcycle in western Canada is that riders cannot allow the cold to deter them from going for a spin. They must ride their bikes until the snow comes. While some race theirs on snow and ice, Antony does not.

He's a bare road kind of guy. He waits for the warm and near-warm days. His goal is to ride once a day during the spring, summer, and fall.

Those last days, however, before he puts the stabilizer in the tank, he checks the weather report and looks to the sky.

"Can I get just one more ride in? I promise, Eema Mother, I'll be good. Be merciful, dearest Grandmother, Granny of Ages. Bless me with thy meteorological grace."

Most would describe Antony as a born-again motorcyclist. A man who reached middle age and rediscovered the riding joy of his youth.

When Antony arrived home from Rolly View on his last ride of the season, exhilarated, his bike all hot, oily, and smelling of gasoline, he rolled it into the garage and parked it over a piece of cardboard, as if it were a Triumph 500 Daytona.

He took his sunglasses off, removed his helmet, and reached into his jacket pocket for his regular glasses, but they weren't there. They had fallen out somewhere on the road, and his heart began to sink.

What was he going to do? Without his glasses, he could hardly see.

He put his sunglasses back on, made sure the petcocks on the bike were turned to the off position, flicked off the master switch he had wired to foil the electrical gremlins that kept draining his battery, and walked into the house to face the music.

What a day. It had started so sweet and ended so bitterly. Antony found out that the wise are poor because the lessons that they learn are so expensive.

"The next time I go riding," he promised Eleanor, "I'll put my glasses in a pocket that zips shut."

At least Cordelia loves him and is happy to let him sleep in the garage with her. When he said his goodnight prayers to Eema Mother above, he asked Her how much She loved him.

"Nothing, my son," She replied, quoting the youngest daughter's bare-to-the-bones honesty in *King Lear*. "According to my bond. Nothing more."

Part Five

29

Family Man

Married for twenty-three years, the husband of one wife and father of two daughters, Antony was forty-eight years old the day he sat in the coffee shop on Calgary Trail in south Edmonton at sunrise. The sun shone golden over the horizon.

Heavy, black-bottomed clouds lofted in the wind. Men and women hurried to work. Muffled sounds of stop-and-go traffic filled the air. Leaves clung to trees along the boulevard and in the median.

A plastic bag, trapped in the branches, snapped and crackled as the wind gusted every which way but up.

Cars and trucks floored it from one red light to the next, and Antony sipped his coffee.

Good to be inside, thinking, not scrambling on a construction site, Antony thought.

Lately, he had been out of work more times than he cared to remember. This time, though, he quit because his employer hadn't given him a paycheque in six weeks.

The pain of separation was acute. Even in work, human beings bond in relationships. They develop an emotional commitment to one another.

Alone again, he wondered if he'd ever fit in.

Unemployment was not so much a case of being out of work as it was a shunting to the side. In spite of his general good health, and his optimism, his age made him an unlikely hire. He couldn't compete with all the sharp-edged young Turks swarming the pavement.

Forty-eight and wiser than ever, Antony thought he saw the sunrise over the horizon. *It can only get better, not any worse,* he surmised. Little

180

did he dream, thanks be to Eema Mother, of what would occur in a year or so.

She had something else in store for him.

He had come to this day of employment self-termination with his eyes wide open. He had seen it approach. He knew the signs and cleaned out his desk well in advance and hauled his stuff home from the shop weeks ago.

Even when he accepted the job as a manager, helping with the start-up of a new ethnic bakery, producing delicious naan, a flat bread from Central Asia, hot from the oven. Like its shelf-life that is measured in hours, he knew his days were numbered.

He took the job because the challenge and the adventure of something new interested him. He saw it as an exciting opportunity that he couldn't refuse. He realized that "selling" is not a dirty word. Rather it is the offering of a service to solve a problem. Selling is helping people find solutions.

When the time came for him to quit, he grabbed his jacket off the hook and walked out the door. Both easy and hard, he was prepared.

Reclining in his chair, sipping his coffee, and watching the traffic made him realize once again just how lucky he was. A day like this freed him to thank Eema Mother for his topsy-turvy life.

It could be a lot worse, Antony chided himself.

A guy could be just as miserable with a clear title to his house, a car that he owned outright, and a positive bank balance at the end of every month. Antony's investment portfolio was thin.

Maybe this week's 6/49 or Super 7?

His Golden Years certainly wouldn't be like those promised to the Freedom Fifty-Fivers.

Resolutely, he took another sip of his coffee and attacked the morning's crossword puzzle.

Twenty-Six Down, a five-letter word beginning with S, a river in Berlin.

Ha!

He knew that one.

He was halfway through Günter Grass's impenetrable *Too Far Afield.*

If it's this hard in English, what's it like in German? He didn't bother finishing it.

Excuse me, Herr Grass, your prose is too difficult. I can't understand it.

Antony looked up from his crossword. He saw the plastic bag hanging from the branch. The sun was now above the clouds and the wind was still.

The traffic, though heavy, was no longer a steady stream. Cars, trucks, buses, and motorcycles surged ahead like waves on the river, cresting, ebbing, and then pushing forward. An assault of vehicles from the suburbs, acreages, and bedroom communities outside the city limits, one person at a time.

Spree! he announced as he reached for his pen. He checked. The five letters fit perfectly.

Crossword puzzles require a long memory. Various clues are Wagnerian *leitmotifs,* Antony philosophized. They appear in one puzzle, submerge, recede, and disappear only to reappear in another several months later. Not that Antony ever listened to a complete Wagner, but he had seen *Apocalypse Now.*

He could hum those famous bars from the *Ride of the Valkyries.* He could also imagine what napalm smelt like in the morning. Gasoline and burning villages. The sound of people screaming.

His life could be a lot worse.

He didn't have to look far to know how good he had it.

Even with its huge lexicon of words, English has only a finite number of variations to draw from, making a crossword puzzle challenging, yet still accessible. The Saturday morning one in *The Journal* was his baby. On a good day, he could usually complete half of it, but the Thursday *New York Times*? That one was way out of his reach. He couldn't even pick up his pen. It felled him with its wit and clever humour.

He worked his way methodically through the Across clues, then he went over the Downs, filling in whatever answers he could. Sometimes he would whirl in a vortex of familiarity, rapidly writing one word after another. When he'd finish what he could, he'd pause, look up, and smile.

He did a double-check on Thirty-Three Across before he filled in Twenty-Six Down, *Glacial Boulder*, seven letters. *Spree*, he wrote first, then *Erratic* triumphantly. Tattooed in black or blue, each letter stood strong and true, secure in its place.

He didn't like making mistakes. Errors make the work doubly hard. First you have to back track from all the false leads that you followed. Then try to solve the original problem. It usually ended in a smudge of ink blots and scratched-out illegible squares.

He was too experienced a crossworder to need the safety net of an *HB* pencil. Filling in the clues in ink was an extreme sport for him—that, and drinking coffee mugs filled with espresso, not to mention eating red-hot Thai chilli peppers any chance he could.

He relished the subtle citrusy nuances that habañeros added to the dishes he cooked, though not the fire that came into the eyes of The One He Loved The Most when she bit into a piece he hadn't chopped finely enough.

Making mistakes is not always a bad thing. Progress can occur even though you follow a false lead. As you gingerly step forth in the darkness, you might happen upon a consonant or a fortunate vowel that draws you in the right direction. Such purchase is hard-won, but effective. You're going the wrong way, come across part of the answer, make a few reversals, then continue forward.

It's not like you have any choice. It's do or not do. And the latter is not an option if you want to live.

Your mistake helps you. You learn, loop back, and press forward. That's all there's to it.

There's no life like it.

Even though Antony tried to confirm his responses before he committed himself, he often inked in his hunches with a blue or black pen. Periodically, they worked in his favour.

He would rather mess up a crossword puzzle, attempting to solve it than to leave it blank. It was the act, the process, not the final destination that counted, or so Antony liked to think. One word at a time.

Suddenly, Antony noticed that the plastic bag was gone. This morning's morning minion, kingdom of daylight's dauphin, dapple-dawn-drawn Falcon, it somersaulted through the air, pell-mell and hurly-burly, only to freefall into an eddy behind a cement block building down the road.

Trucks with long, empty trailers hauled into the city. Train cars off-loaded in the rail yard behind the berm. Containers weighing thousands upon thousands of kilos, stacked one on the other, waited for the lift to grab their four corners and shift them to the stalled line of trucks.

Everything in this country moved by truck. Espresso makers from Italy, pipe organs from Quebec, grapefruit from Florida, and cedar shakes from the Coast.

Maybe he should get his Class One license and hit the road? That old Grateful Dead "Truckin" tune played in the jukebox of his mind.

He took another sip of coffee and scribbled *Radiant*, a seven-letter word for Type of Heater. Though generally a happy man, he was rather embarrassed and chagrined at the descent of his academic career.

It was quite something for him to walk in the shadow of the buildings at the university near his house and realize how insignificant he was. The world continued on, whether he was on top of it or not. Whether he had tenure or not. He could not let defeat and humiliation keep him from living his life. He simply had to keep on going. Life was what it was.

Regardless.

During liminal moments like this one, some might call them epiphanal, when the door behind has shut but the one ahead still hasn't opened, Antony was stranded in the vestibule, reflecting on what was, and what was about to be.

It is both an airless claustrophobic place, more like Jonah's Belly of The Whale where the world crashes in from all sides, epic, heroic, and at other times, a freeing sort of place. Out in the open, the fresh air blowing, the horizon is as broad and as distant as Alberta.

That's the way Antony felt.

He breathed easily, even though the days were ambiguous.

30

Cooking With Spice

In spite of the uncertainty in life, Antony learned a long time ago that one of the best ways to keep a woman happy was to feed her really well. A good supper covered a multitude of sins.

And losing at Scrabble.

That was absolutely critical. Not that Antony ever intentionally threw a game. He fought ruthlessly to win, a two-letter word here, a three-letter there. His downfall was that he saved his Xs, Qs, and Js for the perfect placement, the coveted triple-word squares. He'd forgo opportunities at hand and miss by a turn those double letters.

His clearheaded strategy for winning by losing was to open up huge sections of the board with low-scoring words. Then he'd forget the long game and go straight for the jugular.

"Rats," he'd say as he'd place "oxyphenbutazone" on the board and miss getting laid for a month of Saturdays.

In this marriage, Antony did his best to lose at Scrabble and win with Minute Miracles at supper.

He could have a fish dinner, stir-fry, or plate of pasta ready to eat in thirty minutes from start to finish. Olive oil, garlic, fresh vegetables, and red wine were the armaments he depended upon in this domestic warfare. Beef, chicken, and pickerel were his weaponry.

"If you need a cream sauce," Antony intoned whenever anyone would listen, "a tablespoon of flour, a teaspoon of corn starch, a cup of milk with a dollop of extra-virgin olive oil, and a twist of black pepper are all you need. Whisked quickly together and without a lump. Healthy, too. Vine-ripened tomatoes from the Farmer's Market, crushed oregano from the Italian Centre, and garlic sautéed in grape-seed oil are the only way to go when you need to bring to her knees, the woman who bore your children."

Since working at the bakery in Edmonton's Little India, situated near 34th Avenue and 96th Street, he'd developed a taste for toor and kali dal and Indian curries. He even bought a few cookbooks.

Lately, he was experimenting with what was left of the four-hundred-pound front-quarter of a bison he bought from a farmer on the 36 east of Vegreville and split with Prester John.

Butter Bison, Bison Tikka Masala, Bison Madras and his favourite, Do Piaza.

His daughters were sick of bison before they had chewed their way through the first twenty-five pounds.

"Not again!" they'd yowl.

"Only another 175 to go," Antony said encouragingly.

One of the girls' boyfriends dropped out of the picture when he heard what was on the menu for the next six months. *There's a lesson to be had for the learning*, Antony thought. Cook meals for the boys in your daughters' lives with food so bad, they run out the door and never come back.

Antony figured that he'd move on to Greek recipes next. That was sure to get rid of the next one.

"Sayonara, lads," Antony said as they peeled out of his life.

He imagined that a bison *Kota Me Bizelia* or a *Htapothi Me Tomata* would be quite lovely if the meat were cooked properly. Indian first, Greek next, and then perhaps German, if he still had any bison left in the freezer or daughters left in the house.

What he would give for a Hungarian goulash with lots of paprika.

He learned to bake bread, using squeezed lemon juice as a natural dough conditioner. No woman can stay mad at you for long, if she smells a loaf of multigrain cooling on the counter. In the Battle for Love, Antony washed dishes, hung pictures on walls, and kept the car full of gas, at least most of the time.

He was a survivor who cherished the sweet savour of a happy home. Domestic hero, happyfamilyman.

What got him into trouble, though, was his high tolerance for dust and the habit he had of leaving all his shirts on the drying rack in the laundry room. When he needed one, he'd simply iron the shirt that he wanted for the day.

Then there was his tendency for smothering everything he cooked with cumin. He had the temerity to add an extra teaspoon of the Queen of Spices to the refried beans he was making for his world famous Tex-Mex casserole.

"A scant teaspoon is better than a heaping tablespoon, don't you think?" Eleanor would vainly suggest.

While Antony would go the second mile for the sake of his marriage, there is a line he would never cross again.

He made the mistake one day of shopping with Eleanor for foundation. What a piece of folly that was! Before then, the only foundation colours Antony knew about were the greenish lime of newly-poured cement and the grey of it once it cured.

Women's foundation is a morass and a quagmire.

There are as many colours as there are skin hues. The different shades and subtleties take up more room in a Wal-Mart than fishing supplies, if you can believe it. You enter the makeup section and suddenly you're in a time warp.

Time's passage becomes glacial and is measured in eras, not hours. A guy could mummify looking at Maybelline and pondering L'Oréal. It's an aisle Antony will never knowingly go down again.

The one thing that Antony was more than willing to do, however, but was not allowed to, upon pain of death, was the laundry.

He was supposed to check the water temperature, separate the colours, hang the under-nothings to dry, lay out sweaters, turn jeans inside-out, and read labels to determine which detergent to use.

You need a Ph.D. in Chemistry and years of experience in Materials Management to capture the nuances of women's laundry.

As a new husband, Antony assumed that dirty clothes could be jumbled in the machine and washed *holus bolus*. Oh, the darks must be separated from the whites. That's a given. And woollens must be washed in cold water and never put in the dryer. He understood that much.

The rest, though, was a mystery.

With grown daughters, he now just has to reach for the laundry basket and whoever is home at the time will lunge at him, screaming.

His life, through no fault of his own, had suddenly become easier.

He should have thought about this a lot sooner.

If Antony were honest, he'd have to confess that whatever he knew about women, he learned the hard way.

Like the time, on his second anniversary, when he gave his young bride a bouquet of flowers, then dropped her off at the intersection a block from their house, so he could attend his last sailing class of the year.

He had to get to the Glenmore Reservoir in south Calgary before the wind died down. He was writing a test. He couldn't miss it. There'd be other anniversaries.

But never his second, and quite possibly not a third, if he didn't shape up.

Every day that summer, the wind blew furiously the whole time he was at work. He'd mix mortar for the bricklayers, carry buckets of water up and down twenty-four flights of stairs. He was slim, fit, and always hungry.

He'd rush home, have a quick shower, and eat a quicker supper. Trying not to speed or run any reds, he'd race to the boathouse, and sit through the thirty-minute lecture on why boats did what and when. He'd drag his down to the water, pull the sail up the mast, and, if he was lucky, get the boat out onto the water before the wind died down.

One minute, there'd be whitecaps cresting the water, the next the lake was mirror-like, the sun beating down on him as he held the flaccid rope in his hands.

Impotent, he'd be stranded and alone in the middle of a man-made, land-locked lake.

Alone, just like Eleanor back on Rundlehorn Drive, marooned, walking to her empty house, the bouquet of flowers trailing in her hand.

Something's wrong with this picture, she thought, as a quick gust of wind pushed her homeward. That very same gust of wind caught Antony's sail.

The boom swung and hit him in the face, knocking his glasses into the water. He couldn't watch as they sank to the bottom. He had to sail his boat, or it would capsize. The one time the wind blew with any force, he couldn't see a thing.

I could be having some fun, he thought.

Then the rain started to fall. He turned the boat to the shore and managed to get the sail down and the boat stowed away before the lightning and the thunder rolled in.

He drove home in the pouring rain, windshield wipers slapping time, his eyes straining to see the taillights ahead of him. Luckily, the blurring made everything larger than life.

Brake lights, turn signals, and reds, greens, and yellows, refracting and kaleidoscopic.

They could have been the fireworks, he thought he was going to face when he stepped into the house. But as blind and as sorry and as contrite as he could be, His *Learn to Sail Level 1 Sailing Certificate* in his hand, he was completely unprepared for the reception awaiting him.

Eleanor was so sad and heartbroken, he never sailed again.

Some Kind of Blue

His marriage surprisingly still intact after twenty-four years, Antony woke before sunrise to walk to the university hospital, so that he could accompany Eleanor home after her night shift. The street was long, dark, and empty. The sky was black, heavy, and bleak. The air was as cold as the frost on the ground.

He adjusted his scarf and zipped his jacket closed. He pulled up his ten-year-old leather gloves. No cold air seeped in anywhere. While he wasn't yet warm from his brisk walk, he knew he would soon be. He hurried his pace. Groggy from another sleepless night, he breathed in and looked ahead. This was another new day.

Ready or not, he was up to meet it.

Walking in the dim half-light of the pre-dawn, he reflected on the neighbourhood he and his family had moved into. Light pooled at the base of lampposts spaced too far apart for relaxed night-time strolling alone.

In the dark, it is always better when two people are side by side. He hurried uneasily from one light to the next. Old wartime houses, small-dilapidated homes cowered near monstrous in-fills, one huge *Casa Ticino* after another squatting heavily on lots too small for them.

Mortgaged to the hilt and empty as caverns during the day, Antony assumed. Must be something to carry that kind of monthly obligation, two new cars in the driveway, a Yellow Lab chained to the front step, and a baby in childcare, but at what cost?

It was easy for Antony to forget that this neighbourhood was in the midst of the city. Over on 114th Street, a tumult of cars and trucks, carpooling be damned, headed northward. Across 82nd Avenue lay one of the largest universities in the country, with 34,000 students on the ground, construction cranes in the sky, and cement trucks holding up traffic as they lumbered towards building sites, incisions that cut deep into the heart of the campus.

East of 109th Street was one of the hippest parts of the city. Not particularly pedestrian friendly, though, Whyte Avenue came to life when families went home. Cars, motorcycles, and gleaming pickup trucks pulsated with boom boxes and straight pipes that throbbed with anticipation, looking for happy endings.

Up the avenue and back down, single men trolled for available women, hoping for a little catch and release. Women cast alluringly into the eddies yearning to attract a tasty delight.

Pubs, clubs, and restaurants spilled patrons onto the streets and filled up again. People came and went. Theatres screened foreign films. Cafés served vegetarian samosas and chai. Buskers sang the blues. The only time Whyte Avenue settled down was on a Sunday morning. Then it was as quiet as an empty church.

Sheltered from urban storms, cocooned by traffic barriers, one-way streets, and vigilant community association members, Antony's neighbourhood during the day was as comfortable as his favourite chair. Tall trees stood sentinel in every yard. Heavy leaves blanketed the lawns and streets, and clogged the gutters.

The sweet, acrid smell of autumn filled his nostrils as he walked toward the hospital. He came to the tiny supermarket, the used bookstore, Maurice's Pharmacy, the acupuncturist's office, barbershop, and pizza parlour on the corner.

A bachelor suite in the apartment across the street was for rent. *This was urban village life at its best*, Antony decided. People could walk to the store for their groceries. They could stroll to church for a Sunday service. Their kids could even run home from school for lunch, if there was a parent to meet them.

Shortly after moving into their little house on 112th Street, Antony put together an IKEA wardrobe in Rosalita's bedroom. A forty-eight-year-old guy in the throes of a mid-life crisis, he listened to Miles Davis' *Kind of Blue*, twisted an IKEA-supplied Allan wrench, and pored over the instructions that he had laid out on the floor, page after multi-lingual page as inscrutable as the writing of a Swedish theologian named Lars Johansson.

Antony tried to lose himself in the task at hand, yet he could not help but wonder how his life could have taken a turn for the worse, those few short years ago?

He was forty-five the year he walked out of the classroom for the last time. The evaluation committee said that they were doing him a favour.

"We're making a decision that you could not make for yourself. It's time for you to do something different. We're setting you free."

If Antony could have spoken the words at the time, he would have said that he was a writer first and a teacher second, acknowledging that his classroom duties frustrated him completely, especially when they kept him from his heart's work.

But he couldn't.

He would have been the last to admit that he was unhappy. Yet he knew it without a doubt.

It had never occurred to him that he might have to redefine what he thought success was. That he might have to develop a sense of purpose in the midst of loss.

That he might fail.

32

Vienna or Bust

Antony loved to go walking. It got him out of the house and into the fresh air. Exercise was better than anti-depressants, and walking was cheaper than a membership at the YMCA, although he did miss the social outing that lifting weights with others offered him.

Not that there was much talking as people worked through their training regimes. It was just that being around other people who were concerned about health and had positive attitudes about their bodies and lives was a good thing. Nothing's worse than being trapped at home with the television on.

He went out two or three times a day. The exercise was invigorating, winter bearing down with a vengeance. *That's the secret*, Antony knew from experience as he laced up his boots.

Get out of the house, enjoy the fresh air, but be prepared. *When the earth is covered in a blanket of snow, a person has to wear long johns.* East of Eden, Antony learned that there was no such thing as bad weather, only poor clothing.

If he dressed in layers, he could do anything, go anywhere. He didn't have to stick close to home, waiting for the telephone to ring or Outlook Express to beep. He was as free as he could be.

When he wasn't outside, he was in the house reading more history of Austria. This time it was Metternich. Antony still remembered the day he discovered that he had an Austrian heritage worth knowing. Up until that point, he hadn't given central Europe much thought.

As a kid, he read war comics about the Allies defeating the Nazis. When he went to university, he discovered that not all Germans were in the SS. Many were, and they will be judged for their part in making the twentieth century the bloodiest in human history. Austria, other than its patina of *Sound of Music*, had not captured his attention.

Now, he dreamt of singing the blues and busking on the streets of Vienna.

Antony'd owned a guitar for thirty years. He couldn't strum to the rhythm of a good drummer. He didn't bother to learn the notes up and down the neck. Now that he had time to noodle, learn to read music, play scales, he yearned for a less taxing instrument to master.

He'd heard that the ukulele was the last, best hope for the middle-aged musician. Four strong strings perfectly tuned and three chords, the world could be his oyster.

"Here I come," he swore. "Vienna or bust!"

Was it '82 or '83? Antony couldn't recall. After he finished his B.A., or was it his B.Ed.? That was how he demarcated the phases of his life— by the degrees on his wall: 1973 High School, 1982 Honours in English, 1983 B.Ed., 1988 M.A., 1991 Ph.D.

An education does that to a guy, he thought. *It enables him to learn a thing or two.* It trains him to question firmly held but unexamined assumptions.

To be honest, though, Antony had gone to university to get a girl. Learning was incidental. He didn't do it for a corner office or a cubicle. Why would an arts major do that? When an education that is broad and wide-ranging, miles wide and canyon-deep, hands you the world on a platter.

"You've got the whole world in your hands," Eema Mother sang. "Teach the nations everything I have commanded you. Love your parents, respect your children, and be kind to your neighbours."

What with the imminent return and no one knowing the hour, he wasn't about to waste his time laying up treasures when the fields were ripe for the harvest.

Then he'd met a stunner.

When he tried to marry her, her family put his strengths and weaknesses onto a balance sheet. They calculated that the goodness in his heart wasn't sufficient. It left a little something to be desired.

They sent him packing. He'd need a career before he came calling.

Back on Canadian soil, while reading *Calvin's Institutes*, he came across an old nugget he'd heard before but didn't understand.

"If I knew the Lord was returning tomorrow, I'd plant an apple tree today."

Once he got going, there was no stopping, this late-blooming overcomer of Eema Mother's lifelong hurdles.

It was 1983! Antony suddenly remembered, the year blonde-haired, Teutonic Heinz, older friend and mentor, laughed when Antony pronounced his mother's maiden name.

Antony, Eleanor, and Heinz, and Elsie had just finished eating supper.

They were drinking strong, freshly-dripped coffee in delicate Rosenthal cups, a membrane of oil on the surface of the coffee. As they ate their desserts, they joked about heart attacks and arrhythmias. They were happy, the young undergraduate student, his beautiful wife, and their older friends. They laughed, talked, and wished for nothing more.

"Gutrat," Antony replied, exactly the way his family pronounced it: Gut and Rat.

"Gut-rat?" Heinz echoed, Canadian-like.

"No, Heinz, Goot-rot," Elsie said, opening Antony's eyes to a completely new way of viewing what had hitherto been the familiar and quickly passed-over.

Gutrater, pronouncing the vowels the way an Austrian would, with an oo and an ah.

The name had always been locked shut, closed and forbidding for Antony's family. Now it clicked open, the pins and tumblers falling into place, the shackle free and swinging clear.

"Your family is Austrian. You need to speak your name properly," Elsie said, pointing Antony in the direction Eema Mother wanted him to go. "Learn their story. Learn their language."

Then 1990 rolled around. Antony was an eager doctoral student looking for some relief from his studies deep in the heart of the North Rutherford Library at the University of Alberta. He pulled books from the shelves, one at a time, trying to uncover his past and learn about his family. He yearned to know.

He pleaded to Eema Mother for some sense of who he was, for the purpose of his existence.

He was prosperous. He was lucky. He was grateful, Yet he felt rootless, friendless, a stranger in the very land where he was born.

How could he be an outsider in the city of his birth? He didn't know. He wished he belonged. Where was his home if this wasn't it?

He opened one book at a time from the shelf. Dust-covered, the binding brittle, their pages unread in decades. He sneezed. His hands filmy, he needed to wash them.

He felt unworthy in Rutherford North, this library where lovers snuggle, where students eat and drink and hide their lunches whenever someone official comes by. Where people discover who they really are.

Yet this womb-like sacred space nurtured him. He was Ulysses with the Lotus-Eaters. The hours evaporated before him. He should be up in PR3329 working on his dissertation.

Instead, he was down in DB85, dallying, learning about Austria. He knew nothing about that little country. He couldn't even read the books he was holding.

His nose running and his hands filthy, his eyes were red from scanning the index.

There was so little about Austria that he actually knew. He could stay down in DB for the rest of his life. Why had he started his studies up in PR in the first place?

Now he was stranded in the Bruce Peel Special Collections Library, climate-controlled, humidity constant. Reading one well-preserved book after another, hands in white gloves, taking notes with a pencil.

Antony went into English literature, not history, because of the latter's math requirement. He couldn't add or subtract if his life depended on it, let alone do the higher calculations of multiplication or division. His writing gave him the grades he needed.

Another life choice made on a whim with consequences unforeseen.

He could barely read the German. Yet here he was, once again on the outside, a Hercules fighting to get in. The stacks were quiet. A pall settled over him. What a lovely, lovely place to hide.

Antony had long thought that there is nothing more attractive than a well-mouthed German vowel or a lovely-figured German woman onscreen, those distant stars or the very recent.

He began studying German all those years ago to get a girl who would no longer talk to him. By all rights, he should have studied French. After all, real Canadians are bilingual, fluent in both official languages.

But for Antony, German is the language of love. Its sibilants and film stars: Marlene Dietrich, Brigitte Helm, Julia Jentsch, Sibel Kekilli, Franke Potente. They lured him down a road less travelled.

He didn't get very far, memorizing a grammar rule a day. But still, his studies made a difference. The glitter and the glitz, the soft, malleable contours of its sentences, the position of its verbs, fluid and dynamic, well-spoken German drew him like no other language could.

Then he discovered Käthe Gold, Liane Haid, Hedy Lamarr, and Romy Schneider. Their Viennese was the language of love whispered into the ear.

Then his mother, with whom he had recently become reacquainted, started making annual trips to Austria to visit her two Viennese cousins, Hertha and Walther. She'd send Antony postcards from Salzburg, Schwanberg, Gleichenburg, Laufen, and Vienna, of course.

She collected things, photos, train passes, Mozart chocolates, *Sound of Music* souvenirs. Tourist kitsch. She tucked them away, along with the hurt she had received and meted out.

Their shared past and pain was *Verboten*! Only the present was allowed!

Then she sent him a newspaper clipping from the *Salzburger Landes Zeitung* It clarified for him the puzzle he wanted to solve.

Schenkung für das Landesarchiv

Gutrater Wappenscheibe: Hinweis auf historisches Privileg

Dkfm. Walther Hetzer aus Wien, ein Nachfahre der ehemaligen Salzburger Adelsfamilie Gutrater, schenkte dem Landesarchiv einen historischen Ring und eine Wappenscheibe aus Glas, die sich auf das ehemalige Salzburger Privileg der Erb-Ausfergen bezieht. Diese Personen (der Kreis war auf 40 beschränkt) waren seit dem 13. Jahrhundert vom Erzbischof dazu berechtigt, die Salzschiffe von Hallein nach Laufen zu kommandieren. Bei der Neuordnung dieses Vorrechtes im Jahr 1531 wurde das Erbausfergen-Amt eingerichtet, das mit der Schiffahrt nichts mehr zu tun hatte. Es war dann eine Einkunftsquelle, mit dem verdienten Beamtem des erzbischöflichen Hofes ausgezeichnet wurden. Eine der letzten Familien, die den Titel des—Hochfürstlich salzburgisch Erb-Ausfergen— führte, waren die Gutrater.

Donation to the State Archive

Gutrater coat of arms: reference to historical privilege

Business Graduate Walther Hetzer from Vienna, a descendant of the noble Gutrater family, gave to the provincial museum in Salzburg a historical ring and a pair of memorial glass plates, commemorating the noble Salzburgian title of Erbausferge. Since the thirteenth century, the archbishop gave these people (originally numbering 40) the right to command the boats that transported salt from Hallein to Laufen. In 1531, the archbishop issued a decree stating that the Erbausfergen no longer had to travel personally on the boats. The Gutraters were one of the last families to bear the title Noble Salzburgian Erbausfergen.

He went through agony trying to decipher this. His heart leapt for joy as this universe of information about his family unfolded. His German-English dictionary was well-thumbed. He wrote down each word and the possible definitions for them.

More often than not, after he finished making a pass over each sentence with his dictionary open before him, the words wouldn't make any sense. As he continued, starting at the beginning with each successive reading, editing, and defining, he'd develop a sense of what the whole was trying to convey, even if the individual words were as difficult and as obscure as ever.

The sense of what the writer was saying grew. It may not have been an exact translation, but it was a close approximation of the original.

Then he drank in Robert Kann's *History of the Habsburg Empire*. He couldn't put it down. He read it and took that history as his own. It became his. He devoured his Great-Uncle Walther's genealogical history of the Gutrater family.

Vienna captured Antony's attention. He needed to get home, he needed to get writing, he needed to take control.

Part Six

33

The Hairless Hand

Wan and tousled, Antony tumbled into his doctor's office. Falling heavily into the leatherette and chrome chair, he squeezed in beside the sink and medicine cabinet and the door. Antony flushed red. He looked up and saw an empty jar of marmalade on the shelf. Curious and curiouser. Robertson's Seville Orange. By Appointment to Her Majesty the Queen.

The label's in French and English, he observed. *Can't be any more Canadian than that.*

He yearned for the golden times when everything was straightforward and simple. Like patriotism and maple syrup. Things are no longer what they seem.

Antony's face was drawn and worried as he waited for his family doctor to examine him. Fair-skinned, red-haired Dr. Ross knocked lightly on the door before he entered. He didn't want to startle his patient. Once inside, he checked Antony's shoulder.

"To be honest, Antony, I don't know why you have this injury. Where did it come from? I haven't seen the x-ray from Emerg yet. Is it true what the tech said? That you should get your clavicle checked? It could be fractured. But you are healthy, young, and barely middle-aged. We'll have to order some tests to figure out why."

Antony's shoulders sagged as he slumped against the back of the chair. For a week he had struggled to keep calm despite the uncertainty of this mysterious pain that was disrupting his life. He couldn't sleep on his side. He couldn't drive without using a small pillow to support his arm. He needed a sling when he went walking with Eleanor. The pain was increasing daily.

"What do you mean, you don't know?" Antony blurted. "Isn't this just a rotator cuff injury? I've taken up fly fishing and wasn't prepared for its specialized physical activity. That's all this is, isn't it? From the casting of a six-weight fly rod?"

"The fact is," Dr. Ross continued. "We need to figure out what's going on. This could take time, and we do not want it to get out of hand."

Antony squeezed forward in the unforgiving chair, designed for quick and easy ten-minute consultations, not prolonged therapeutic and philosophical discussions on the triune mysteries of the nature of pain, the beginning of life, and the exact point of death.

A sense of impending doom and fear moiled within him.

"This is not at all the news I was expecting. A torn muscle, perhaps, a strained ligament from not enough stretching."

Antony's imagination began to run wild. He assumed the worst. This is something that should never have happened to him. A portent? A genetic accident? The Hairless Hand of Eema Mother God? He didn't know, and his fear grew.

Smaller and smaller, Antony wound his way, disoriented and lost, through the warren of hallways and examining rooms to the door that finally opened to the outside. If it weren't for the large, hand-written exit signs with arrows in faded red permanent marker on white Bristol board, he wouldn't have made his way out to the blazing noon sun.

Not a cloud was in the sky. The sun's glare pounded his body and assaulted his mind. He fumbled for his keys and tried to pay attention as he drove home. Impatient sufferer. The traffic worried him.

Storm warnings besieged Antony's brow. After he pulled into the garage, he named his worst fear and wrote it on a legal pad the size of tomorrow.

Cancer.

Black ink on stark white paper and the line demarcating the margin as red as Judgement Day. It made Antony despair as he anticipated the days ahead.

This is a hell of a cross to bear. But how am I going to tell Eleanor and our daughters?

Nicola was a blond-haired German major at the university, and Rosalita, a brunette who was sixteen going on seventeen. He wondered if they would ever read *King Lear* and ever get the joke he had been playing on them for years.

"Another sister for you?" he would reply. "I'd name her Cordelia."

Eleanor was a blue-eyed descendant of Vikings, elegant and practical-minded.

"Let me remind you," she often said. "My ancestors conquered most of Europe. They travelled in long ships on open waters and inland rivers. No castle keep was safe from their eyes."

How Antony loved and feared her!

When he was a graduate student, he and Eleanor saved $1000 a month to buy their first house. They struggled, but the determination to have their own home high on a hill steeled their resolve. It was only when Antony was working full-time, and they lived in a small house in the suburbs, that they began to carry a credit card balance at the end of every month.

Once it started, there was just no stopping. Antony learned that debt is a tyrant whose kingdom is without grace or mercy. It is like those Vikings, relentless in their besieging. Assaulting spendthrifts and frugals alike until they are completely in the red, leaving no room to maneuver their way to a firm financial footing.

A week before the visit to his doctor's office, Antony had been standing in the river. He was casting his rod quickly and then more slowly, learning to let his line out over the water. The movement back and forth, his arm raised above his head from the eleven o'clock position to the one o'clock, began to hurt.

Like a watchman on the seacoast looking to the horizon and sounding an alarm, warning of a danger that was already moving towards him, fly fishing saved Antony's life.

It forced him to pay attention when his right shoulder began to ache. It compelled him to see his doctor.

Eleanor was adamant. "I know about little things. Warning lights, symptoms. Signs. Ignore them at your peril."

Long before that, however, when the fly fishing idea was just beginning to formulate in his mind, Antony needed to talk to someone about where to begin.

It was a matter of choice, this fly fishing adventure. One day Antony decided that he was going to fish with flies.

He needed to know what the accoutrements were. Once he acquired the necessary things, he could then focus on gaining the skills. It would be a slow and convoluted spiritualizing of a material process. A western consumer, he needed to buy the stuff before he became authentically one with the universe.

While eating lunch with his pal Gerry Lee, Antony asked a few questions about what he would need to be outfitted properly as a complete angler.

Gerry Lee, however, attended to the matter that was first and foremost in his mind. He needed to know exactly what items on the menu didn't have onions or garlic.

The restaurant on 109th Street was Lebanese. The ingredients he was concerned about were central to every dish on the menu. But Gerry Lee was adamant.

He was deathly allergic to the Allium family.

While he had an Epi-pen on his person, he didn't trust Antony to treat him for anaphylactic shock. He did not relish the prospect of dying as a side order to an entrée.

After they settled on an emasculated vegetarian pizza, with a special request to the chef to hold the garlic and onions, Gerry Lee answered all of Antony's questions. He took care because that was the way he was, a fretless bass-playing jazz musician with perfect pitch.

Gerry Lee also had a penchant for preaching long sermons that invariably stuck Antony somewhere between the fourth and the fifth rib. His words went straight to Antony's heart.

Gerry Lee was Antony's spiritual advisor. A jazzman who loved Eema Mother, fly fishing, and the sanctified life, one day at a time. He was a fisher of men.

On the Crowsnest, Gerry Lee could land sixty trout on any given day.

"Catch and release," he intoned to Antony's exclamation. "Barbless hooks make you efficient. They come out as easily as they go in. You don't waste time, and you reduce the trauma to your catch."

Antony enjoyed another mouthful of the best pizza Edmonton had to offer.

"A beginner's fly rod and reel," Gerry Lee continued. "You'll want some wet and dry flies. A floating line for river fishing."

They spent the better part of an hour together. Antony figured that while he'd like to start now, he'd have to go slow, getting his gear together.

I don't need to buy everything all at once, he concluded.

On a fine spring day, the following year, he was racing down Fox Drive in southwest Edmonton. Antony followed the ravine road towards the river. On the north side of the traffic artery was the stable with its white-fenced paddock, where yuppie parents in glistening matador red SUVs took their children for horseback riding lessons. Fancy jackets, black boots, spandex pants, bowler-style riding helmets and light gear. Nothing western for these young riders. Their parents had eastern aspirations and were about as far from Antony's experience as he could imagine.

Edmonton, Queen on the North Saskatchewan River, was exactly where he wanted to be.

Home is where your sweetheart is. Eleanor, goddess, lover, gardener, mother of his children, and friend for life. She chose him for his promise. He chose her for her looks, smarts, humour, and family. The two became one, and that settled that. They were here for good and ill, whatever befell them in their life together.

On the north side of the road was the original homestead. The Keillor family deeded their land to the City of Edmonton for its citizens to use in perpetuity. The practical effect was that this one-time sleepy hollow became a corridor for commuters who needed to get from their homes in the wealthiest postal code in the city to their work at the university, hospital, or downtown.

Gridlock traffic. Red brake lights blinking, white-hot halogen daytime running lights burning brightly, morning and late afternoon. Carbon monoxide and diesel fouling the air. Into the forest and throughout the night.

On weekdays, Filipino nannies watched their employers' children posting in the saddle and acculturating to the lives they would inevitably lead as adults.

The parents would wait in air-conditioned isolation for the stop light on Belgravia to turn green, so they could inch closer to their work in the city core.

On weekends, the nannies would bus their own children to Superstore for groceries. A Canadian dream. They didn't complain about how hard their lives were. They were grateful for the little that they had.

In the middle of the afternoon during the middle of the week, Antony saw a sign that caught his eye.

FLY FISHING FOR BEGINNERS. MONDAY AND WEDNESDAY

Phone number a blur. Call for more details. His heart in his throat, he drove past in a hurry. The number didn't set. The next time he went by, he was prepared. He entered the first three digits into his cell and memorized the last four. As he entered them, he pressed Send, then downshifted from fourth to third gear.

He had an appointment he didn't want to miss.

Antony hurried home to make supper for his wife and daughters. They were his pleasure. Feeding them the food he loved to cook. Red-hot chilli peppers, freshly-peeled cloves of garlic, stir-fried vegetables, tossed in olive oil. Just what the doctor ordered.

34

The Elk River

With the motivation and the means, Antony could finally take up fly fishing on his own. When he exited stage left from the bakery that went bankrupt the day it opened, he took up real estate and needed to broaden his circle of influence.

"It's busy in the spring and summer but slows down in the fall and hibernates in the winter," his friend Arni told him. "But you need to find creative ways to meet people. Get on a first-name basis with everyone within a handshake and give them a business card. If you want to make money selling houses, you have to have six real-estate conversations a day. Can you phone up your friends and acquaintances? Cold-call strangers?

"The best is to start a conversation with someone you know or is somehow connected to you. What are your hobbies? Find something you're genuinely interested in. Get involved in that community."

Antony thought fly fishing might be the thing.

It'd be better than standing in line at the grocery store, riding the elevator, or pumping iron at the gym.

Making small talk to strangers is key. Swimming's no good for networking, at least not in the fifty-metre lanes at the Kinsmen. There's always talking to strangers in the hot tub or sauna, but you'd need waterproof business cards. His most creative was a Circle of Fifths beer coaster. Didn't make him any money, though. He should have thought it through a bit more. Drinking musicians don't buy houses. They buy guitars and amplifiers.

Fly fishing it is, then.

Antony jumped when Eleanor suggested in her own sweet you-can't-refuse-her way that it was time for them to make a trip to the folks'.

The days in that mountain town on the Elk were as long as the nights were hot. He needed an escape from the house his in-laws built. He was cut from coarser cloth than they. He needed room to breathe, and they needed space.

Fly fishing would give him a reason for getting out.

In the year since his talk over an allium-free pizza, he had been accumulating the gear he needed. He started with the list Gerry Lee rattled off between mouthfuls. He picked up some of the other, less well-known, but equally essential, items that were on his shopping list: leader, tippet, fly box, magnifier, and forceps. Of course, there was more, but next year would be soon enough for him to start another buying spree.

He calculated, without detailing each and every one of his purchases, that with the money he had spent on this new diversion from the pain and the sorrow of the real world, he could have bought an old motorcycle and not gone riding instead.

He would have enjoyed the fresh morning air on a vintage machine flying down the highway at 100 km/h. He would have loved the *phlaat* of insects against the face screen on his helmet. But he had chosen, for better or worse, to take up fly fishing, acquiring the gear first and the skill after.

He wanted to accommodate Eleanor's Intensive Care nursing sensibilities. That was his desire. He fly-fished to keep her happy. And to get out of the house. It also kept him off a motorbike, which was her desire.

Not that Eleanor minded him owning a bike. Having one in a garage was one thing, but riding it another. She was a woman who cared deeply for the people in her heart. She did not hold their lives lightly.

Antony assumed for Eleanor's sake that fly fishing would be a whole lot safer than motorcycling. He picked fishing because it was akin to one of the few activities that were available to him as a young lad back in Manitoba.

On the Canadian prairie, three-down football, baseball, biking, hockey, and curling were the only sports summer and winter that were available to a boy of his proclivities and economic standing. The other two, fishing and motorcycling, were a stretch because of the cost.

Later on, billiards entered the picture, but it required a level of skill he never fully acquired. He and his Risk-playing arch-nemesis B.S. were the worst snooker players this side of the Great Divide.

As a grown man in middle age, Antony was too cranky and individualistic to be a team player ever again. He took up solitary pastimes that didn't involve secret understandings, unspoken pacts, and promises not to invade where you're most vulnerable.

Fishing on the Elk River was safer than playing Risk.

Antony's father-in-law, a soft-spoken man who always knew which way was north, urged him to be careful.

"You know," he called down from upstairs. "A man died fly fishing last week on the Elk. He was trying to cross to a sandbar when he slipped on a rock and fell into a sinkhole. His waders filled with water, and he drowned."

Antony paused for a second.

He then gathered his rod and the day pack that carried a water bottle, polarized sunglasses, catch-and-release net, hook hone, barb squisher, fly floatant, nail knot tier, and the like.

He put on his hat, a Canadian-made Ranger, not a wonder-working Tilley, but just as durable, without the marketing hype or the lifetime warranty. He speculated as he opened the front door that maybe he should have spent the extra thirty dollars. That might have given him the edge.

At least he could have looked something like Brad Pitt (on a bad day) in *A River Runs Through It*.

"Catch ya later," he yelled back as he shut the door a little more forcefully than he needed to; the hinges were lubricated to perfection.

Would the proper hat help me catch my first trout with a fly? he asked himself.

"Probably not," Eema Mother replied. "With it being the middle of the morning and the caddis larvae long hatched and flown. The trout have eaten their morning's fill.

"You'd be better off dozing in the shade with a good book. You did bring that John Irving along, didn't you? I'd like to borrow it when you're done."

Or maybe, just maybe, he replied as he crossed the threshold to Paradise, *Mordechai Richler's Barney's Version would be more to Your liking, another messy, complicated account of a life hard lived.*

Antony clambered over the dike and down to the river's edge.

Family, fly fishing, snooker, and motorcycling were a few of Antony's favourite things. Along with reading.

Reading can't be dangerous, he asserted when he reached an eddying pool. Paper cuts, too much caffeine, not enough physical activity are its perils.

What else could turn reading into a blood sport? He tied a caddis fly to his tippet. He wasn't sure. He made his first cast and tangled the line.

His second was a little better.

The danger in a book, Antony theorized, his rod vibrating and shivering as a sparrow on a wire in the middle of January, *was in the thinking, the ideas, and the book as artefact.*

Reading kept him from engaging, and a man did not want to forget his place when Eleanor was around.

Reading got a man to thinking, and thinking sure got him into a whole heap of trouble when he was supposed to be doing something like making a phone call or plugging in the toaster.

Reading led to buying, especially when Antony was in a bookstore, and he found a missing Chaim Potok for his collection.

"Where are we going to put this one?" Eleanor asked, her frustration barely noticeable.

Antony smiled.

"I'll just have to ask your father, the nicest man in Fernie, to build us another set of bookshelves."

Eleanor would have ploughed him right in the breadbasket, but the prospect of another trip home eased her spirit considerably.

That Antony had her figured out, she knew.

Then all of a sudden Antony noticed his rod a-shaking and a-twitching. A river-born trout as wild as wild could be, was playing with his fly.

But too late, Antony was too late.

He tried to set the hook, jerking the line and taking up the slack. But the fish was already gone, and Antony once again was alone with his thoughts.

Thinking.

A dangerous act.

It must be the actual buying of the book that made reading a blood sport. There was the thrill and the illicitness of it all. There is nothing more tempting for him than the purchase of a good book. The dust jacket is like the scent of a woman, her perfume, her décolletage, and the tease of her beauty.

There is a sensuality in the unveiling that reveals all, but there is also the delight in the promise of mystery, of hidden knowledge, the solitude of writer and reader alone in secret, leafing through the sheets, the two becoming one.

"Now that's a text worth the effort!" Antony shouted, startling the trout feeding near his fly.

Readerwriterloverfriends, together, hand in hand, turning the page, until they both come home. Breathless.

Antony yearned deeply whenever he entered a bookstore, Audrey's on Jasper, Greenwood's on Calgary Trail, Chapters, Indigo. Why, he'd even done a Coles and bought books at Costco, Superstore, and the Salvation Army.

There was (another) line he refused to cross, though.

He hoped he still had a shred of moral fortitude.

It'd take a heart of gold, pure and unalloyed to see Ted Bishop's *Riding with Rilke* in a Wal-Mart store and not buy it at their everyday low prices.

If Antony were honest, and if he were there and did see a book about motorcycles, take Ernesto Guevara's *Motorcycle Diaries,* for example, he'd have to put it in his shopping cart.

The thought of a book by Che being sold in a Wal-Mart was a paradox that defied words to describe it, Antony concluded.

Antony would have to confess, first to himself and then to Eleanor, the only woman in this world with a reservoir of patience deep enough to tolerate his angled-out elbows, sharp tongue, and risible nature that didn't know when to stop joking, that he was too weak for words, the giants of modern literature, and most clearly defined convictions.

He would enter the Bower of Earthly Bliss and would most assuredly fail the test. He would drive his Corolla into the parking lot and sell his soul to the world's largest, most profitable, non-unionized, town-centre destroying retailer and buy a socialist's book about motorcycling, travelling, and reading.

Yes, Antony admitted, when his fly snagged a branch on the backward arch of the most picturesque cast he had made all day. *Book-buying is a blood sport, and it alarms me.*

After the visit to his doctor's office and the dismal year that followed, Antony decided he would read books that made him feel good at their conclusion. A sad ending and a lack of redemption in a narrative of suffering and woe were no longer worth the time, effort, or money. The cost was too personal for words. That was why he liked *King Lear. A happy tragedy*, he thought.

Virtually everyone may end up dead on the stage, but the audience member knows that after the curtain falls, all will eventually turn out well. For Antony, Edgar's words rang true. They ring true:

The weight of this sad time we must obey.

Speak what we feel, not what we ought to say.

The oldest hath borne most: we that are young

Shall never see so much, nor live so long.

Chilled to the bone on the hottest day of the year, Antony decided to return the five hundred metres to reality. He was a mortal man and there was just no way of getting around it.

I am booking a motorcycle with a sidecar and saving an empty coffee can for my ashes. At least, then, my final journey will bring a smile to the faces of all who witness my funeral procession.

People will giggle as I pass on (by).

"What a hoot!" they will say to each other. "He must have been full of beans."

35

Catch and Release

Antony remembered the first and only time he talked to his father about fly fishing.

It was on a cool autumn day shortly after he and Eleanor were married in 1979. The sun was brilliantly warm, the air holding in its hand a precursor of the season to come. They needed to wear heavy jackets and sunglasses as the boat they were in chopped through the waves on Lake Worthington, north of Lloydminster on the Saskatchewan side of the Alberta border.

Eleanor brought a book along with her in the boat. She hoped to have a leisurely read while Antony and his father fished, except the jackfish were biting and taking any lure that could be found in the tackle box. She didn't get a moment's respite.

"Hand me that net, will ya, Eleanor? It's right by your feet."

. . . .

"Where are those pliers, sweetie? Are they in that red tackle box?"

. . . .

"How about those Oilers, Eleanor? Will they ever make it to the playoffs again?"

She slapped her book shut and stared blue-eyed daggers at Antony's chest.

"All right, I get the hint. I'll finish this book tonight before you fall asleep."

When they got to shore, Antony roped the unwitting Eleanor into following him to the cleaning station. That was a moment before she knew in sport fishing that gutting was the man's job.

"You could always go back to the camper. I'm sure there's a *National Inquirer* for you to read if you don't want to help. Catch up on your current events."

Antony hadn't yet learned that there were times in his new marriage when he needed to shut his mouth. That it was better for him to acquiesce than to make a palpable hit. After all, marriage was about living together in relative harmony, not in trying to one-up the other. Poor lad, he had a long way to go.

Sure, Eleanor believed in equal opportunity and women's liberation. She also believed in a clear division of labour. Eema Mother created husbands to serve their wives.

"Love women with kindness," she explained whenever she had a band of young fellows wrapped around her finger. "Make them happy and do what they want."

It became immediately clear to her on the shore of the shallow, reedy Worthington that fish entrails had nothing to do with a woman's God-given right to life, liberty, and happiness.

"You've got to be kidding, Antony," she said.

She left him there, wandered off to a bit of shade, and pulled out her book.

Antony thought he got off rather lightly. When he realized that there would be no nookie in Canada for him that night, however, he felt as if he had been cross-checked straight into the boards.

The joke fell flat in his mouth.

"Catch and release?" James George snorted. "Why would anyone go to the bother and expense of catching a fish and then releasing it? I intend to fry every single one I catch and eat until I'm full."

Antony's father was a heavy-set man who wore gloves whenever he did anything that required getting his hands dirty, like changing the oil in a pickup truck, gassing up the lawn mower, or hilling potatoes in the garden.

"Nobody throws a big fish away," he insisted.

Antony and his father, however, did toss the small ones back into the lake. That was a given, even with their mouths mangled from the three-pronged hooks and barbs.

Once a pike swallowed the lure, a guy would have to decapitate it to get the hook out. Long, needle-nosed pliers in one hand, slimy, green fish body in the other; organ-crushing grip squeezing tight to hold the panicking fish still.

Antony performed thoracic surgery with Craftsman tools. They are Mastercraft delicate. Snap-On with a lifetime warranty. Fish writhing, slippery with blood and scales. *Might as well knock them on the head and get it over with. This fish is going to die, anyway.*

Antony rinsed the blood and shiny mica-coloured fish scales from his hands. There may have been a lifetime warranty for his pliers, but certainly not for the fish.

"What about fly fishing, Dad?"

"What? Fly fishing?"

His years of listening to the roar of big diesel engines while working on the oil rigs in northern Alberta made him hard of hearing.

"Too expensive."

Antony left it there, in the back of his mind.

Over the years, the lure of fly fishing resurfaced again and again. It'd slip away when he didn't bite, and then return, every five years or so. His ears would perk up. The fly fishing antennae would tingle whenever he saw something on television.

He'd notice a guy casting on the river as they drove through the Crowsnest Pass with his family. *Someday*, he yearned without words. Or he'd mention something to Eleanor, but the timing'd be all wrong.

"You know, dear, I'd like to take that up before I die."

She'd pass him one of their two toddlers or start picking up the toys scattered around the townhouse that they moved to in 1988.

On Friday nights, they'd go to Superstore to buy groceries. That'd be their family night out, two kids in two shopping carts and the best life had to offer.

Eleanor would have the shopping list in her hand: bread, milk, eggs, fruit, vegetables, macaroni and cheese, some margarine, and coffee. *Don't forget the coffee!* The family that shopped together stayed together. Eleanor scoured the aisles for staples.

But Antony and the girls? They screamed. They had a shopping cart named *Desirée*. Olives, dill pickles, and salt n' vinegar potato chips. And butter, dream-come-true real butter, not oleo, the budget-conscious, non-dairy spread.

"And cereal, Daddy! Don't forget Shreddies!"

Then the other would cry.

"It's my turn for Cheerios. Last week, you got to choose."

Eleanor frowned when she saw the booty her crew of marauding Vikings brought her.

"Laid the junk food aisle to waste, I see. You could make a mortgage payment on the amount we pay for cold cereal! No soda pop or chips, though."

Eleanor steered her brood toward the essentials.

And Antony?

He took his daughters on a flight of fancy. They careened around corners and squealed with delight, terrified and laughing.

"Dad!" Rosalita yelled.

"Look, Mom!" Nichola cried.

Father and daughters, so excited and happy, they had to pee.

Now!

36

An Arc of Pain

Graduating in 1991 from the university; his ailing mother dying on a hospital bed in 1992; his father capsizing his boat and nearly drowning; establishing a teaching career when all he wanted to do was write; and, of course, pleasing Eleanor for all the wonder she brought to their family.

They lived one day at a time and found pleasure in their children, going for walks in the ravine and taking their kids to soccer, piano, ringette, hockey, and church. Life was like a bird that flew into a room through an open window and out through another. The 1990s went by in a blur.

Finally in the middle of May 2004, Antony had his opportunity to take up fly fishing. His eldest daughter Nicola was in Europe on her second student exchange, studying the German Imperative at the *Frei Universität* in Berlin, and Rosalita was away for a weekend youth retreat.

Teenagers. Teen Angels.

"Venus in Blue Jeans" came on the radio. Antony hadn't heard that song since Miss Lightly walked the halls at Clearwater Collegiate back in 1971.

Rosalita's preparing for a summer of counselling at a camp, an hour's drive north of the city.

"The goal I have set," she said, as she sipped a Timmie's iced capp, "is to make the week my campers spend with me the best of their entire year."

Then Antony found himself on Fox Drive, entering the phone number he had seen on the sign. He pressed Send. A few days later, an envelope arrived from the City of Edmonton.

He registered and showed up for class. It was held in an implement shed up by Victoria Trail along the bank of the silt-laden North Saskatchewan River. The students sat on orange plastic chairs around a plywood table, among snowmobiles, lawnmowers, and a couple of pickup trucks.

Antony met the instructor Jason and the other students. Jason talked entomology, wet and dry flies, sinking lines and leaders, Gunk, and rod weights.

"You need different rods for different conditions and different flies for different times of the day. It all depends on what the fish are eating," Jason emphasized. He pulled out a turkey baster.

"You use this to pump out the stomach. Then you know what fly to use."

Fish on subsistence made hungrier, just so fishermen can succeed at their leisure. That's just the nature of sport, though.

What's one man's pleasure is another species' nightmare.

Antony began casting with one of the rods Jason gave him.

"Eleven to one, eleven to one," Jason kept repeating.

Antony remembered his father's comment about fly fishing. What he really meant was complicated, not expensive.

James George had ten grand tied up in fishing gear, not including the boat, and he fished for fun, not profit.

No wonder the provincial government nurtured its sports fishery. Fishermen had money to burn, and Antony's father didn't mind spending it. However, he had no intention of devoting his evening hours tying flies to catch a fish he couldn't eat, especially when there were *Star Trek* reruns, John Wayne films, and *A Fistful of Dollars* to watch on his big-screen television.

After an evening of casting, Antony's shoulder began to hurt.

This is odd, he thought. *I'm fit. I go to the gym. I push weights, I stretch, and I do sit-ups on an exercise ball. I follow a regime of trunk strengthening exercises, so I won't develop a biker's paunch.* The elliptical trainer he spent forty-five minutes a day on cost as much as a new motorcycle. His arms, back, and heart were strong and healthy, he believed.

Antony and Eleanor lounged on the couch after he got home from an evening of casting a six-weight fly rod. They watched a travel show on OLN. Antony had always thought that Megan the winsome presenter from New York as his third daughter. She's cute and watchable. She's a gas, eating snake in Vietnam, scorpion in China, caterpillar in Australia, and bat in Oceania. Antony loved her wit, her burst of laughter, her bravery, and her ease in front of the camera.

Antony snuggled with Eleanor on their couch. Their adult children were away, and they had a few moments of privacy to themselves. Antony shifted his weight, and an arc of pain cracked his chest apart.

"Eema Mother, this hurts." He could hardly breathe. "You had better take me to the hospital. Something's wrong."

Eleanor gathered their things together, her heart beating with fear. She marshalled her forces and struggled to keep calm, but this was her husband, not some nameless patient.

For the first time in nearly thirty years of nursing, she found herself on the patient's side of the equation. This time not a caregiver, but a receiver of care. It was not an easy reversal of roles.

She helped Antony into the car and drove him to the Emergency. They parked, gave the admitting clerk their information, and waited, interminably, for a doctor to see them and explain what was happening.

"A sporting injury," he surmised from Antony's account. "Your rotator cuff," he concluded as he ordered an x-ray. "Just to be safe."

The tech recognised Antony from church. The machine whirred and clicked.

"You're a good father," she said. "The way you're involved in your kids' lives. Not many dads are as caring as you."

She viewed the film before sending it back to the doctor, seeing a hairline crack in the collarbone.

"You'll want to get this checked," she said, her eyes full of concern.

They returned to the waiting room. When the doctor finally saw them, he gave Antony a shot to lessen the pain and sent them home. He spoke directly to Eleanor.

"You better phone your family doctor right away." He looked her straight in the eye, and she knew exactly what he was really saying.

That night, Antony rolled onto his side. The pain, so sudden and acute, made him want to throw up. He stumbled toward the bathroom door and passed out, naked.

Eleanor could hardly pull him from the corner he had wedged himself into. She managed, somehow, to help him up. While he was in the bathroom, she called the hospital, wife-like, worried, upset. They talked her through an over-the-telephone diagnosis. She checked his pulse, nurse-like, and his respirations.

"A vasovagal response to pain slowed his heart," the nurse on the telephone said. "But you already know this."

Antony's vital signs gradually returned to normal, as did his pulse, colour, and breathing.

The nurse told Eleanor that her husband, the man she'd been married to for twenty-five years, should be fine until morning.

"He'd be more comfortable in his bed than in Emerg," the nurse tried to comfort Eleanor.

They crawled back into bed. Each faced the dawn alone, and together, they spooned and wondered what the future held for them.

Just when Antony finally reached the apex of his existence, not while landing some trout with his fly-fishing gear, not while riding a motorcycle down a long and winding road, and certainly not while besting his arch-nemesis that Risk-Playing-Double-Crossing Infuriator with his armies in Iceland, but when he was finally winning at something he truly enjoyed, making pots and pots of money, Eema Mother threw a surprise his way. Surprised by pain, a new narrative about Antony's life journey.

It wasn't an unexpected vista on a long and familiar road, a pleasant valley beside still waters, or you've-won-the-lottery kind of experience that won't change your life in the slightest.

It was more of a "wrestle with the angel until she breaks your hip, and you spend the rest of your life walking with a limp kind of encounter with the Divine." The sort that teaches you more about the fear of Eema Mother than about Her loving kindness and good nature.

"Females," Antony said. "You love and fear 'em. It'd have been so much easier if God had been a guy," he said, sidestepping another thunderbolt shot down from on high.

It shook Antony, Eleanor, and their two daughters to the core.

It forced them to retrench in order to survive, to muddle through each day as it came along. One slow, miserable step at a time. Descending into the darkness.

After his visit to Emergency, he made an appointment to see his particular, slight, caring family doctor, Swedish and full of compassion. They shared a love for Nordic Noir.

Antony wanted to avoid the discussion they were about to have. He took evasive action and asked if his good doctor knew about the Icelandic settlement on Lake Winnipeg. He wondered if Dr. Ross grew up in Gimli.

"Are you from Manitoba?"

"No," Dr. Ross replied. "But I have an aunt who used to teach piano there. She lived in Quickfall, a small farming...."

"Quickfall, on the #7? In the Interlake?" Antony interrupted. "I lived there for five years. Was your aunt really Mrs. Mann?"

Antony didn't give Dr. Ross time to reply.

"I took lessons from her for a year. I've never forgotten what she taught me. She changed my life. Discovered that I had an ear for music, if not the opportunity to develop it. The old, out-of-tune player piano was in our living room. I wasn't allowed to practise when the television was on, which was from after school until bedtime. I tried practising early in the morning, but the rest of the family complained when I woke them. Then I tried over the noon hour, which I loved because I didn't have any friends at school, but Flora put her foot down:

"'Antony, you have to be more sociable. You have to play with the other kids.'

"I just wanted to retreat and hide myself away. Piano was my refuge.

"Mrs. Mann introduced me to a whole new world, a beautiful universe next door. What a woman! So elegant and cultured and kind. The half-hour I spent in her music room was the best part of my week. I could forget who I was and where I was living.

"I dreamt about what could be, not what was.

"Her piano was a portal to the heavenly spheres.

"The music I have with me today is because of her."

"She had a hard life in that small town," Dr. Ross confided. "Her husband was a fine clarinetist but committed suicide in his fifties. She never recovered. The whole family was traumatized by his untimely death.

"We still are."

"If it's any consolation," Antony said. "She taught me how to find beauty in this miserable world. I'm grateful for her presence in my life."

Antony sat in the small, close room, resting in the chair by the sink. Unexplained pain filled his heart, body, and soul. His doctor stood, leaning against the examining table. There wasn't enough room for them both to sit or stand in that confined, claustrophobic space where Antony's world crashed in upon him. He felt like Jonah on a journey of his own choosing, whom the crew threw overboard to drown in the dark, angry sea.

"Antony, the news I have for you. It's not good," Dr. Ross said. "You have been diagnosed with cancer."

"Cancer?" Antony cried out. He breathed in quickly. "Does this mean I'm going to die?"

"We don't know what kind," Dr. Ross explained. "It isn't always the end of the road. The advances in treatment have been incredible. You could still have a long and productive life."

Antony sat back, terrified of the diagnosis, and strangely relieved. The unknowing that he had been living with was worse than the knowing that he now possessed. Now that he knew there was a monster within, he could begin to marshal his forces. Knowing was better than simply waiting.

Dr. Ross was more than a physician. He was a friend, but then, all of his patients must have felt the way Antony did. The two of them always talked about books for part of the examination.

"What are you reading these days?" Dr. Ross asked.

"A Fine Balance. A Suitable Boy. The Gift of Asher Lev. The Emigrants. The Memory Man. The Green Library. Kate Vaiden."

"You might try shorter works for a while, ones with happy endings. Characters who get the girl and ride off into the sunset. Tragedies might be too much for you right now. Too close to home. Give short stories a go; I have a collection from National Public Radio in the States that might interest you, one or two pages long and written by people across America. Only read the ones you like, ones that make you feel good. Next time you're in, I'll have it for you.

"Remember, Antony, you are more than your cancer. It's only a small part of your life. Don't let it define or consume you."

The burden of this doctor's practice grew heavier and heavier as his patients aged. The issues they faced were pretty easy when they were young, but as they grew older? Surely, they got more and more burdensome. Aging is not for the faint of heart. It takes endurance to live as long as some people do.

When Nicola and Rosalita were born, Antony and Eleanor became friends with Bill and Lorraine, an older couple with grandchildren. They had a gift of hospitality and a zest for life that knew no bounds. Over the years, they came up with various howlers that helped Eleanor and Antony make it through each day.

"The reason our marriage succeeded? We decided early on that whoever leaves first takes the kids, and neither one of us ever wanted to be saddled alone with the four of them."

Or, when Eleanor and Antony yearned for the joys and the wonders of the empty nest.

"Adult children are just great, so are grandchildren. Babies are highly overrated."

The one that really helped Antony.

"One day, you'll get your love life back."

Thanks be to Eema Mother for older friends, Antony prayed. They put his life into perspective.

"Antony," his doctor continued. "Now you know you have cancer. The worst is ahead: realizing you are ill, but waiting in agony for the treatment."

He was right, this doctorphysicianfellowreaderfriend. He prepared Antony and he waited through the long summer, knowing something was terribly wrong and not knowing what to do about it.

37

Floodgates of Heaven

Antony watched the Euro Cup soccer matches on television. Blitzed out on Tylenol and codeine, he cheered first for Austria, then Germany. He loved the Dutch games. Their fans sang in the stands. Wave after wave of songs reverberated throughout the stadium.

What a way to conquer the world! Through beer-fueled harmony, unity in diversity.

Antony spent his days going for x-rays, helping his clients with their possession dates, making suppers. He tested out the Indian cookbooks he had been collecting. Made a vindaloo that went over quite well, froze the leftovers, one day after another, time dragging slowly on.

Late one July afternoon, the floodgates of Heaven opened wide. Rain poured down. Gutters filled. Streets flooded. Their sewer backed up. He pailed bucket after bucket after bucket into containers that Eleanor and Rosalita hauled up the stairs and emptied onto their neighbour's lawn. They weren't home, those renters.

Antony had been mowing their lawn, anyway, and shovelling their walk in winter.

They'll have the greenest grass in the neighbourhood, and I'll be left with the consequences, mowing it twice a week, Antony mused whenever he could catch his breath.

Will Nicola ever get back from Berlin? She now spoke German with a Scandinavian accent. It filled Antony with pride, the thought that she could converse in the same language as his grandparents.

His life was complete.

That and the fact that Eleanor and their daughters learned how to drive a standard in spite of his un-Eema, un-mother like teaching methods. Lightning bolts and deprecations, words blasted in the heat, heavy judgements out of the blue, their consequences scathing and instant.

I said ease the clutch out, not pop it. Sheesh!

Touch the gas! Not floor it!

Grind me another pound, why don't you?

Better get a move on! There's a car coming behind you.

Now! I said. Now!

"Learn a standard and you'll never be stuck," he insisted when they stopped sobbing. "You can drive any vehicle then."

They maintain to this day, however, that he browbeat and terrorized them the whole time. He was more of a hindrance than a help. It was really his friend B.S. who showed them how to rev the engine and let out the clutch, and drive off without a hitch.

When they sold their Camry with its automatic transmission, they were left with their Corolla and its five-speed standard. Since Eleanor no longer had any choice in the matter, she did what she had to do. She shifted from first into second, her left foot clutching and unclutching, from third into fourth, and finally into fifth, driving it like she stole it. Show off.

Shortly after, he bought a Tercel station wagon with a stick for the girls that he named "Dexter." Even he had to admit that saying he had taught them how to drive would have been a gross misrepresentation. The truth is that they learned in spite of him. He was too emotional, too excitable, too unstable to have the equitable calm driving instructors need when teaching their students.

Nicola and Rosalita were as smart as their mother, and just as capable. Soon they were teaching the boys who came calling how to drive a standard. They were in control and had the upper hand. That's what all fathers should do, Antony knew. Teach their daughters well. And when

Antony failed? He learned to apologize. To admit his failing. To try harder. To be better. To be.

And never run away.

A man of sorrows, acquainted with grief. His children gave meaning to his life. He used his words to keep them close.

"I am sorry. Forgive me. I am wrong."

When they were young, he read stories to them back to front, the sentences in reverse, from right to left, starting with the period, and ending with the capital. They were puzzled and confused. He'd get a page or two in before they figured it out. Then they'd yell, "Dad!" and stand on the sofa or the bed and wrestle with him until he promised to read from Once Upon a Time to Happily Ever After.

Kids are resilient and tough. They survived his inept parenting.

There was love and grace and inconsistency in their home. He was there for them and made it up as he went along.

"You'll get the hang of it," his older friend Heidi said. "Make mistakes, change your mind, cut them some slack, and back off. They'll eventually love you in return. There's no right way to raise your children."

Antony loved every stage of fathering, from the birth of his daughters to their maturing into grown women.

The rains stopped, the sewage receded, and their basement was spared. Their bucket brigade was able to keep up. No lasting damage ensued, just a little sanitization needed, some bleach here and there.

Eleanor and Antony went on a walk-about to survey the neighbourhood. Some houses were devastated. They saw a young couple in Spandex and on bicycles. They'd been standing under a garage eave for the last hour, blue, hypothermic, and shivering.

Antony and Eleanor brought them into the house, wrapped them in blankets, and served them hot tea. When they were warm enough and the water level receded so that it was safe on the road, they cycled home.

Antony used his real-estate skills to discover their names and address. The next day, he wrote them a note and included his business card. He knew that if he didn't ask the question, he would never get their business.

"Do you know anyone who is thinking of buying or selling a house in the next six months?"

He and Eleanor headed back out onto the street. Nothing brings neighbours closer than a natural disaster. Righteous and unrighteous. The rain fell on both. One woman mourned the loss of her garden. Another was exultant.

"We'll finally get the basement of our dreams, courtesy of insurance. A windfall from the deluge of the century."

On the first Tuesday after Thanksgiving, Dr. Andrew, the wispy-haired oncologist from the Cross Cancer Institute, said, "It's Multiple Myeloma, the rarest of cancers, and incurable."

Unable to comprehend the weight of these words, Antony was so loaded on morphine his guts turned to concrete. For a former academic who prided himself on the grace of his prose and the elegance of his punctuation, this brutal introduction to physiology was way too biological for him.

What he wanted more than anything else in this world was a really good shit, with a turd so large it went twice around the bowl and plugged the toilet. That's all he could think about.

Loosen my bowels, Eema Mother, and I will devote the rest of my life to your service, Antony prayed. *Otherwise, let me die quickly.*

It was hard for him to pay attention to the oncologist when all he could think about was how he had to hurry home and writhe on the bathroom floor, stuffing an enema up his rear, so he could do something he had never really spent much time contemplating in the past.

How best to relieve himself.

Eema Mother, give me this day My Daily Waste. Cancer may be fatal but constipation stinks. Come, Sweet Death, just let me go!

"We've had good success with our treatments," Dr. Andrew continued, unaware of what was foremost in Antony's mind. "Most of our patients survive. You can, too, if your body responds as anticipated. The odds are in your favour.

"What I don't understand, though, is why aren't you sicker? How come you look so good, Golden Boy?"

Antony thought that maybe Eema Mother in Her great mercy was answering his prayers. Others thought it was his relative youth. Someone else, the glassfuls of execrable vegetable juice he drank every day.

It's an Olympic sport, making vegetable juice without a recipe, Antony discovered the hard way.

Carrots, spinach, beets, cabbage, ground up willy-nilly in a midnight-black Champion Professional 5000 variable-speed dual-auger masticating juicer, to produce a potent, revolting goop that was worse than Buckley's but twice as effective. Three times a day and no skipping.

"For some reason," Antony learned as Dr. Andrew persisted in his explanation, "the marrow produces cancerous blood cells that congregate in tumours on the bones.

"They erode. Starting with small lesions. Pitting first, and then total destruction. But it gets worse, slowly, and yet very quickly. One day a hairline crack, a month later a tumour that breaks bones. Like your clavicle. Or they can eat right through."

Multiple in layman's terms, Antony translated, means many places. *Myeloma* means bad news. Bad news in many places. Doesn't translate worth beans into everyday English. *Must be an idiom*, Antony thought.

Doctors use Latinate phrasing to communicate directly with their colleagues, without fear of miscommunication. Sounds positively medieval. On the outside of Eema Mother's musk-filled and ever-loving embrace, Antony was drugged up, delirious, and afraid for his life. Deeply paranoid, he suspected the doctors were distancing themselves from their patients.

Incoherent, he came to the hazy conclusion that the latinizing of medical language is an attempt to codify the uncodifiable, to fit into precise clinical categories the oozy slipperiness of living tissue, live cells. Life is indefinable, mysterious, and ultimately unknowable.

Doctors are physicians who deal with the crap their patients' bodies produce. They are practitioners. They need to communicate clearly. Their words signify life or death.

"What do you mean, if my body responds as anticipated?" Antony squinted through the miasma rising from his bowels.

"Most patients worry about the side effects of chemo. We doctors aren't concerned about that at all. What we worry about is whether or not the treatment works. Will the drugs do their job? The side effects are hard, but cancer is fatal. You could die from this, Antony. That's what worries me."

Antony suddenly realized that Eema Mother was playing hardball with him. There weren't any walks in this game. Three strikes and you're out. Would he get out of this alive? Would he escape scot-free? He didn't know.

He ate bitter apricot pits, eleven a day, drank juiced wheat grass, black walnut elixir, and bought organic cherries from the health food store down the street. He drank red wine and ate dark chocolate, fighting cancer with an arsenal of prayer, folk remedies, and alternative medicine. Foods that fight cancer. Medical proclamations from Google that guaranteed good health in three easy steps. Suggestions from well-meaning friends.

Antony settled on acupuncture, *Tai Chi*, ancient Chinese herbals, green tea, and intercessory prayer. When he felt sorry for himself, when he couldn't sleep at night, he prayed for his friend who was recently widowed and for another who lived with chronic pain. He prayed for all the kids he knew.

"Keep them safe. Give them hope in their suffering. Help them to keep fighting. Call them by name, oh, Eema Mother. Bless them with goodness, shaken down and overflowing." He tried to survive by focussing on the needs of others.

When he finally got home, he ran for the bathroom. He turned on the fan and locked the door.

"I'll be a while" he yelled, clenching his teeth and stripping as quickly as he could. "Don't come knocking anytime soon."

38

Muscular Faith

Side-by-side, Antony and Eleanor faced their eternity, alone and together. After the first face-to-face meeting with Dr. Andrew, Antony had a bone marrow aspiration. Like all women who had borne children, he could now say without hesitation that he knew pain. Granted, Antony did not experience twenty-four hours of labour and delivery, just a few seconds' worth of agony that was through the roof. The consequence? Not the birth of a longed-for child, but a confirmation of a diagnosis.

Nevertheless, Antony could now sit in an anteroom knowingly, a fellow traveller down a pain-filled road of no return. Been there. Done that. No whelp, though. Just his own life. His own. That was worth three excruciating seconds. For sure. But more pain was on the way.

Dr. Andrew wanted to know why Antony couldn't get out of bed at night, the pain was so agonizing. He'd lie flat on his stomach, inch his legs over the mattress and onto the floor. With his hands on the side of the bed, he'd slowly stand and totter to the dresser. Balance. Shuffle. One foot forward. The next. A hand on the dresser, the other reaching for the doorknob. Lean against the doorframe. Steady himself and lurch towards the bathroom. Sit on the toilet, catch his breath. And up again. So much effort for so little relief. Just a dribble. And up again and again. To the bed? To the sofa?

He'd rather sit up all night than suffer through that ordeal again.

What Antony would give for a good night's sleep! His soul to Eema Mother.

Then Eleanor bought him a Medi-Chair that lifted him to a standing position. Antony didn't have to hurt himself every time he needed to pee.

The chair also reclined. He could doze there all night long, reading, writing, praying for others, and crying. The night times were the worst. He dreaded the darkness. Dr. Andrew wanted to know why.

"What's causing all this pain, Antony?"

They needed to go on a search-and-destroy mission.

Suddenly, a spot on the MRI waiting list became available. Antony jumped the queue. Somebody else's misfortune became his answer to prayer. The medical professionals led him through the procedure, clinically, step by step. The pain in his back made lying on the narrow stretcher-like table nearly impossible. It was torture. The pressure was exactly where he felt it worst. Someone put a set of headphones on him and let him listen to CBC FM, the Mother Corp of publicly-funded Canadian radio stations.

Antony wanted the new French station, but the nurse couldn't find it. A woman with soft caring hands, warm and welcoming, her touch reassured him. Her voice reached out to him. She spoke Antony's name as he surrendered himself to the wonders of medical wizardry that made the invisible visible. He needed this woman's humanity to ground him, to help him get through to the other side.

The MRI whirred, clicked, and spun. Sometimes it even roared. Antony nearly fell asleep, a little Mozart to soothe the soul. Except he couldn't. The lump of toxic waste, a globe the size of the earth grew in his back. Kafka's Gregor. Gregor Mendel. Supine, legs and arms flailing, a metamorphosis of pain. All of his qualifications, publications, degrees, and achievements meant nothing. Nada.

He was a biological being besieged from within and probed from without. The dragon was fighting over his prize and Antony's life was in peril.

"Soon you will be no more," the monster gloated.

The table rolled forward then backward without warning. The sudden movement woke him from his misery. At one point, the nurse asked if he was okay. She knew his name and spoke it with care.

Lovely sopranos, Antony heard their voices on the radio. *Lift me out of my misery,* his prayer soaring.

Oh, thou Cecilia Bartoli, thou Isabel Bayrakdarian, take me to Italy, Armenia, or Toronto. Any which city but here.

The tumour was trans-continental, trans-national, and trans-awful. Trans-scented, it reached to the depth, reeking to hell.

Fine. I'm fine, Antony murmured. *Just get me out of here.*

He chose to ignore the unignorable. The light in the chamber was as bright as the sun at Surveyor's Lake, south of Fernie on the 93 towards Eureka, Montana. The air was just as hot, hot, hot.

He was drawn to a mirage of young women in bikinis, tanning on towels, and skittering over blinding sand to cool in the lake before returning to repose in all their resplendent glory.

They piqued his interest.

For a moment Antony forgot where he was.

I am okay, but not, he rued. His world was falling apart. Falling to pieces. But not for lost love, just lost.

I hurt, therefore I cannot. Contemplate or even desire.

He was no Priapus in the MRI chamber.

The MRI showed a nine-centimetre tumour along his spine. Dr. Andrew ordered five days of emergency radiation the weekend after Thanksgiving.

The first treatment went fine until Eleanor heated the bison vindaloo that he had made and frozen. The smell was enough to send Antony diving headfirst to the toilet. So began the worst week of his life. He heaved from one wave of nausea to the next.

After the second treatment, Antony woke in the morning without pain for the first time in months. By the third, he had the nausea under control with drugs, travel bands on his wrists, breathing exercises, and weak apple juice diluted with water. He hadn't eaten in days, and lost fourteen pounds. Faster than Atkins or South Beach. *He was never dieting the hard way again,* he decided when he was just a few radiation treatments from his ideal weight.

By the last one, he was ravenous, and even had enough energy to play a few scales on his guitar that he'd named Juliette—after sweet, lovely Juliette Binoche.

Then the chemo, three treatments, each twenty-eight days apart. Harsh chemicals pumped into his veins, designed to kill cancer cells, but causing collateral damage. They killed healthy ones, too. Around American Thanksgiving, his hair fell out in clumps while he was showering.

"Eleanor!" he called out for help. She came running, nurse-like, marshalling her forces, preparing for the worst. Antony stood in the shower, naked. Hair clogged the drain.

"What do I do now?"

He was bawling and helpless.

Oh, Eema Mother, I could use some of Your tender loving right now.

"One step at a time," Eleanor said. "We'll get through this one, too."

She turned the water off and helped him step out of the shower.

He towelled off.

She handed him his clothes and phoned Prester John, his dearest friend. He had his back, and they helped each other when life turned hellish. One man's pain is another man's loss.

We need each other when there's nowhere else to turn.

Prester John had a hair clipper and buzzed Antony's head with a number three.

Eleanor and Prester John made a joke, and he laughed from the heart for the first time in months.

Antony had always wanted to shave his head. Now he had the chance.

His friend Bruce came home from Australia with a shaven head after working in a gold mine for a year. He paid cash for a Marantz stereo system and JBL speakers. It had a top-of-the-line receiver with a volume control that went past eleven in the day when a ten could peel a woman's clothes off. One afternoon, Antony knocked all of Bruce's LPs off the shelf, yards of vinyl, lined one after another from here to eternity. Bald Bruce and clumsy Antony.

"You tipped my entire collection over," Bruce said, smiling. "No damage, though." The LPs were close enough to the floor. Not a scratch. They listened to The Doors.

"Is this the end?" Antony asked. "My only bald friend?"

Not for them, anyway. It was a long and winding road that they were on.

Prestor John laughed. Eleanor rubbed Antony's head for good luck. "Your skull is perfectly round!"

"Rather suitable," Antony replied, "given my studies. I'm a Roundhead. One of Cromwell's boys. Trust in Eema Mother, but keep your powder dry."

An apt saying, as Antony prayed for healing and was hit with another whack of chemotherapy. It takes muscular faith, the kind we need. Sturdy roundheads. Not longhaired Cavaliers, but heroes who will face their Apollyon without flinching. Take their chemo sitting down. Survive the worst cancer has to offer.

And still glorify Eema Mother with their thoughts, words, and deeds. At least do their level best.

"That's all I ask," Eema Mother said. "Do what needs to be done. One day at a time. I'm not asking for miracles. You are, after all, just a man."

Antony felt an immediate reduction of pain. While he still needed loads of morphine at night, his dose was half of what he took before the radiation and chemo started. And he was no longer bunged-up tighter than a frozen barrel of bitumen from Fort McMurray.

He could finally go. Man, he could. Sweet Eema Mother!

There was no stopping once he started.

39

Road of Bones

There was more to suffering than pain, Antony decided. Learning, change, and transformation, an expansion of human feeling for fellow travellers, empathy, and sympathy were all part of his pilgrimage.

Antony retreated into his inner universe; crossing the River Lethe into darkness and isolation with no companion other than Eema Mother, he came upon an open line of communication to a hurting world.

I suffer, therefore I am.

Unbearable pain enabled him to reach out. Made him honest with himself, Eema Mother, others.

The otherness of cancer brought him into oneness with the universe.

Everyone who lives must down a full draught of suffering.

And then, there were practical humiliations at the front of the war against that old dragon. Financial considerations. Antony lost his ability to work and bring in a paycheque, to pay his part of the bills. He had just started work as a realtor. In three months, he had sold seven properties, and this after five years of being under-employed. It took a long time to redefine himself.

Five years, in fact, to move from an academically-minded researcher, writer, critic, and reluctant teacher to entrepreneur. Five years to realize that all he learned in the study hall, the classroom, and the library could be used to build a business. Five years of questioning Eema Mother and doubting himself. Five years to understand that the world needs more than beautifully suited desks jobs to make it go round and round. Hand work, back work, arm and brawn, and skilled craftsmanship with an eye for detail. Essential services that enable people to live, raise their families, and have their being.

242

He and Eleanor conferred.

"Shouldn't be that difficult to adjust our budget so we can live on one income, just a little discipline, financial clarity. Sell our second car. Cancel our subscriptions. Discontinue cable. Stop eating out. Consolidate credit card balances and somehow, somehow cut two thousand dollars a month out of our expenses."

Cancer, credit cards, and debts. Anyone else caught short of cash when serious illness strikes? One day at a time, one bill at a time, don't look at the whole picture. Little things add up.

Then the mail arrived. Gift cards from family and friends. Cheques from cousins. Dollars from Heaven. Never underestimate the efficacy of hard cash, given freely to those who have been sideswiped and brought low, to heal the spirit and pull the body back from the grave.

Cheerful givers are Eema Mother's gift to those wracked in pain. Home-cooked meals, lawns mowed, walks shovelled, houses cleaned, laundry folded. The gift of live music shared with one who can no longer sing. Like the time his friends Gary and Stefan riffed on a medley of jazz standards. They reached into his soul and brought him back to life.

I'm gonna love you

Stars shining

A valley green

Red roses too

Nothing but blue skies

Get your hat

I can hardly speak.

These words gave him hope. That this was not all that was meant to be. *That a new day was coming.*

Nicola and Rosalita's church friends helped load the truck when Antony and Eleanor found a larger house along an old-abandoned railroad line. It was a wreck when they signed on the dotted line, but from one realtor to the next, a good deal cannot easily be ignored.

"Must be loaded on morphine," Darwyn the cousin said to James Eadie the brother-in-law. "If he thinks all that can fit in there."

"Ativan," James Eadie said to Darwyn. "He clearly doesn't know what he's got himself into. Us neither."

"You got plans for the next few weekends?" Darwyn asked.

"Not anymore," James Eadie replied. "Unless Red Molly has written something in ink on the calendar that I don't know about."

"Then we're good to go."

And with that, the two started breaking apart the concrete floor and framing up the walls.

With relatives like that at his back, Antony knew that he could survive anything. He gave them his heart.

Tiling and plumbing and electrical and drywalling and painting, the old house became a home that a hope-filled community built.

J'espère—I hope. Therefore I am.

They lived from sunrise to sunset to sunrise, doing all that needed to be done in the short, few hours between them. They hoped that all would eventually turn out well. Hoped there wouldn't be any more unpleasant surprises.

And then it happened.

Early one morning in the hunker-down-and-recuperate week between Christmas and New Year's, Antony sat at the kitchen table to do some journaling. The eastern sun poured through the frost-rimed window and warmed his soul. Antony stretched out his arms and rubbed his hands together. Only then did he realize that his wedding ring was missing.

It had slipped off somewhere without him realizing it. He didn't remember taking it off. A man, who had fallen in love with his wife again, after twenty-five years of marriage, did not lightly remove it. He pawed his way through the deplorable leftovers of the worst vegetarian meal he had ever attempted to make. He moved furniture. He looked behind his grandmother's broken-handled rolling pin, and still no ring.

Cancer, he could accept as a force that invaded his body, compelling him to dig deeper than he had ever dug before. Cancer he could understand. It demanded that he change his diet, make healthy choices, exercise daily, and search for opportunities to serve others. Cancer he could understand. But this?

To lose his wedding ring when his whole world was turned upside down? This was over the top. Insufferable! One trial too far. An unnecessary dose of divine vindictiveness in a long, sad story. *Eema Mother God, shame on you!* He seethed.

Antony was not a holy man, no-one out of the ordinary, just a white, heterosexual, middle-aged male deprived of his livelihood. Losing the ring that Eleanor gave him as a token of her plighted troth was unbearably heartless and cruel.

It made him see red.

On New Year's Day, he and Eleanor went to People's Jewelry in the mall and bought a band of gold to ring in their dreams of better days and welcome nights.

Slowly and imperceptible, quickly and readily apparent, Antony lost his attention span. Couldn't concentrate. Simply couldn't stay the course. He watched television commercials and chose to read stories with happy endings. He turned to the east and squinted into the brilliant winter sun and lost his sight.

Old and tired and completely broken, Antony sat at the kitchen table, looking at pictures of his much younger wife and small children. They were healthy and happy. He smiled.

What a wonderful, busy, exhausting time they shared.

How Eleanor and Antony then wished for a moment's respite, some peace and quiet, never quite realizing just how quickly the years would pass.

Their youngest daughter was almost twenty, and their house more peaceful and still than they could ever have imagined. Someone once said that human memory was like a grammar lesson.

We find the past perfect and the present tense.

When Antony looked back on those days that had flown by, he could now say that they truly were present perfect. Hindsight has a short memory for hard times. Things are never as bad as they once appeared.

He loved raising his daughters. Giving them the kind of childhood he never had. He learned from his older friends. They mentored him in the art of fathering. Henry, Heinz, and Arni. That's why Eleanor married him. For the qualities of the people who were there when he needed them, Marge, Elsie, and Heidi.

They spoke their truth, and he listened. Guardians of his heart, they were the reason Eleanor said yes.

Antony yearned for those glorious days when cancer was not part of his present reality. What an awful place this new world had become, this fallen Eden. He felt like Adam, thrust out of the Garden, walking hand-in-hand with Eve towards the dawning of a new day, a day of judgement.

The sorrow Antony carried was great enough to break his heart. Cancer was a disease that felled others, and if people like him got it, they were healed completely. They received Eema Mother's touch, and their strength was renewed. Cancer does not strike the blessed, and it certainly does not return to people like him!

When cancer invaded his body, Antony read the entire Book of the People through. It took a year to claim all the promises of renewal and harvest and to skim all the passages of bondage, captivity, and tyranny that make up its bulk.

The Songs were most enriching, fully expressing his anguish, pain, and profound disappointment. The one or two promises in each of The Prophets were as precious gold nuggets that needed to be hydraulic-ed out of a ton of overburden. Powerful fire-hose jets of water wash soil and gravel off the bedrock and into sluice boxes. Screens of varying gauges and rippled bottoms capture the dust and nuggets and flecks of gold that settle to the bottom.

The Good News was increasingly foreboding, as they descended towards Sheol with no resurrection or redemption yet in sight.

"Cancer may be your enemy," Mrs. Wiebe said when she and her husband were visiting Antony and Eleanor, "but Eema Mother is your Helper amid this flood of mortal ills prevailing." Then Mr. Wiebe sang in German the words she had just proclaimed. "*Sie hilft uns frei aus all Not, / Die uns jetzt hat betroffen.*"

"A mighty fortress in my weakness," Antony said.

"After all you've been through," they insisted. "Call us Henry and Marge."

"I'd rather call you Mum and Dad," Antony confessed.

And Eema Mother God drenched them with Her tears.

They prayed and anointed the lintels of the doors with extra-virgin, cold-pressed olive oil. This was the closest that Antony would ever come to using lamb's blood in a ritual sacrificial offering to his loving Eema Mother.

They commanded the Angel of Death to pass over this house. It had been marked with transubstantiated olive oil, the blood of the lamb.

Death could not enter this home.

"To hell with Cancer," they prayed as they cried out in worship and woe.

The ritual strengthened his heart and resolve as he faced a demon greater than he. Of his own accord, Antony chose to enter into communion with other sufferers. This was the way of faith along the sorrowful way.

Did Antony receive healing the day the elders of the church, male and female, laid hands on him and prayed out his woe? Did Eema Mother take control of his life as he confessed a litany of present sins and asked Her forgiveness? Did he go through a refiner's fire of purification?

Yes, on many levels.

Antony entered the church every week for the next year and was loved. People cared for him and his family. They provided meals, money, and practical help of all sorts. Eleanor and he flourished.

Cancer was on the wane and his health slowly returned.

It is an insufferable plague that doesn't go away. It is a constant reminder of one's mortality.

Antony's theological certitudes were both shaken and stirred. Who dared to counsel him with platitudes that Eema Mother was allowing this for a reason? To teach him a lesson? To purify him of a private, hidden sin? Will people avert their eyes and shun him, or embrace him in spite of it all?

Cancer had made him vulnerable, dependent, and unsure of the future. His hands were down at his side and his shoulders were slumped.

As his strength returned, people often asked, "Are you healed, Antony?"

He learned to accept a heightened sense of his own mortality. That we will all die one day on this road of bones is a certainty he could no longer deny. Antony did not have the assurance that he would enjoy a long and pain-free retirement. Antony dared not, simply could not, state that he was healed.

Cancer taught Antony that he was an ordinary man. It liberated him from any illusion that he was chosen or elect. The faith he had embraced since a child had not inured him from suffering. He was not deserving of special treatment.

He came to the church and offered his sacrifice of woe on the altar in praise to Eema Mother. He chose to believe that She loved him and called him the apple of her eye. He ran towards Her and sought shelter under the shadow of Her wing. He sought Her refuge and waited for this calamity to pass.40

Fool's Gold

On the hottest day of the summer, heavy thunder clouds far off on the horizon, the snow in the mountains long melted and gone, the river gentle and sweet, ambled its merry way across the western provinces. Antony packed up his fishing gear and drove to a sheltered spot on the North Saskatchewan River near Lamoureux just outside the city.

Cancer had indeed returned and robbed him of his joy. It had not, however, destroyed his hope of catching a fish that he could release back into the water.

He walked down to the cooling river's edge and tied a fly to his line. He noticed what looked to be a nugget of gold nestled in the gravel and chose to leave it there.

Probably Fool's Gold, he thought.

Under no circumstances was he going to unleash any more of Eema Mother's great bounty upon his life.

He had more than enough of Her blessing.

Sufficient to the day is the evil thereof. He wasn't under any circumstances going to look for any more trouble.

Sometimes it's better not to be noticed. Sometimes it's better not to take advantage of exciting new opportunities that suddenly become available. Sometimes it's better just to be.

Eleanor, Nicola, and Rosalita were happy as clams. Antony was well enough to go out fishing for the afternoon. They had the house all to themselves. They could enjoy a spa day.

What could be better? A cup of tea and a slice of lemon meringue pie.

Antony stepped into the water, waded up to his hips, and began to cast. There was nothing that he could do to hold his cancer in check or to add one more day to his life. He settled into a rhythm of casting out his line and drawing it in. One small cast at a time. There were fish in that river, and one of them was hungry enough to strike at the fly on his line. Of this, he was sure.

The current out past the eddy pushed and pulled and tugged and drew and heaved a half-submerged log north and eastward beyond the land of Eden.

Golden in the afternoon sun, Antony did the best he could with the life he was given. One day at a time. Mostly.

I grow old...I grow old. I will grill a *paella mixte* for my family's supper.

Now that's something to live for. That and my grandchildren.

Thank you to Josephine Blefare, Heidi Breitkreuz,

Mary Davis, Edith Evans, Irma McCue, Florence Meyers,

Elsie Schönhoff, Marion Starcher, and Marge Wiebe.

You were there when my mother wasn't.

Thank you to Sandy, Jillian, and Kara

You have taught me more than you will ever know.

Thank you to my sons-in-law Christopher and Nathaniel.

I am grateful for the way you treat my daughters.

Thank you to my grandchildren Tessa, Luca, and Willa

You give me bright hope for tomorrow.

Also by James Gregory Randall

Available at

aospublishing.com

amazon.ca

gregrandall.ca

Special order from your favourite bookstore